"He's Here, Kate . . . Right Over There, and He's Been Watching You,"

Kate's friend Josie whispered at the Irish Arts Festival.

Kate's heart slowed and seemed to stop. She looked up and Flynn's black eyes met her gaze. Then she noticed the young boy standing next to him, and she turned away, her eyes filling with tears. When she looked up again, he was walking away.

All day, those black eyes followed Kate, watching her photograph the festival and joke with her friends. Finally, she wandered off alone . . . looking for him.

She rounded the corner of the deserted bandstand. He was standing there, silently, in the shadows.

A shuddering excitement passed through her, and all the strength seemed to ebb from her body.

They stood there in the gathering dusk just staring at each other; then he reached out his hand for hers. He took it firmly but gently into his and coaxed her toward the dark woods.

As she followed him, Kate felt an unbearable joy . . .

FLYNN'S LOVER

MARY McSHANE

PUBLISHED BY POCKET BOOKS NEW YORK

Another *Original* publication of POCKET BOOKS

POCKET BOOKS, a division of Simon & Schuster, Inc.
1230 Avenue of the Americas, New York, N.Y. 10020

ISBN: 0-671-45276-2

First Pocket Books printing December, 1986

10 9 8 7 6 5 4 3 2 1

POCKET and colophon are registered trademarks
of Simon & Schuster, Inc.

Printed in the U.S.A.

This book is dedicated, with love, to all the tight-lipped, hard-faced, tender-hearted, deeply loving men of my family . . . but most especially to my beloved father, Thomas Llewellyn Owens. We miss you, Dad, very much.

FLYNN'S LOVER

{ *Chapter 1* }

The sound of the warm spring rain pelting against the gallery windows drew Kate's eyes to the huge panes of glass holding up under the rainy assault and to her reflection.

Large dark eyes gazed back at her: a calm, level gaze in a face unmarked by the emotions warring within her. The face with question-mark eyebrows was crowned by long, cascading waves of heavy auburn hair. Her white wool dress took on an eerie glow. All in all, she resembled one of her own portraits, done with the infrared technique for which she was becoming famous.

Behind Kate was her work, most of which had little "sold" tickets decorating their frames.

Eileen, her agent, was winding up a sale with the last customer in the gallery, an unusually garrulous man in his mid-forties.

Throughout the long evening of her first show, the man who was now buying one of her favorite studies had commented on the beautiful color of her hair, her figure, her graceful hands, but not once on her work.

It had been a triumphant night and a depressing one. Her face ached from smiling and talking. Eileen had dragged her around all evening to meet with reviewers and potential buyers. And one by one, her work was sold. Photographs of the past seven years that represented her life. A part of her was appreciated, paid for, and sent off to live in someone else's house.

She had seen the elegantly dressed woman who bought "His" black and white. Kate had almost stopped Eileen from selling it as they bent their heads in conversation. She watched as Eileen nodded, confirming whatever the woman was saying, and when Eileen looked up at Kate, she had a sad smile that seemed to ask, "Are you sure?"

Kate had nodded yes to her and turned away from the scene.

She sighed to herself and turned to the now empty gallery. At least the talker had bought the Jamaica study. Eileen in a hot, red raw-silk dress was busy writing and absent-mindedly running the fingers of her other hand through her short, curly black hair.

Drained and exhausted, Kate was still elated over the success of her show. She chose to ignore the underlying depression.

Her eyes wandered to the huge black and white with handpainted pockets of color. "His." He was one man in a crowd of handsome, virile men, dressed in a kilt and playing a war pipe, surrounded by an even larger crowd of people laughing and dancing and staring.

Eileen caught her eye.

"You know you don't have to sell it if you don't want to."

Kate stood perfectly still and nodded slowly to Eileen. She could feel the pain catch in her chest and tears start to well in her eyes.

She took a deep, shaky breath, coughed, and cleared her throat.

"Eileen, I *have* to sell it. That night was five years ago. A lost weekend that is gone from everyone's memory except mine. I have to let the man in the picture go. Every time I look at it I remember, and every time I remember I push everyone away from me. Then I turn and move back into my memories of him and try to live there, hoping some day he'll join me in the present."

Kate stood up and brushed nonexistent crumbs from her soft wool dress. She was fighting the impulse to throw herself down on the couch and cry.

"Eileen." She turned, her eyes glistening with tears. "I'll never hold Tom Flynn in my arms again. I'll never rest my body against his. I'll never look into his eyes again and see tears there. He'll never join me in the present. It's time I sold it, long past the time I should have kept it."

Eileen pushed back her chair and hurried to her friend and client. She put her arms around Kate and held her as only true friends can hold and comfort one another.

After the wave of tears had passed, Kate straightened herself and pulled away from Eileen, sniffing, trying to smile. In shaky voice Kate declared that they should break out the last bottle of champagne and celebrate with a toast to each other. It had been a long, hard haul for both of them.

The worry and concern in Eileen's eyes receded, and she went for the champagne.

Tonight had been Kate's crowning success, over in a matter of hours. Eileen's had come earlier, clients and commissions rolling in, in ever greater numbers.

Kate was the professional photographer she had started out to be when she was pregnant with her son, Kevin.

Eileen was her agent. Eileen was anybody-who-was-anybody's agent.

During the past seven years they had become close friends. Eileen had seen Kate through the birth of her son, her ensuing divorce, and then the gruesome death of her ex-husband, Felipe.

And it had been Kate, nearly seven years ago, who had talked Eileen into becoming an agent. After a series of soul-wrenching jobs, Eileen had collapsed onto Kate's couch declaring that she would kill herself before she would ever humble herself to another employer. Kate decided that Eileen should be an agent, and she would be her first client.

They had seen each other through the lean and despairing years, congratulated each other on their first successes, and rallied one another to keep on trying.

And Eileen had been there after that weekend with Tom Flynn.

The first few days she had listened to a wildly happy Kate.

She had listened to Kate's frightened voice making excuses for why he hadn't called.

She had been there when Kate's voice became slow and quiet, torn with agony.

Eileen had listened to her pleas and dried her tears, and felt helpless as she watched her friend suffer.

Eileen had been there from the start and to what seemed like the end. She prayed it was the end. She prayed Kate would finally be rid of her torturous obsession.

Maybe Kate is right; maybe selling the picture will break her last and final link to that moment in time, Eileen thought.

She raised her overflowing goblet of champagne to make a toast.

"To new beginnings for both of us. To your smashing success tonight. And," she finished with a chuckle, "to my commission." Silently, she added, "And please, Mother of God, let this wonderful woman finally be happy."

Kate never drove into the short, maple-shaded drive in front of her house without pausing there to view her home with pleasure. The house was white stucco with a rust-colored tile roof, surrounded by birch and maple trees burgeoning with the pale green promise of spring. It was still raining hard, and Kate sighed with relief at the sight of her home through the rhythmic slap of the windshield wipers. The drive up the Palisades Interstate Parkway had been harrowing in the rain and fog.

She opened the car door and dashed through the deluge to the garage, vowing that this time she would buy an electronic garage-door opener. Half soaked, she ran back to the Porsche, her first indulgence, and drove it into the dry, warm garage.

Shivering, she hurriedly closed the garage door, her cherished Porsche secure and removed from the elements. Kate entered the house through the side door. Her favorite lamp was pouring soft yellow light over the paprika rug in her study/studio. A remnant of her disastrous marriage to Felipe Zandt, she prized the piece of Zuñi pottery Felipe had turned into a lamp.

Alone in the house, Kate stripped all the wet clothes from her body and moved naked through all its dark rooms. Kevin was spending the long weekend with her parents. Going nude in her world was a luxury Kate, the mother, very rarely had.

Her world, her house. She loved it. Remembering all the care and work she had put into every detail, she savored each room as she passed through. The front entrance hall had a high-beamed ceiling and darkly stained parquet floor contrasting with white stucco walls.

The parquet floors had been the best surprise, a secret of perfectly inlaid oak under layers of ugly, scratched paint.

Felipe bought the house for her during their divorce. She had left him after he had openly started seeing an old flame from Holland. Berthe was one of those international butterflies without conscience, money, or a legitimate profession. She had called Kate one horrible afternoon and suggested in loud tones that she leave Felipe so that she, Berthe, could move in with him. She went on outlining how Kate was interfering with the social aspects of Felipe's position at the museum, that the happy little homemaker and mother role didn't go over well with the director.

Kate had listened and tried to be angry, tried to be hurt, but hung up overwhelmed with defeat. The pain came later that evening with Felipe. She left him the next day, taking her baby and her ravenous hurt home to her parents.

After Kate's mother, Nora Gallagher, managed to restrain Kate's father, the Judge, from having his daughter's errant husband drawn, quartered, castrated, and ruined, Kate got her divorce.

Felipe disappointed the Judge. He simply handed over everything he was asked to and bought Kate her house. The Judge wanted to punish him, rip him to shreds, and Felipe thwarted him by being totally cooperative.

She had found the house on a cold fall day when she was out driving, getting away from her family and their ardent, loving sympathy.

It sat there, looking empty and sad to her. The maple trees were a brilliant mixture of orange and red, the birch trees an almost translucent yellow in the harsh sunlight.

She drove up to the front door eagerly, then became excited when she found it open. It was obvious even under the heavy neglect that it had once been a beautiful house.

As she wandered through its damaged, debris-strewn rooms, Kate slowly filled with a happy impatience that began to replace the pain.

She stood there in the house's heart, a neglected, much-the-worse-for-wear house and a woman in much the same condition. She decided to rebuild the house and her life.

The price was right, and after a little "you don't know how to remodel a house" arguing with her parents, they threw in the towel and helped her.

She wiggled her toes in the soft plush carpet under her feet and ran her hand over the smooth surface of the antique oak dining-room table. Speaking aloud in the dark, she remarked on how strange it had been that she had closed the mortgage, moved into the clean but not yet remodeled house, and received her divorce papers in the mail all on the same day.

Her dining room, which once had gigantic punchholes in the plaster and lath walls, had been spackled by Kate herself.

She looked around in the dim light at the forsythiafilled calligraphic vase, the leather Indonesian chests filled with Kevin's toys, and the French Provincial armoire replete with Felipe's Chinese porcelains and the remnants of her Belleek service for twelve.

She moved into the living room. The curtains were drawn over the French doors that led to her iris and daffodil spring garden. The long expanse of her black linen couch on the huge Chinese Oriental rug beckoned to her. She was tempted to light the wood, stacked and ready in the lacquered manteled fireplace, but moved on.

She avoided Kevin's room. She never went into it when he wasn't there. His room, complete with a sky-and-cloud ceiling and crammed with toys and stuffed animals and sporting equipment, was barren when he was not in it. She realized that tonight she missed him sharply. Her little boy, who wasn't so little anymore. He was too big to cuddle and hold and kiss—at least that's what he told her. She smiled to herself, thinking it was a shame that the only time she ever got to cuddle him was when he was sick.

Kate decided against a late-night snack and passed by the brick-floored kitchen and the family room with wall-to-wall books, a Parsons table, and an old wing-back chair for serious bill paying. Photographs had been pinned to the walls when she started to take herself seriously as a photographer. The family room had been added four years after Felipe was killed.

Even though they had been divorced, Felipe had never changed his will. In fact, he had made it very clear that he wanted Kevin and Kate to inherit . . . and no one else. His estate had been sizable, as had his art, book, and record collections. Berthe never got a dime.

Sometimes when Kate was browsing through one of Felipe's art books, she would come upon a note he had written to himself all those years ago. Kate understood some of them; some she didn't.

Some brought quick hot tears to her eyes, like the one reminding him to buy Enfamil for Kevin or the one mentioning a time and a lady he was seeing on the side.

She passed by the family room, which was rife with bitter memories, went on to her room, pressed on the soft recessed lights, and dimmed them. She walked to the French doors, drew back the heavy black-and-white print drapes, then opened the doors. The overhang of the roof protected that part of the patio outside her bedroom doors from the rain, and she stood outside in the dark, naked, listening to it drum on the tile roof above her. There was a heavy, dense fog in the wet forest that surrounded her house. She stared into it.

Finally, the pain that was tearing at her chest roared out of her in great, gasping sobs. Tom had been here, long before she had finished the house. On this patio. In that bed.

He had stood, naked beside her! It had been raining on the second night. It was a summer storm—deep, rumbling thunder in the distance, great sheets of cold rain cooling the land, raising a mist in the green, lush woods around them.

Shivering, Kate turned back into her room and made her way to the oversized adjoining bathroom. A torrent of hot water rushed into her cherished sunken tub, blending with the sounds of the rushing rain outside.

She moved across the white rug in her bedroom to the gleaming black lacquer Oriental chests. She opened one and pulled out a brilliant red afghan. She moved to the banks of mirrored closet doors, an elegant figure repeated seven times in reflection, to hang up her wool dress.

Sleepy from her hot bath and the ceaseless murmur of the rain, Kate stretched out on embroidered sheets. The red afghan lay like a puddle of blood on the starkly white carpet, tossed there carelessly by an unhappy and exhausted Kate. Her creamy white body was reflected in the gleaming black chests as she tossed restlessly.

She moaned, "Tom," and tossed her head from side to side on the damp pillow.

The high, lonely wail of pipes, caught up and carried by a gust of wind filled with cold spring rain, passed from the tops of the tallest evergreens to the graceful white birches of her woods. Then, in a last dying effort, the wind threw the notes through the open French doors to her.

She looked back up at him. His shoulders were hunched over, almost pleading with her for something.

Then he swallowed, shifted from foot to foot, and looking down at the floor he asked her to dance.

When he took her into his arms, he was trembling violently, and she was astonished. Such a big man trembling like a boy?

He crushed her to him when they started to dance, and she could feel him grow against her. He stared, shaking again, and pulled back from her, still holding her, bent over, leaving a pocket of air between their thundering hearts.

Halfway through the second song, he stopped dancing. He stood still and without a word put both of his hands to her face, and gently, very deliberately, put his lips to hers. Then he brushed her lips slowly with his, back and forth, savoring them sweetly, tenderly.

He gathered her into his great arms and opened her mouth with his, and her breath seemed to fail her when his tongue entered her mouth.

They had stopped dancing; they had even stopped swaying. Her trembling body flowed against his as they explored each other's mouth. Their fingers traced tender lines on each other's face and neck. They stopped to look into each other's eyes. His face was flushed with a look of delight and wonder, as was hers.

Things like this don't happen to adults. But they did. My God, how they happened!

When they finally pulled apart, they were alone on the dance floor. The party was going on around them, ignoring them, but for the occasional solemn glance from Tom's fellow pipers.

They must have sensed what was happening, and they knew what Kate didn't . . . that Tom was married.

Then he ran his fingers through her hair and bunched it up behind her head. He looked somber and centered, and kissed her on her eyes, nose, and lips.

She felt flushed, her throat was tightly caught with desire, and Kate leaned into him, her legs against his, her breasts crushed against his chest.

She pulled back to look into his face. It was open and warm and full of longing. She rubbed her nose alongside his. The tenderness and desire were unbearable. When she put her fingers to his lips, his face hardened, then fell, and as if to stop feeling more, he kissed her again. A long, deep kiss, and when he ran his hands down the sides of her body his thumbs brushed her nipples.

It felt like someone had thrown a billion-volt switch somewhere in the universe and they were the conductors.

They couldn't get out of there fast enough. Flynn asked Kate where she lived and didn't seem to care that it was a forty-five-minute drive.

He held her hand in silence and didn't stop the car until they had driven over the George Washington Bridge.

He reached for her hungrily then, touching and caressing her. Tom rolled her nipples between his fingers and moved his hands down her body. Trembling, he thrust his fingers deep inside her, stroking her everywhere as her hands fondled him. She wanted to make love to him, to do everything with him, more than she had ever wanted to with any other man.

He bent his head and began kissing and tonguing her breasts. His breathing was ragged.

Their moans and breathless whispers filled the night, and she moved her lips up his neck and put her tongue into his ear. Flynn groaned, pulled away from her, and put the car in gear.

She thought the drive up the Palisades would never end, but finally he pulled up in front of her house.

As they hurried from the car, Kate fumbled nervously for her keys. She remembered feeling panicked.

What if he hates my house? It was only half finished then, and she tried to remember if she had cleaned it before she left.

It was then that she realized that she had left both her cameras and her car back in New York.

Oh God!

And that was when Flynn began to fondle her again, and Kate forgot everything else.

The house was completely dark as she led him through it to her bedroom. She went to the French doors and opened them wide. It was the dead of night, the woods were sleeping, and a rustling breeze broke the summer's green silence. The moon threw long rectangles of light across the rug and her bed.

Kate turned to Flynn, afraid. What if he didn't like her body? What about the stretch marks from her pregnancy?

He stood and looked at her and started to undress. She looked down at the floor, too afraid to meet his eyes, and undressed too.

Finally they both stood there naked, and Kate looked up. His eyes were hungry, and his face was full of desire. He lowered his head and put his arms to his sides, hands open, palms up, and whispered, "Please."

She could still hear his pleading voice, and it tormented her. And in her dreams she cried back, "Don't you ever hear *my* pleading voice?"

He stood there, tall and powerfully built, engorged and very vulnerable.

He was totally open to her, and he wanted her as much as she wanted him. It didn't seem possible.

Oh, that fleeting, bittersweet power women have over men. She went to him and rested against his body. She moved her hands over his chest and then down his back and felt the muscles ripple as he moved, picking her up and carrying her to the bed.

Flynn moved over her, then down, and merged with her. All of him, with all of her, their eyes and breasts, hands clasping hands. Then he drew her to him, one hand under her shoulders, the other under her buttocks, holding her tightly in.

All the while he had been slowly rocking, flooding her as she came and came again. Then he started to tremble again, this time more violently. His mouth was over hers, consuming her as they moved faster, and then he went even deeper as she felt her whole body open to him.

As they shared that exquisite, timeless release, a sob broke free from his lungs, and her eyes filled with years of unshed tears.

She looked into his very dark eyes, vaguely aware that the deep pinks and yellows of the dawn had splashed them with its colors. Then she lost herself in him again, as he lost himself in her, over and over.

The early morning light washed over their tangled legs and casually meandered up her body, insistently poking at her eyes with young white light until it woke her.

The musk of Flynn's maleness mingled potently with her femaleness. The sounds they had made, making love the night before, assaulted her mind. The groans, moans, and breathy whispers, deep sighs, and not one spoken word.

Kate closed her eyes again and buried her face under his chin as he held her close, his leg thrown over hers.

He stirred, and Kate held her breath, lying absolutely still, afraid to wake him. His breathing became even again, as her fingers went wandering over every line, facet, and texture of Flynn's body, and she didn't know when he awoke.

She had been caressing him, marveling at the sight of him, and as her lips closed around him, she knew he was awake.

Flynn moaned, "No, no, don't do that!" but he made no move to stop her.

He put his hands on either side of her head, kneading her hair. As she made love to his body, she thought she would die from desire.

Later he moved his body down over hers, tracing pathways with his tongue, whispering a poem by Yeats as he made love to her.

> Shy one, shy one,
> Shy one of my heart,
> She moves in the firelight
> Pensively apart.

She carries in the dishes,
And lays them in a row.
To an isle in the water
With her would I go.

She carries in the candles,
And lights the curtained room,
Shy in the doorway
And shy in the gloom;

And shy as a rabbit,
Helpful and shy.
To an isle in the water
With her would I fly.

He made love to her tenderly, every touch
gentle as he moved his massive body effortlessly,
as she responded with hers. When they stopped,
he was loving her with his eyes, shaking his head
in disbelief, and asking her if she knew when they
had begun to love each other. Did she know the moment?

Diamond tears spilled down her cheeks, and she
shook her head no. She reached out for him, and he
held her close, tightly to his body, whispering, "I love a
stranger. I love a stranger."

They dozed, and when she awoke he was kissing her
face gently, holding her hands in one of his. He started
to talk again about how he had never felt this way about
himself or anyone else in his life. He told her that when
he read Yeats he was always embarrassed for the man
when he came to a love poem. He told her that now he
was embarrassed for himself for never having loved

before, and then he smiled a smile that ached at her in the dark.

The days flowed into one another. They talked, made love, and talked. He talked about death and despair, how he had become afraid of dying like his father. She talked about Felipe, how he had lived and died, and her hurt. He got angry for her and talked to her about her worries about her son. He reassured her. He had gone to college for a semester and stopped because his father had been shot on the job and was pensioned off early. He tested for the department and became a cop.

He told her that after his father died he started taking night courses at Hunter and over the years had finally earned a B.A. in English Literature. She had been surprised and asked him why literature. He told her that after his father died he didn't have anyone to talk to, that now he didn't have anyone to talk to except his partner, Tim McBride. He explained that Tim was kind of a philosophical guy and didn't kid him about all his reading. He started to read his way through his father's books, and then he read one that said it the way he felt it, said his feelings for him. He continued to read because it was the only way he could feel close to his father. After he came across *Dubliners* he read everything that Joyce had written.

Then he explained to her about *Finnegan's Wake*, how first you had to be Irish and had to have been to a wake. You had to read it with a drink in one hand and out loud in a brogue; after that it made perfect sense.

She had run and gotten her copy, made him a drink on the way, and he read it, stark naked, aloud with a drink, and, indeed, it finally made sense to her.

They had laughed a great deal about that, then started to exchange favorite writers. He liked Thomas Hardy and dismissed Fitzgerald as self-indulgent. She brought up D. H. Lawrence, and he liked *Sons and Lovers* best. She admitted liking *Lady Chatterly's Lover* best, and then they made love again. They went through Irving Stone and James Clavell, J. M. Synge and Edna O'Brien, and he surprised her with quotes from the more erotic passages of the Song of Songs from the Bible. She brought up Isaac B. Singer and *The Slave,* and he got serious and told her how Singer and Chaim Potok had helped him deal with the elderly Jews in his precinct.

He continued to amaze her. She had spent her whole life looking for a regular guy with a screaming intellect, and she had found what her friends called the impossible. They told her there was no such thing as a modest Renaissance man.

They were wrong.

They had moved on to American politics and into the kitchen, where she was making eggs benedict with chilled white wine and asparagus, without Hollandaise sauce because when she bent over to find the mayonnaise, Flynn mounted her, pulling her back by her hair, and she loved it.

And on Sunday morning Flynn went out and bought the *Daily News* and the *Times*. She read Jimmy Breslin and the funnies, and he read the Week in Review.

And later . . . when she awoke . . . she found his note. All she had of him:

Dearest Kate, my only love,
I'll be back for you.
Wait for me.

Flynn

But he never came back. No, not for days, or
for weeks, or for months, or for years. He left her
lying there . . . dying there, waiting for him in her
dreams.

{ Chapter 2 }

The morning light hit Kate's eyes like a jackhammer. They were all puffy and painful from crying and pleading with Flynn and God.

The telephone beside her bed trilled, and Kate, after pausing to take a very deep breath, answered.

"Hello?"

"Hello, Mommy. What are you doing?"

"Well, hello, my love. How are you?"

"I'm fine, Mommy. Can I come home now? Grandpa is still sleeping, and Grandma says she isn't interested in super heroes. She says they are reactionary. Mommy, what's reactionary?"

"Well, Kevin, it's a little early in the morning for me to explain what Grandma means by reactionary. I'll explain it to you sometime when you're a little older."

"I love you, Mommy. Mommy, did you know that Spiderman is radioactive? Grandpa said he was going to drop me off at two o'clock, after lunch. Grandma wants to talk to you. Hold on a minute."

Kate heard her mother and Kevin exchange rustling early morning dialogue.

"No, Grandma . . ."

"Kevin! Do as you are told, and don't wake your grandfather."

"Yes, Grandma. Can I eat my bacon and butter sandwich in the TV room?"

"Good morning, dear . . . Yes, Kevin, you may . . . How did your show go last night?"

"Good morning, Mom. From all I could tell, it was a screaming success." Kate rolled over on her side, propped her head in her hand, and got comfortable for the long conversation she knew she would have with her mother.

"Well, dear, if it was such a screaming success, as you put it, why do you sound so depressed?" Nora Gallagher's warmth and love for her daughter flowed over Kate.

Kate paused and then answered in a quiet, controlled voice. "I don't know, Mom, I guess it's the calm after the storm."

Depressed and drained even after her conversation with her mother and her son, Kate sank back into the pillows and into her thoughts.

"Memories, memories. So many painful memories. Begone, pain, I banish you." Kate smiled to herself. "If only it could be that easy."

She stretched and shuddered. She stared at the

23

sunlight playing off the raindrops dripping from the new spring leaves and let her mind drift. The small birds outside her doors made gossipy sounds while huge crows flew overhead. The sun rose higher, drying her back patio, raising a steamy cloud, conjuring up memories of Felipe.

At first she couldn't recall his face, and then the coarse, curly blond hair and the smiling blue eyes came into focus, and she remembered. She remembered the first years they had been married and the house at the beach—rolling themselves up in a quilt and snuggling deep into a bowl in a high sand dune, lying there warm and safe as angry Atlantic winds howled over and past them. Kate always believed that was when she had conceived Kevin.

They had fallen asleep like two burrowing animals, and when they awoke they were covered with a fine layer of the purest white sand.

Kate rolled over onto her stomach, tears welling in her already stinging eyes. She punched her pillows up and buried her face deep into them, trying to force her mind to think of other things. But the memories crept out of their dark corners and forced themselves on her. Light little scenarios of their crazy ground-floor apartment on the Upper West Side of Manhattan, of Glasses, Indiana and Wilbur, the resident black street philosophers helping her work the nearly dead soil of her garden, heavily pregnant while Felipe carefully planted her precious hybrid tea roses. Oh, her roses—Sterling Silver, Fragrant Cloud, Garden Party, Angel Face, Crimson Glory—and her beautiful baby boy, pink and budlike in the garden, surrounded by their fragrance and his parents' love. Felipe's eyes filling with tender tears as he held Kevin high up in his arms, close to his lips, whispering promises to his beloved son that he was never to keep.

Kate rolled over onto her back again as the scenes from the past began to degenerate and grow shorter, full of ugliness and shouting and pain.

Careening out of control, her thoughts rushed toward the crash as tears slid painfully down the sides of her head into her ears.

Kevin was still a baby then, safely asleep in his room. Muffled traffic noises and a ticking clock were the only sounds that broke the near perfect stillness.

The sound of a car's brakes squealing on the road outside her house reminded her of the sounds of New York City and of Felipe's tortured scream shattering the stillness, followed by a sobbing moan.

"Kate, Kate, you've got to help me get to sleep."

Felipe Zandt was having a manic breakdown.

He had kept Kate up for nearly two days, and she was nearly crazy herself. He had been awake for six days. She called her mother and begged her to come and take Kevin. She explained that Felipe was having a problem that she was trying to help him work out and that it would be better if the baby wasn't there.

Her mother agreed to come, and asked her in a very worried voice if there was anything she could do.

"Just this . . . and thank you, Mom."

Felipe was pacing the apartment when Kate's mother arrived, and he didn't even look up when Kevin was taken to the door and handed to his grandmother.

Kate's mother pleaded with her to come too, but

Kate refused. "I'm Felipe's wife, and I have to stay here with him and help him in any way I can. I'll call you, Mom."

Shutting the door quietly, Kate edged her way past Felipe, who seemed oblivious to everyone and everything around him. She sat down in a living-room chair and tried to sneak in some sleep.

Felipe came in and woke her up, screaming, "I told you not to go to sleep!"

He was on his knees in front of her, and he grabbed her face in his hands and was shaking her head violently. He kept screaming, screaming at her, and Kate begged him to let her go back to sleep, just for a little while.

He had been awake six days, and he was getting crazier . . . and violent. He slapped her a few times, and Kate really woke up and, sobbing, begged him to leave her alone.

He snarled at her and said, "Come here, you fat tub of lard. I'm going to give it to you like you've never had it before."

He wrestled her out of the chair, pulling her to the floor, then rolled her over onto her stomach and pulled her exhausted body back onto his, brutally piercing her as he tore into her rectum.

The scream she screamed that morning and the rage she felt were the last things she allowed her mind to experience of that nightmare time before she shifted to the final memory.

The time of Felipe's death.

She was in her house. She and Felipe were divorced then. The telephone rang, and it was a Sergeant Clarke from the Elmira, New York, state police substation. He told her in a very grave and awkward voice that her husband had been injured in a hang-gliding accident.

She asked him to tell her how seriously Felipe was hurt, but he refused, saying that he would meet her at St. Lucy's Hospital in Elmira.

When she arrived at the hospital, she was escorted to Felipe's bed in the intensive care unit.

She was shocked and horrified by what she saw. The people around her shook their heads and talked about all the nuts who have been critically injured and killed, hang gliding off the cliffs of Elmira.

Felipe was a gruesome sight, his face horribly distorted and bruised. It was obvious that it was very painful for him to breathe. He tried to smile at Kate when he saw her, but the effort only distorted his face even more. As she sat down beside him, Kate breathed a silent thanks that she couldn't see his broken body covered by the sheet.

He directed a labored whisper up at her, and she bent down to hear what he was saying.

"I'm sorry, Kate . . . I've been lying here thinking . . . and I'm sorry for everything we lost, that went bad between us. I love you.

"Please tell my little boy that I loved him. Please tell him that I have always loved him. All those times when I didn't show up, they were because I couldn't bear bringing him back to you, and home, and not being a part of it. That I had to leave and go away . . ."

Kate saw the tears form in Felipe's pain-racked eyes, and she broke down, sobbing, "Felipe, Felipe, please don't die.

"Please try to live. If not for me or just for yourself, please fight for Kevin's sake. Felipe, fight for Kevin's sake. If you die . . . he won't understand. He needs you too much. You can't leave us alone."

Felipe was whispering again. And again she bent down to hear what he was trying to say.

"Please kiss me, Kate." He smiled his broken smile. "Please kiss me one more time and be my Kate."

With tears blinding her, cries tearing at her chest trying to come out, Kate brought her lips gently to his battered ones. And while their lips clung together for the last time, she could feel the breath of his life leave his body and enter her lungs.

Felipe did not breathe in again, and pandemonium broke out in the intensive care unit. Someone pushed Kate roughly aside, and she stumbled away, not wanting to look at the scene behind her. People pounding on him, shouting and giving orders, sticking gigantic needles into his chest, straight to his heart and into his then dead body.

Kate leapt from her bed and shook herself fully awake.

I cannot bear this anymore, I simply can't, she thought to herself. *Maybe a shower and some hard back-breaking work in the garden will help.*

She padded to the bathroom and onto the cold marble floor and shivered as she made her way to the mirror.

With a groan, she turned away from her pain-ravaged image, flipped on a torrent of hot rushing water in the shower, and stood under it until she felt all the muscles in her body relax and the lids of her eyes smooth over.

Her mind was mercifully blank.

Deodorant and baby powder, cutoffs, and a top all in

place, Kate slipped on a pair of comfortable sandals and headed outdoors into the sun. Her wet auburn hair gleamed as she bent over the tall purple and white Dutch iris, sunny yellow daffodils, and brilliant red fire-spray tulips that swayed in the breeze like silent bells, trying to attract her attention as she weeded the garden bed.

The rich odor of the earth beneath her hands rose up as she worked it, digging deep, turning its sleeping winter chill to the warm spring sun. She moved on from the stalwart iris to the daffodils and tulips fairly dancing for her notice. The fragrance of warmed lilacs wafted by her in the quiet.

She looked up.

A huge black crow had flapped down in front of her and was silently observing her at work. His hard agate eyes never blinked, and Kate was possessed by an unreasonable fear. A sharp, mean beak surrounded by blue-black feathers stabbed at the ground for grubs and worms.

"All I need now is a little blood, red as my lover's lips, and snow, white as my lover's flesh, to be a full-blown Deirdre of the Sorrows," Kate thought ruefully. "And the black of my lover's hair, only my lover is plain old Tom Flynn, not Oisin, and if eye-cast were still a popular legal covenant among the Irish he would be here now.

"My, my, ain't we waxin' literary this morning," Kate chided herself and went back to her work.

After about an hour she had finished. She stood up and brushed the soil on her hands off onto her old cutoffs. A profusion of flowers, whites and purples, yellows and reds, all skirted with green lawn, stood in their bed for her to admire. She went into the house and made herself a toasted cheese sandwich. Moving to the library, she turned on the TV and looked for a juicy old gangster movie.

Unfortunately, *Back Street* was on, and as she watched it she started thinking again.

Years ago she had been alone with Kevin on a dark, stormy night. Lightning ripped across the night sky, frightening her. The wind was making a hissing sound as it blew through the pine branches. The cellar door was open, and she was too afraid to go downstairs and shut it. She decided to wait until morning and the sunlight. The neighbor's dog was barking, and she could hear the sounds of car doors closing and voices, and in the far distance the cars on the parkway.

But that night she had felt he was there with her, erasing the everyday fear of being alone in a storm.

So she went down to the cellar and shut and locked the door, then checked on Kevin asleep in his bed, and went to hers.

It was the only time she could remember that the love she had for Flynn was not the abusing, tearing emotion her heart was so used to. That night she was content with it. It was warm and comforting. She went to her bed and her dreams, imagining herself in his arms again, and slept deeply.

The telephone rang and pulled her into reality again.

"Coming . . . I'm coming," she shouted to the empty house.

"Hello, it's me. I heard the show went very well last night . . ."

It was her friend, sometime date, and constant

admirer, Bob Scanlon, the managing editor of the local newspaper.

"I'm serious, Kate. The show was a great success, and I'm not the only newspaper that leveled some critical acclaim at you." He continued, laughing.

"It seems you didn't catch me among all the monied dignitaries clustered around you."

"Really, Bob," Kate teased back, "wasn't I the one who told you where the men's room was? You small-town newspaper guys simply have to be better informed."

"Enough, enough, I surrender . . ." and he continued by asking her out to dinner.

Kate turned him down pleading work, and he countered by warning her that even though he was a persistent man, four years of this was getting him down.

And before she had a chance to think of a friendly retort, he strong-armed her into covering a local Irish-American festival of the arts.

Kate hesitated. The image of Flynn overwhelmed her as Bob talked on. Taking advantage of her hesitation, he thanked-her-very-much for agreeing to do it.

"I'll even run a little box. Famous local photographer remembers her roots and covers not-so-famous local festival."

Kate cradled the telephone gently, then shook her head at her reaction, and said to herself, "No, Kate, he won't be there. It would be a million-to-one shot if he were."

{ Chapter 3 }

"'You're right, Mrs. Beaver,' said her husband, 'we must get away from here. There's not a moment to lose.'" Kate put the marker in the book she was reading to Kevin and closed it.

"Please, Mommy, just one more chapter . . . please!"

"No way José. That's not our deal. A chapter a night until we have read all the way through the *Chronicles of Narnia*. It's way past your bedtime, and we have a very busy day ahead of us tomorrow."

Kate stood up and tucked the blanket under the mattress. Bending over, she kissed Kevin under his ear lobe, whispering, "I love you very much."

Kevin sleepily mumbled back at his mother.

"I wish I had a lion like Aslan, Mom . . . A lion like Aslan and my daddy."

FLYNN'S LOVER

Kevin's one long-lost love was his daddy, and whenever he reminded her that he still loved and remembered him, Kate felt the pain of her son's loss. She wondered if her love would ever be enough. She wondered if there was anything she could do to help him.

Saddened, she left his room and in the dark made her way to the kitchen. She mixed herself a very stiff gin and tonic, wandered into the study, and flipped on the stereo.

Debussy rushed in on the quiet space and over Kate lounging on the couch. The music paused and pulled her thoughts in a direction she would have preferred to avoid.

A time she had felt she had shamed herself. A time she had tried to find Flynn. A walking-around-in-the-world regular woman trying to track down a cop on duty.

Ridiculous.

She had found out a lot about cops, but she had never found him.

She had found out where he worked, where he had an occasional beer after work, even where he parked his car, but she had never put herself in the right place at the right time to find him.

That was the first year.

Full of small elations as she found out more and more about him, she hoarded the bits and pieces, and it made her feel as if she was moving closer and closer to him. She was sure that one day, she would be in the right place at the right time and they would meet and he would, once again, love her.

That was the first year.

The second year of her search began when she realized she had learned all she could without actually being with him again. She came to understand how protective the New York Police Department was of their own.

She had never learned where or how he lived.

The second year was the worst. On the advice and urgings of her friends and family, she started dating.

She dated three men from her background and three cops. The men from her background just to appease her worried family, the cops to find out what it was like to be a cop . . . and maybe, just maybe, they would lead her to Flynn.

It was at the end of the second year that she told her brother, Brian, the story and begged him to help her find Flynn. She had begged, and he had refused. That was when she had stopped talking to Brian for a year and began begging her friends to help her.

The third year was better. She became more immersed in her work, and Kevin had grown into a little thinking, questioning person. She tried to let go of her terrible hurt.

She also stopped dating the three men from her background because one of them had fallen in love with her. Confused and ashamed of herself, she realized she had used him as a diversion and he was really in love with her. She felt she had done a terrible thing. So she let her family go unappeased and stopped dating the three cops too.

Then God came roaring in out of left field and let her have it.

It was at the end of the third year. Kate was in Central Park, busy and happy and photographing an outdoor concert for a New York magazine. She took hundreds of pictures of people dreaming to music under the stars and moonlight on that very beautiful summer night.

She started developing what she had shot the very next day. On the evening of the second day, she came to the rolls she had done of faces with a telephoto lens . . . and his face was one she had shot.

She had caught his image, his face at rest, really listening to the music. A small smile played on his lips as he leaned back against a patrol car, his hat pushed back, dreaming with his eyes closed.

He was part of the crowd on the other side of the field. Her camera had seen him, but her eyes hadn't.

The night was in the past, but his face smiled softly back up at her.

She left her darkroom in hysterics.

After that day she poured herself into her work and her son and tried harder to forget him. She stopped walking in the neighborhood he patrolled, stopped trying to place herself in his path. She tried to stop talking to her friends about him, stopped trying to find him.

Josie and Eileen, her two closest friends, worried. They formed a private pact, agreeing they would both, from time to time, get her to talk about her feelings and try to help her deal with them.

She started seeing a psychiatrist, to help her with both her love for Flynn and her terrible hurt over her divorce and Felipe's death. Kevin was growing up, and his questions and probings were getting more pointed.

There were times when she almost forgot, when she

would experience herself as a young, vital woman, alive and attractive.

High, wide, and absolutely gorgeous, she would get into a dancing, prancing, and partying mood, feeling her sexuality and loving the attention and desire, and sometimes love, that men offered her.

Then the crucible.

The man of the hour, of the moment, would want her, and her soul would stop and turn, and Flynn would come flooding back in, stronger than ever. She would go home alone and suffer through the cruel sleepless night, as the anguish slowly released its grip on her heart. She would sleep, and the morning would always come too soon.

She made it through those terrible times with the help of Josie and Eileen, the joy and love that her son filled her with, and the quiet, never wavering support of her family.

Sometimes she even got angry with herself. She would question everything through again, demanding an answer from her heart and her mind that never came.

It was during one such phase that her family made an effort to exorcise Flynn.

All the Gallaghers had packed up and gone to the family compound on Greene Point, Lake Ontario.

Three hundred miles from New York, Lake Ontario lay placidly like a crystal-clear glass, huge table rocks scattered carelessly in its depths, silent testimony to the glaciers that had rumbled over North America before the dawn of man. Lake Ontario was like an ocean with breakers you could surf on, and on stormy days, mean and gray, with an undertow that could kill.

Sam Feeny was the son of one of her father's old political cronies. He was a widower with a daughter named Maeve, and naturally a lawyer. Everyone thought it a perfect match. Sam was tall, husky, and hairy. A blond man of wit, intellect, honor, and the proper family background. Her mother and father held their breath.

Her entire family adored him, especially Kevin.

Maeve was a sparkling little pixie. She had been alone with her very masculine father for a very long time. She took one look at the Gallagher women, nestled down right in the middle of their warmth and femininity, and proclaimed it home. In one week she went from sandals, shorts, and a tee-shirt to ruffles, Mary Janes, and a frilly bathing suit. And during that week she decided Kate, not Kate's sister Deirdre, was going to be her mommy.

For a while Kate thought it might work.

Sam the Man, Kevin called him. Sam the Man invented the Zantelumpus Sea Monster for the delight of the children and her. Kevin laughed and really smiled for the first time since his daddy had died. He rode on Sam's shoulders and hung on his every word. He adored him.

Kate's "mother's heart" ached with joy at the sight of her son's happiness, and she warmed to Sam the Man Feeny.

The shadow of Felipe's death seemed to lift from Kevin, and Flynn's dark presence receded from her mind. The shadows under Kate's eyes faded, replaced by a healthier, tanned, smiling face. She swam and ran, her body became thinner and supple, her voice hinted laughter and high spirits.

Sam the Man would look at her with his calm, warm brown eyes, crinkled at the corners from years of driving to and from work into the sun, and wonder if he could make this lady love him.

He tried, and she did come to love him, with a grateful mother's love, a sisterly love. But Sam wanted what Flynn had, what she couldn't give to him.

The Judge, Brian, and Sam had driven to and from New York countless times at the beginning of their stay at the lake. Early on in August they declared a moratorium on work and stayed and vacationed. After endless sailing trips, barbecues, and small friendly parties with other families along the beach, the whole thing came to a head between Kate and Sam.

They had gone for a walk on the beach. The water was a dark, inky calm, reflecting a blood-red sunset. It became a mysterious, unknown, dangerous body of water to Kate.

She shivered, Sam gave her his sweater and his arm, and they continued their walk in companionable silence.

Kate's imagination waxed macabre, and as the moon rose and stars sprinkled themselves across the vaulted deep-blue sky, she imagined sly Chagall sea creatures swimming just below the surface of the lake. Lying there in wait with huge saber teeth for an unwary swimmer.

She shuddered, and Sam stopped.

"Do you want to go back to the house?" He tried to read her face in the darkness. "Are you really cold?"

"No, Sam," Kate responded in a vague tone. "I'm just having the most incredible morbid thoughts. Chagall sea monsters waiting in the water to eat me up . . . even this beautiful night sky . . ."—Kate gestured with a sweep of her arm—"seems threatening."

"Maybe," she added in a forced laugh, "I shouldn't have eaten so many raw mushrooms."

They continued their walk down the beach. The sound of music floated across the water. They could hear the door of Bennett's Bar and Hotel open and close, then the sounds of cars starting and the roar of a motorboat as the DeNoto kids water-skied in the dark with torches.

They stopped and sat on a low dune and watched the lights on the boats in the distance. It became very quiet, with only the sounds of crickets intruding.

Sam put his arms around her and lay back, holding her to him. Kate knew even before they had started their walk that he was going to try. She had decided to let him.

Let him? It was more like letting herself. She needed to know if she could be with another man, and Sam was the man she was going to try to be with.

She knew she cared a great deal for him, that if any man could replace Flynn it would be Sam.

He started by kissing her gently on her lips, then her neck. He brought her hands to his mouth and kissed the fingertips and her open palm.

Kate forced herself to relax in his arms.

He began to whisper her name hoarsely, telling her how sweet she was, how beautiful, how beguiling. Then she felt his body change when he started to tell her how desirable she was, and his lips moved down her neck to her breasts.

Her throat tightened. She breathed deeply, trying to relax. His hand moved up her leg slowly. He gently stroked her thigh, but Kate only felt a rising tide of panic.

No, no, she thought to herself, *this isn't working.*

She was too aware of everything around her in the night, of Sam's blond head bent over her now open body. It was as if she was floating above herself, observing the whole scene and not feeling anything.

Sam began to touch her roughly, and when she brought her hands back to push him away, he caught her right hand and drew it down to his naked erection. He was going to devour her, and Kate froze in panic and disgust.

He forced her onto her back and, ripping her underpants off, pushed her skirt up around her waist and tried to enter her.

She was as dry as the sand they were lying on, and he got angry. Kate began to fight him, moaning, "No, Sam, no."

Suddenly her very cold voice reached him.

"The Judge doesn't like men who rape his daughters, Sam." And she breathed a thanksgiving to her powerful father when Sam pulled back from her.

Maeve and her father left the following morning. The whole family bade him a confused and worried goodbye.

Kate stayed in her room, her feelings alternating between grief, guilt, and rage.

She knew Sam really loved her and that she had been driving him nuts.

And now she knew she still loved Flynn, that no other man could touch her, love her, or bring her to a point where she forgot all else except him. It was a memory that both caressed and taunted her, and it wouldn't go away.

The ice in her glass had melted when Kate reached for it. The record clicked dully on the turntable. She heaved herself up from the couch and headed for the darkroom. She wanted to finish her work before the family came over for dinner tomorrow night. She decided on a sirloin roast, white and sweet potatoes, salad, and green beans with almonds, onions, and mushrooms. Everything her father liked, and maybe if there was enough time she'd make a trifle—he loved trifle.

She conjured up the image of her father as she walked down the hall to her darkroom.

It always warmed her and made her smile.

"Cat the brat" he would call her and kiss her on the forehead, hug her, love and approval beaming down on her from his eyes.

He had been like a rock for her when Felipe had died, and when Sam told him what had happened that night on the beach he was angry but understanding. He talked to Kate about the incident, helping her release her anger and guilt. She and Sam were even able to be friends.

Unfortunately, he was not there for her when she needed to talk about Flynn. It probably would have helped, but her hurt was so deep, so thorough, that it made him feel helpless and enraged him. The Judge was a father who loved his children, and Flynn was the man who had hurt his "Cat" so deeply that even he, with all his love, couldn't ease her pain.

He hated the man passionately.

{ Chapter 4 }

Kate finished enlarging the photographs of Deirdre she had taken at the parade. She had been promising to do it for months. She would give them to her sister tomorrow at dinner.

The last image came clear in the developer, and Kate picked it up with the tongs and put it in the fix. There was her sister's face, awash with tears, her right arm raised in salute as the controversial grand marshal strode by.

Behind her head was a sea of shoulders covered with buttons.

"Bobby Sands, Free at Last," "England Get Out of Ireland," "End the Death Camps in Northern Ireland," and above her head the banner her group had made, "Saint Patrick Drove the Snakes Out of Ireland, Michael Drove Them Out of the Parade."

Deirdre would love it.

The wording in the banner had been her idea, and as her group marched up Fifth Avenue the crowds had cheered even louder when they caught sight of it.

Her sister was the firebrand in the family. Kate was the romantic. Their gran had spent hours telling them both tales from the Tain. Kate absorbed the romance and the tragic strain, Deirdre the politics and the seemingly infinite tragedy of a divided Ireland.

She rinsed the print and put it in the dryer. She would frame it tomorrow.

Stretching and yawning, Kate made her way to Kevin's room. He was curled up in a ball, sound asleep. She decided to soothe herself to dreamland and went into the family room, stacked four Chieftains records on top of each other, and turned the stereo on in her room only.

"I'll dream a dream of the mighty Ard Rì, Brian Boroihme at the battle of Clontarf as he drove the Danes into the sea. I'll dream myself into his golden arms as he carries me through the salty mist to Tara."

Kate smiled to herself as she made her way down the hallway to her bedroom.

"Or perhaps the Owen Rua will carry me off to the wild wild West and make passionate, red-haired love to me."

Kate laughed out loud and, just then, "Dònall Òg," a slow Connemara air, came on, and Kate reminded herself of the story.

The song expressed, in music, one of the most beautiful poems in the Gaelic language. The poem, a part of Irish culture, tenderly, simply, and sincerely expressed the feelings of the girl Dònall wronged. To her, he was everything that is beautiful:

He was the most handsome to be seen at the fair;
his skin was whiter than the limewashed walls of
a castle, his eyes were like the dew drops in
April and his breath had the fragrance of fresh
apples—he was blest because he had died young,
before he humiliated himself to marriage.

Kate resisted a surge of melancholy and drifted off to sleep as "Brian Boru's March" ended.
And then the dream came.

"I am the crazy old woman who lives on the strand in a tumble-down cottage in Mayo. I am assaulted by the winds from the wild westerly sea.

"I went from a deep laughing woman, tall and red-headed, to this silent old hag with a mouth set in a bitter line, bent and gray, but I still wait for you.

"Years ago when the straw boys came to torment me in this cottage, I tried to eat peat and burn out my eyes, but the universe filled my loins with remembering you, and filled my head with visions of you . . . and I stopped.

"I have rubbed ashes in my hair to no avail. The howling winds and the promise of my lover blow the ashes out of my hair.

"In the deep dark silence of winter, there is always one golden light burning in the window and one fire, bright orange and yellow, hot in the stones waiting for a lost love of decades.

"I would have you come in and shake the snow from your shoulders, sending drops hissing into the flames. You would be young and dark and frowning, and I old and bent from waiting for you. You would mumble inanities and finally touch my papery wrinkled cheek and transform me into a young woman again, vibrant and alive and in love.

"Oh, so in love with you.

"I would ask this of you so we could live what should have been lived at length with graciousness over slow moving time, erasing our fear and loneliness. I have waited for you through eternity, and I despair of finishing with you in this lifetime.

"I am tired. You are a stubborn old man. Could you not hobble into my tumble-down cottage and cackle out your love for me so I can go to my eternity, and you to yours?

"Your beautiful black hair is shot with iron gray, and I look at you now a cranky old woman, and in the frigid steel of my loins I feel a warmth. You move in on me in my sleep. In on a wave of heat from the fire that slices the cold around me, making my eyes watery and tired, and then I see you. Your face above me, below me, around me, pleading with no clues.

"I cry out to you. Where are you, to live the loving and the children and the growth and the building and the immense grace of age? And finally where are you to hold my hand at death with your love obliterating my fear?

"Where are your old eyes? Seen by any other I am ancient. But only your young eyes saw me at the moment of first love.

"We were the man and the woman, meant to be seeing each other through all our human times. My young girl's face laughing in exult when I knew you loved me, overlaid with my woman's face in ecstasy at your touch, overlaid with my face in pain and fear at childbirth, overlaid with the gracious loving care I would have had for you.

"Where are your eyes? Where are your old eyes to see my beauty?

"My eyes, my eyes would have seen you young and shy and awkward and nervous, then ecstatic when you realized how I loved you, then struck with ecstasy, then your face wrinkled with tender disbelief at our childbirths. I would have seen your face, a man content and in love and in great satisfaction and comfort.

"Thousands of sparks fly up as I bend and stir the fire, searching there for a vision.

"They say I am an old woman who dreams her dreams of a young lover and waits as she had waited through eternity for him to reach out and touch her once more before death.

"Take care, take care, you cannot cheat your destiny too many times; you have cheated mine, overly much."

Flynn could not bear the stench of his wife's clothes in the closet next to his, so he moved his possessions into the closet in the spare bedroom. After a time the uneasy odor of her body became too much for him too, and he moved himself into the spare bedroom, and after a time it became his room.

It was a smaller room. The double bed he slept on had an uncomfortable wooden headboard. When he stayed up late, reading, it gave him a crick in his neck. The nicked metal gooseneck lamp he had found in a West Side junk shop spread even yellow light over the endless pages of the books and magazines he read. He and his room held all the discarded furniture and memories of the beginning of his marriage to Joan.

Now in his bitterness memories crouched in dusty corners waiting to hurt him in the darkness. The long scratch in the dresser top at the foot of his bed was made years ago. The rookie cop and husband had shot a man, wounded him. He had been crying and feeling ill.

He had picked up Joan's nail file and gouged the wood of the dresser top with it. He hadn't intended to let himself go. It just happened. When he looked up he saw Joan's frightened face in reflection.

The rookie husband stopped his feelings and his tears and decided that he was being unmanly. He tried to explain what had happened and how it made him feel. Joan had listened quietly, her face impassive, completely without expression.

When he finished, relieved at being able to unburden himself to his understanding wife, she responded, "Tom, it's your *job!* I'm sure you did the right thing. If you shot a man I'm sure he deserved it."

Then, sure she had said the right thing, she kissed him lightly, said, "Not tonight, dear," turned an indifferent back to his dilemma, and promptly went to sleep.

The first scar.

She had never understood, and after a time Flynn, not knowing how to explain himself to her, buried everything deep inside.

Until Kate, when it all came out.

He slept chastely and cleanly and dreamed of Kate. Of a tall, beautiful redhead with a deep, laughing voice.

He was free to dream his hopeless dreams.

He played his pipes until his family begged him to stop and eat dinner, do anything, to keep him from playing the endless laments he unconsciously breathed.

He recently began to think about catching a bullet with his body. He dreamed about the bullet exploding from a junkie's gun, entering his body cleanly, then tearing out his back with his heart on its point. He was sure that the junkie who would kill him had more freedom of feelings than he knew existed.

He dreamed of how sad everyone would be, and of how his wife would weep for the cameras on the six o'clock news on the steps of their church. He saw his sons stolid and his daughters vacant and frightened; then he saw his littlest daughter, Maureen, weeping and alone.

How sad Kate would feel.

He had always known how she had tried to track him down. He was disappointed when either her courage or fate had failed to put them both into an irreversible situation. She had almost managed it once. But that was two years ago, early in November.

Flynn leaned back and stared at the cracked white paint on the ceiling and let his mind reel back.

His friend Jack Kelly had started a small contracting outfit. He was trying to set himself up with a small business he could move into when he retired. Two other cops, Herb Schaeffer, whom Tom knew, and Bob Hannigan, whom he didn't know, were Kelly's partners. All three of them had had different shifts, jobs, and talents.

Herb was the first of the three to retire. He handled the masonry work and hired on extra people when they were needed to finish a job. Mostly cops. Cops always needed the extra money.

Flynn's father had been a cop and did side jobs as a mason, and as a boy Tom had gone out with him from time to time. It wasn't the first time Herb had asked him for some help on a job.

Herb called and explained that they were really up against it. This woman, he said, was putting an extension on her house, a library. The excavation was finished, but Herb's assistant had injured his hand. Herb continued outlining the job, mentioning that they had managed to put up one wall before the accident.

"Look, Tom, I know how you feel about your three-day layovers, but I'm desperate. The job will pay you four hundred bucks, and with the weather getting cold fast I don't want to get stuck mixing concrete with antifreeze to put up the rest of the block. Jack's ready to frame and close up the addition, so the foundation's got to get done, and fast."

He had taken the job. After all, four hundred tax-free dollars was good pay for two, maybe three days' work.

Herb picked him up at 7:30 A.M. It was a gray cold morning, and neither of them was really ready to start the job. So they stopped for coffee and eggs on a hard roll. They bullshitted about the department for a while. Tom filled Herb in on the news. Once a cop always a cop. Tom remembered feeling sorry for Herb that morning. It was passing him by. Herb still thought and felt like a cop, but he wasn't anymore.

They paid up and left.

He hadn't been paying too much attention to where they were going. Herb was driving the van, and Tom was just beginning to get drowsy again.

"Wait till you get a look at this woman, has she got a body . . ." Herb was just beginning to warm to the subject when Tom realized that they had pulled up in front of Kate's house. He didn't hear the rest of Herb's description because the blood rushing through his veins roared through his ears. His heart felt like it had been hit by a freight train.

He started to sputter something to Herb when the front door opened and a trim, medium-sized woman walked through it toward them. She was wearing a simple wool dress, her red hair was shot through with gray, and her eyes were calm behind designer glasses.

Herb eased himself out of the van.

"Good morning. You must be Herb Schaeffer. My daughter asked me to meet you here this morning." She reached out and shook Herb's hand. "I'm Nora Gallagher, Kate's mother."

"Pleased to meet you, Mrs. Gallagher." Herb was all smiles and charm. "And that not-so-ready-for-work man in the van is Tom Flynn."

"Well, I can hardly blame you, on a cold morning like this." Nora Gallagher smiled back at Herb.

"Why don't you both come into the house. Kate made a fresh pot of coffee just before she left this morning. So come on in and have some." She turned and reentered the house ahead of them.

Flynn eased himself out of the van onto shaky legs and caught up to Herb at the door.

Herb turned to him and asked him in a low voice what was wrong.

"You look a little green around the gills. You feeling all right?"

Tom nodded, not trusting his voice to come out normally.

Mrs. Gallagher was in the kitchen pouring steaming hot coffee, thick and rich, into oversized earthenware mugs.

Herb followed the sound of her voice.

Flynn knew the way.

Memories of that weekend washed over him. The house was warm and comfortable. He noted that Kate had done a considerable amount of work. The silence was depressing.

"My daughter, she's a photographer, had an unexpected stroke of luck. A friend of hers, also a photographer, overbooked himself for a commercial and called Kate into town to help him." Mrs. Gallagher moved to the refrigerator and took out some half-and-half.

"She asked me to tell you, Mr. Schaeffer—may I call you Herb? good—that she plans on being home by five, but if she doesn't make it, may she call you at home later?"

"Of course," Herb answered, nodding and sipping his coffee.

Tom was still trying to reconcile his emotions when Mrs. Gallagher handed him a mug of coffee.

"Mr. Flynn, the sugar's in that pot, the one with the man holding his nose. Kate's very antisugar. She calls it refined white poison but keeps it for guests."

She started to turn away from him and stopped herself.

"I hope you don't think I'm being rude, but, Mr. Flynn, are you with the police too?"

Flynn looked up from the safety of his coffee cup at her and answered.

"Yes, ma'am, I am."

Her eyes held his and for an agonizing moment Tom thought she knew.

"Well then," she chuckled, "I suppose it's safe to leave two of New York's finest here alone. Oh, by the way, Herb, my husband, Judge Gallagher, would like you to call him. He, that is, we, have been contemplating some changes on our house . . ."

Flynn tuned their conversation out, absorbing the silence of the house. He sipped his coffee, remembering the sound of her voice, trying to conjure up her image as she stood at the stove with a spatula in her hand, making eggs benedict and talking. Trying to avoid the memory of the look in her eyes when he had pulled her to him in a frenzy of lust.

His eyes swept past the sink, then back again. There was a single mug, half filled with coffee, a lipstick mark on the rim. Suddenly the memory of her mouth under his, full, soft, and pliant, her tongue darting . . .

He looked away as pain and desire stabbed him, into Nora Gallagher's eyes.

She knew. Something in him clicked.

"Well, gentlemen, I have a few chores to do for Kate before I leave, and I expect I have delayed you overmuch." Nora Gallagher knew how to take her leave graciously.

"Right." Herb put his mug into the sink, and Flynn followed suit. His fingers ached to touch where her lips had touched, but he didn't. Such a little thing to not do, but if he had touched the mug, he would have stayed to touch the lips, and the eyes and the body and the heart of the woman whose house he moved in that morning like a grief-crazed man. He had needed that four hundred dollars. Seamus had broken his arm three months earlier, and Maureen's dentist bills were big and they were dunning him.

What did it take to make a man blow his entire world apart for the love festering in his heart?

Flynn rolled over in his bed. The pain hadn't been

that horrible yet. He had his duty to do, both at home and on the job. He had plenty to occupy his mind then. Then . . .

He and Joan had planned to go to Florida with his partner, Tim, and Tim's wife, Margey. Joan didn't let up about Margey when they were alone, but she was all saccharin smiles and personality when they were with them. Besides, Flynn knew that Joan wouldn't blow a trip to Florida in their oversized motor home just because she thought Margey was "a bit of a free-thinking slob." Translation: Tim and Margey had a good sex life.

The cracks on the ceiling began to take on grotesque shapes as he remembered that nightmare trip. Joan had one too many pink squirrels one night and in acid, biting tones told Margey just what she thought of her.

Tom and Joan flew home from Orlando. Tom apologized to them over and over again. He knew Tim felt sorry for him, but he was too proud, then, to accept the succor his friend and partner offered.

Then. That was the last time Tom made any attempt to be alone with his wife.

Flynn rolled over again in the bed and let his mind wander back to that cold November morning. He wanted sleep more than he wanted memory, but he knew that it wouldn't come until he let the whole scenario play itself to the painful ending.

Herb had gone out to the van, and Tom went to the back of the house to look at the job.

He saw Nora Gallagher through the French doors that led to the dining room, struggling with what looked like a huge painting.

He made his way through the garden and into the house.

"Mrs. Gallagher, I saw you fighting with that thing. Let me help you." Tom was making his way toward Kate's mother when her eyes stopped him.

She gave him a quizzical, somehow hard look, and in a cold voice said, "No, thank you, I can manage myself, Mr. Flynn."

He turned and started for the door. She struggled with the painting into Kate's room, and from where he was standing he could see her lay it on the floor before she gently slid it under the bed.

Strange.

A while later the sun had come up and the day was warming. They had just finished mixing the first yard of concrete when Nora Gallagher came out and bade them goodbye. She mentioned that there was some cold chicken in the refrigerator in case they got hungry.

Herb thanked her and promised to call the Judge that evening.

Nora Gallagher left, a mass of jangled nerves. How could she prevent her daughter from coming home early? It had to be him.

The first thing she could do was to arrange for Kevin to spend a few days with Grandma and Grandpa. Then what?

June Halloran. *I'll call June, discreet as ever, and promise her anything, if she'll wander down to the studio and invite Kate to stay at her place.*

She raced home, driving in a way that the Judge would certainly be violent about if he had seen her. She ran into her house, huge and comforting, ignored the housekeeper's questions about dinner, and snatched up the telephone.

June answered on the third ring.

"Of course, Nora. As you know, I've always wanted to know the true story behind Irene's disappearance."

"And you will, *after* you have managed to keep my daughter away from her house for the next three days, you have my word on it."

"Why . . ." June started to interrogate Nora, hoping for an even better tidbit.

"No, June," Nora snapped back, "this is a family matter. All you get is the true story about Irene . . . and I promise you'll love it."

As Nora Gallagher hung up the telephone, dripping with relief, Tom Flynn entered Kate's empty house.

He and Herb had finished the retaining wall, and Herb went out for a cold six-pack and sandwiches. The November day had warmed up quite a bit, and they were sweating.

Flynn made his way to the kitchen, the shadowy silence enveloping him like a lover. He opened the cupboard over the dishwasher and found a half-full bottle of Jameson's Irish. And just as unerringly the ice was in the bin in the freezer. He pulled a Waterford crystal tumbler from the cabinet over the island in the kitchen and made himself a very stiff drink.

He moved into the living room and flipped on the stereo. *Boil the Breakfast Early*, the Chieftains' Nine album, swelled from the speakers and flooded the house with music.

He walked through the rooms, inspecting them,

commenting to himself on the work she had done renovating it. He was half smashed when he entered her room and opened her closet doors. He put his wet glass down on the immaculate black lacquer dresser. The musk of her body still clung to her clothes, and it rolled over him like a tidal wave. He buried his face in an embrace of her clothing and tried to conjure up the real woman for his arms.

He had no idea how long he stood there breathing in the scent of her, but coming out of his stupor he remembered the painting Nora Gallagher had so mysteriously slipped under her daughter's bed. He retrieved his drink, downed the last of it, and moved to the bed.

Fears and tears were choking him as he reached under the brocade coverlet and pulled the frame out.

> I only wanted to be with you.
> Your hands in my hands, kneading
> each other's bones.
>
> The longing I saw in your eyes still
> moves within me.
> I feel a breast-tide filling my stranded
> body
> And in the frost cold night I remember
> the heat of our bodies
> and all the see-through words in bits
> under my body
> as you
> moved yours
> over mine.
> I am falling to pieces.

Flynn felt the tears run down his cheeks into his mouth, wiped his agony into his pillow, and rolled over in his bed one more uncomfortable time for the finish of this memory.

The first shock had been the words. She had penned them carefully and framed them. Apparently they had hung under what he found next.

It was a huge five-by-eight-foot photograph. His own dark eyes stared up at him from the center. He was surrounded by the familiar faces of his friends and then by a crowd of strangers. She had taken it of him when he and the others were warming up for "Amazing Grace." He remembered that he had been eyeing her all night. Thinking how he wanted that woman, and as a kind of madness crept over him, he went after her, captured her, and kept her for a time.

He had suspended his life and everything in it for that weekend he loved her.

She had caught him just before he had put away his pipes, before she surrendered herself to him.

He rested his forehead on the edge of the bed; the empty glass dangled in his hand as he rolled his head from side to side, moaning in impotence and grief. All his yesterdays and tomorrows had started to look the same, too many never-will-be's, only harrowing emptiness and grinning death facing him.

He went into her bathroom and threw up, then splashed cold water on his face and neck. He felt the familiar numbness of his life return as he looked at himself in her vanity mirror, hollow eyes staring back at him.

He took the crystal tumbler into the kitchen, washed it three times over, and put it back into the cupboard.

Zombielike, he made his way back to the excavation and started to lay block. He bent to his task. The muscles of his back and neck strained; sweat dripped down from his hairline, ran down his nose, and fell like tears onto the new concrete.

Herb was delighted with the progress he had made when he came back with cold beer and submarine sandwiches.

"Tom, are you sure you don't want to retire early and go into the business with us? Jesus, you work like a demon." He slapped him on the back good-naturedly.

They finished the work in two days. She never appeared at the house. On the end of the second day, Flynn had all but decided to be there when she came home, waiting for her.

Herb flashed a crisp green check at him.

"She always pays on time. It came in the mail this afternoon. I'll pay you right now, Tom." Herb sat down at her kitchen table, pulled out a check, and made it out for him.

It made him feel uneasy. This would pay for Maureen's teeth and the balance on Seamus's broken arm. The fact that it was her money, money she could part with so easily and that he needed so badly, made him feel resentful and ashamed.

On their way out the telephone rang. It hadn't rung before, a fact he didn't remember until many months later. Automatically he picked it up in the hallway.

"Hello."

"Hello, is Kate Zandt there?" a high-pitched, almost squeaky woman's voice asked.

"No, I'm sorry, she's not here."

"Who is this?"

"Oh, I'm one of the workmen putting an extension on the house." He felt himself flush with embarrassment. *One of the stupid working stiffs is right,* he thought to himself.

"Tell her Junie Halloran called, will you?" Flynn fidgeted with a pencil. He couldn't imagine that Kate would know anyone who called herself Junie.

"And tell her that Jimmy-John Luxor thinks she's a smasher, and tell her to call me immediately."

Flynn snapped the pencil in his hand as he would the neck of Jimmy-John Luxor.

"Have you got that? Tell Kate that Lord Luxor . . . well, just tell her to call Junie Halloran."

In a voice cold as death Flynn assured Junie he would and gently replaced the receiver in the cradle.

He turned to the house and in the twilight rasped, "You god-damned snotty Irish-American bitch princess, rot in hell and in the arms of Jimmy-John, his Lordship Luxor, and may you rot in hell from his disease."

The front door of her house shuddered long after he had slammed it shut.

"Get me the fuck home, Herb!"

"I tell you, Josie." Kate had her friend in hysterics. "I swear Englishmen smell funny. They have a musty put-away-in-the-closet smell to them. And a grown man calling himself Jimmy-John . . ." Kate listened and responded laughing. "I suppose you're right, only a Junie Halloran could know a Jimmy-John. Right. I'll call you tomorrow."

Exhausted yet in high spirits, Kate rolled off her bed and planted her aching bare feet on the plush carpet.

She pulled off her beige cashmere sweater, folded it neatly, and, moving to the dresser, patted it into place in the drawer.

It was then that she noticed the ring on the surface. She ran her fingers over it, wondering how it had gotten there.

Flynn was at home, seething in the grip of an unreasonable jealousy, imagining her lying in the arms of some rich English lord named Jimmy-John.

{ Chapter 5 }

"Ah, the meat's perfect, Kate!" her father said beaming at her over the flat edge of his bifocals. He used them for reading and carving perfect roasts.

"That's what a man likes. A woman who can roast beef, brown potatoes to perfection, and make enough turnips to go around. Not like your sister here." Judge Gallagher raised his bushy eyebrows in mock disapproval as he indicated her younger sister, Deirdre.

"She invited us to her apartment in the big city and made us sit on the floor at a table so low that I couldn't even move my knees. Then she serves us dinner from a pot cooking on a dangerous fire on the table."

"The male chauvinist father speaks." Deirdre raised her glass of burgundy to the Judge.

"My Irish father turns up his nose at a mere brush

with international cuisine. I happen to be one of the finest wok cooks I know, and I . . ."

Laughing, Brian Gallagher interrupted her.

"Finest wok cook is right, Dee. Dad, if you're not careful with your choice of words, she may serve you raw fish the next time."

Ignoring her brother's teasing, Deirdre swore to her father that she would never serve him raw fish, not unless he said he was in the mood to try something different. Kevin asked his grandmother for more potatoes, as did Kathy and John, Betsy and Brian's two children.

The Judge peered over his bifocals and asked Deirdre the family heart-stopping question.

"So, Dee, what's new with you?"

"Oh, Dad, did you have to ask so early on in the evening?" Brian teased. "There's always something new, and it's always political."

The kids begged to be excused and raced off down the hall to watch TV in Kevin's room.

"What's your problem, Brian?" Deirdre shot back. "If Irish politics bore you so much, why don't you stop making all that money off the wetbacks trying to stay in this country?"

"Now, Dee." The Judge flashed her and then Brian a stern look of disapproval. "You've both got to keep your tempers in check. If you're serious about politics, Dee, you'd better get used to men like your brother baiting you. If you get angry when they won't listen, then they'll never listen."

Brian frowned at his sister across the table. The wetback crack bothered him. He knew she classified him with the Pinkertons who broke up the coalminers' strike and persecuted the Mollys, and he didn't like it.

Deirdre was rolling the edges of her napkin, and when she looked down at her hands, her dark hair fell over her eyes, hiding the hurt there. Every time she was called on by her political contemporaries to defend her brother for charging illegal Irish aliens trying to stay in America, she didn't know what to say. Had it been her, she wouldn't charge them at all.

She loved her brother, she knew he cared, if only he didn't charge so much.

She cleared her throat and started to speak very softly, choosing her words carefully.

"Brian, Bobby Sands, Francis Hughes, and all the others starved themselves to death to try to raise the consciousness of the world. They thought their deaths would make the world view Ireland and the captive counties in the north as a serious international political situation."

"I know, Dee," Brian interrupted. "It didn't work, did it? By and large the world, and Ireland too, have forgotten their pitiful deaths, deaths that in some corners of the Vatican are looked upon as suicide."

"Brian, please, listen to me." Deirdre was near tears, and the pleading note in her voice shut her brother up.

"Brian, at any time they could have taken water, but they didn't. They were repeatedly offered food and medical help, and they refused."

She was openly crying now, and Nora Gallagher started to rise and go to her, but Betsy stopped her.

"No, Nora, let her finish." Betsy took her restraining

hand from her mother-in-law's arm and looked at her sister-in-law encouragingly.

"There's a civil war going on in the north and a social and cultural revolution in the south. Here in the United States the Irish want to do something, but they don't know who they are in all this, or what to do, or where to donate their immense energy."

"Not to mention their money," her father interjected.

Deirdre looked up to see if her father had spoken sarcastically and was relieved to see he was very serious.

She went on pleading with Brian.

"Look at us, Brian. We're second-generation American Irish in this nice American home, with American TV, lots of food, all the comforts, a far cry from Derry with all the hate and death and bullets and children with hard, silent eyes."

"Hatred is right, Dee," Brian erupted from his side of the table. "Just what you and your kind are peddling. Hatred and violence and death, Dee."

"No, Brian," Deirdre shot back, "you've got it backward. It's the English who are the purveyors of the hatred, the suppliers of the bullets, the instruments of the dying. The argument between Catholic and Protestant is an economic one created by the British to keep Irish Protestants and Catholics apart."

She was warming up, and her voice became stronger.

"Answer me honestly, Brian. Where in the economically advantaged United States do you see the Catholic Irish at war with the Protestant Irish? Well, Brian?"

"You don't, Dee," Brian grumbled. "I know what

you are going to say. Yes, it's true that the British have denied Catholics the right to vote and own property and have good jobs and, yes, even an equal education, but . . ."

"Right, Brian," Deirdre interrupted. "Equal rights. The British have repressed one segment of the Irish population to make them hate the other."

"That's true, Dee," Kate added. "It's an Irish/English conflict regardless of creed. And I agree the only solution is to make the British leave Ireland. They have been dividing the Irish for hundreds of years."

"My sister, the romantic historian, speaks!" Brian quipped.

"Oh, Brian, shut up." Betsy was getting angry with her husband.

"Oh, I'm not allowed to speak now?" Brian retorted.

"Speak, yes," the Judge said. "Bait, no."

"Thank you, Dad," Deirdre said, and Kate continued.

"Most people don't realize that until James Connelly came along, all the greatest Irish freedom fighters were Presbyterians—Protestants, though not members of the Church of England, an implanted franchised population. Parnell, Wolftone, all of them Protestants, until Connelly, because the Presbyterian gentry could read, could organize and meet without fear of arrest. They were not disenfranchised as the Catholics were. They formed the United Irishmen's Association, and that association welcomed Irish Catholic men. They initiated the modern Irish revolution, and that resulted in the then Free State. The Sinn Fein, the Gaelic League, the IRA, etc., all came out of the United Irishmen's Association."

When Kate paused for breath, Deirdre jumped in and continued the argument.

"It's not a religious struggle. Protestants and Catholics started this together as Irish people. It must finish with the same group, together, as Irish people trying to educate anyone who will listen to the truth. So that they can finish as Irish people, not as decimated, destroyed religious factions.

Betsy interrupted. "What about the reverse repression in the Republic, Dee?"

Deirdre smiled at her sister-in-law. Everyone always underestimated Betsy.

Brian turned sideways and looked at his wife, amazed. "What are you talking about, Bets?"

Deirdre and Betsy shared a smile across the table, and Kate added her voice.

"What repression, Betsy?"

"Go on, this one's all yours." Deirdre relinquished the speaker's chair, and Betsy continued.

"Until recently Ireland was a Catholic state, and even now, for instance, a woman can't buy birth control pills there, get a divorce, or get an abortion. Basically the Church imposed its canon law on an Irish state, where not all the people are Catholic. It's changed now."

The Judge interrupted, amazed at his daughter-in-law's statement.

"Betsy, you of all people, I would think, would approve of that."

"No, Judge, I don't believe anyone has the right to

impose their religious beliefs on anyone else. Just because I'm serious about my Catholicism doesn't mean I've got the right to force people to live, or believe in God, the way I do."

She finished, looking directly at Brian. "Nor does that give anyone the right to take away my power to make decisions about the way I live or believe in God."

Brian turned and looked away from Betsy, obviously very disturbed.

The awkward silence at the table was broken by the sound of screaming, kicking, fighting children in Kevin's room.

After Kate and Betsy had stopped the free-for-all, Brian took Kate into the family room for a little chat. Betsy, Deirdre, and Nora had shooed Kate out of the kitchen and washed the dishes.

"Brian." Kate held out her glass for a refill. "What's going on between you and Bets?"

Brian refilled Kate's glass and handed it back to her. He sank into the overstuffed chair across from his sister's reclining figure on the couch. The Judge had elected to entertain the children with some magic tricks. Brian swirled the ice around in his glass, making it clink, stared down into it, and sighed.

"Betsy and I are coming apart." Kate was stunned and silent. Brian stood up abruptly and started pacing. As he talked, he would stop and sip and examine Kate's photographs on the wall.

The story he was telling her was painful and embarrassing, and she sat stock still, afraid to interrupt him. He would stop from time to time, draw a deep shuddering breath, hold back his emotion, and continue.

"I didn't do it to hurt her, Kate, I did it because I

love her so much." He added in a softer voice, speaking to the faces in Kate's photographs on the wall. "Because I want her so much, I want her all the time."

Brian's back was to Kate when she started speaking. "Let me get this straight. Three years ago you told Betsy you were going on a fishing trip with Sam, when in reality you checked into New York Hospital and had a vasectomy. Five months ago, in the throes of passion, you blurted this out to Betsy. You told your very lovely, smart, liberated, and very seriously devout Catholic wife that you had a vasectomy three years ago?"

Brian covered his face with his hands and, in a miserable voice, said, "Yes."

"And naturally, making love without the purpose of procreation became a religious question for Betsy." Kate took a swallow of her drink and set it down on the table in front of her with exaggerated care.

"And may I ask," Kate questioned in her gentlest voice, "when was the last time you made love to your wife, Brian?"

"Over five months ago," he answered miserably.

"Brian, why did you do this? Why? You have enough money and enough love to support truckloads of children." Kate reached over and took her brother's hand. Brian's hand, her big brother's hand that was always there for her, always supportive of her every choice, except Flynn.

She could see he was crying but made no move to console him. She wanted an answer.

"After John was born—you remember, Kate, how difficult that birth was—the doctor said she would be risking her life to have another baby. So I thought about it for two years." Brian stood up and started pacing again. "My God, Kate! I thought about it for two years! Every time I made love to her, every time I folded her into my arms, her face so beautiful and glowing, I thought this could be the night I am killing my beautiful Betsy . . . I couldn't go on, Kate. I . . ."

Kate got up, went to Brian, and hugged him.

"I'll talk to her. I'll try, Brian. I promise, Brian. I know how much you love her."

{ *Chapter 6* }

Kate heard a car pull into the drive, and she hollered to Kevin to see who it was. He came racing back into the house to her studio to tell her that Jim and Josie, Nicky and Pat had arrived.

Kate stopped loading her cameras and went to greet her lifelong friend.

The Ryan family came tumbling out of their Volkswagen bus, talking and making points, Nicky and Pat asking if they could ride this and have that, and Jim and Josie bellowing at both of them at the same time.

Kate always marveled at Josie.

She wasn't a pretty woman by many people's standards. She wore thick-lens glasses, and her short brown hair crowned her amply freckled, plump body. But her light green eyes were the eyes of a friend who always leveled with you. The inner glow caused by her love of her family and friends and Jim Ryan gave her skin a radiance no other woman had.

And Jim Ryan loved Josie.

All through the years she was trying to get pregnant and got depressed instead. Then through the complications after Patrick was born, and when the doctor had said "no more," and the depression after that had happened.

Then Jim's young business had failed, and Josie had pulled him through that. They had pulled together, and from the casual looks they gave each other, it was obvious that they were both still mad for each other.

"Well, are you ready, Kate? The kids are sending me right up the wall, and I'm getting ready to bash them good."

"Well, bad-tempered as usual, I see," Kate chuckled as she kissed her friend hello, then leaned over and gave Jim's whiskery cheek a kiss too.

"Still not shaving on the weekends, Jimmy?" Kate teased.

Standing there in all his plaid bedecked glory, he answered jokingly, "Well, darlin', if I was married to you, I'd shave twice a day if I'd suit you, but with my old lady . . . well, she doesn't even notice me. I'm lucky if I get a little one in now and again."

Josie retorted, laughing, "A little one's right, you sod." She took a swing at his arm when he pinched her.

"Would you two please stop this disgusting display of marital affection. I've got to finish loading my cameras." Laughing, Kate went back into her house.

Kevin went sprinting by with Nicky and Pat thundering down the hall after him, and she could hear Josie calling to her that they would wait in the bus.

All morning Kate had been in a kind of trance. She tried to sleep past five A.M., but she couldn't. She got up then and started her ritual bath for important occasions.

She started out by giving her thick auburn mane a hot oil pack, guaranteed by the manufacturer to make her hair shiny, silky, and soft. Then she sat with the whole mess wrapped in foil and a towel under her hair dryer, removing her old nail polish and repolishing her fingers and toes, fretting at their not perfectly symmetrical length, and sweating bullets.

All the while she kept telling herself, "Kate, he's not going to be there. Even if he is there, he probably won't remember you. He'll be with a whole crowd of people you don't know. Remember what Brian said. If he really wanted you, he would have come after you. So even if he is there, he'll probably ignore you. He didn't come back. He doesn't want you."

After her nails were done to a mauve perfection, Kate showered, shampooing her hair until it was squeaky clean, and shaved off every hair on her legs.

An exquisite, long-legged tan body emerged from the shower. The lines from her itsy-bitsy bikini looked like a white bathing suit in the early dawn light of her bedroom.

She wrapped herself in a white Indian cotton robe and wandered into the kitchen to make fresh coffee. On the way she turned on the central air conditioning.

She finished her first cup of coffee, standing in the morning sunlight admiring her garden. She was particularly fond of the pansies. Finally it was time to wake Kevin.

He got up, grouchy as usual, and sulked his way into the kitchen for breakfast. He sat in an early morning stupor on a high stool at the breakfast bar, his skinny legs dangling down toward the brick floor.

Kate couldn't help thinking how like Felipe he was, but too little to have that first cup of coffee in the morning that his father always said made him human.

Kate decided a glass of freezing cold orange juice would jolt him awake.

"Mommy?"

"Yes, Kevin?"

"Mommy . . . I think I want to make the bacon. Grandma always lets me make the bacon at her house," he ended, challenging his mother to prove that she loved him even more than Grandma, by letting him make the bacon.

"Kevin, the last time you tried, you spilled the grease all over the bricks, and the floor is still slippery from it. Why don't you go in and watch cartoons, and I'll call you when breakfast is ready, okay?"

"Boy, Mom! You never let me do anything!" was the response as he stamped his way to his room to watch TV.

"Brother," she muttered to herself, "is this going to be some day!"

After a good deal of haggling over whether Kevin would or would not eat his breakfast, Kate abandoned her child-psychology techniques and told him, "If you don't eat that, and eat it right now, I'm going to smack you silly!"

Without another word, he started shoveling in the

pancakes and long strips of bacon, while Kate watched him, a second cup of coffee in her hand.

"Mommy, why do I have to eat breakfast and you don't? It's not fair. If I eat breakfast, then you should have to eat breakfast too."

"Kevin, just shut up and eat your breakfast so we can get ready to go. When you're seventeen, I promise you I will give you a detailed and honest answer to that question. Until then, I am the mommy and you are the little boy, and that means you do what I tell you to do." It would be just like him to demand an answer on the morning of his seventeenth birthday, she thought.

"Boy, Mom, you're grouchy this morning," Kevin complained.

You're right. I'm irritable and tired and edgy and worried, Kate thought to herself. *He's not going to be there, Kate, and even if he is he'll ignore you. You're going to go. You're going to be nice to Bob's mother, even though dear Mrs. Scanlon makes you crazy. You are going to take your cameras and take nice pictures for the nice paper of the nice people. You are going to have a nice time with your friends, and then you are going to leave and go home to bed with an empty heart. Right? Right!*

The telephone rang, and it was Josie calling to say that they would be there in about two hours. Then Nicky got on the telephone.

He and Kevin had a long, drawn-out conversation about how much money they had to spend for the day; about the cotton candy and the rides and the games and the prizes they could win.

Kate half listened to the conversation as she cleaned up the breakfast dishes. She wondered about the paradox of Irish America putting on a festival of Irish arts, and all the children seemed to care about were the rides and the games and the candy and how much money they had to spend.

They are so American.

They don't know about the dancing and the music and the fight generations of people fought, to even have *a festival of Irish arts at all.*

I wonder if Kevin even knows what a tin whistle is? she asked herself.

After he had hung up the telephone, Kate turned to him and asked if he knew what a tin whistle was.

"Sure, Mommy. It's a whistle made of tin." And he left the kitchen. "Great," she mumbled. "Does he know about the great Fenian Rising, about Parnell, about the Gaelic League, about the Sinn Fein or about Collins or Dev . . . Boy, is my Irish up today."

He won't be there . . . he won't be there. This will be just another one of those pleasant, maybe boring things that you'll have to get through. He won't be there . . . he won't be there . . .

Kate retreated to her bedroom amid the sounds of Superman fighting off another attack from evil alien invaders.

After about an hour of pulling out what appeared to be every summer outfit from her closet, Kate selected an embroidered peasant skirt with attached lawn petticoats and a matching embroidered peasant blouse with front lacing.

She checked the clock by her bed. Just enough time to load the cameras . . . and take another bath.

She started running cool water into the sunken tub and added some perfumed oil.

Cool, with her hair perfectly curled, Kate slipped into her blouse and skirt. Eyeing her reflection in the mirrors on her closet doors, she pronounced herself well turned out . . . and overdressed.

Normally she would have worn blue jeans and a shirt promoting a cause. But today she thought she would overdress, just in case. She compromised and pushed her perfectly manicured toes into a pair of comfortable sandals.

She stopped by Kevin's room to see if he was ready. He was dressed in shorts, tee-shirt, socks, and new sneakers, all cleaned up and glued to the TV.

She moved on to her studio to load up.

"You know he won't be there, Kate."

Startled, she turned to Jim, who had been standing in the doorway to her studio, watching her as she stood transfixed, staring at something far, far away.

"I know, Jim, I know," she whispered back.

"It's a pity. You look very beautiful today, Kate."

She thanked him and put a few more rolls of black-and-white film in her bag with the cameras. She left the house with him, locking it behind her.

The kids were going at it in the bus, and Josie was bellowing at them to pipe down. A knowing look passed between Jim and Josie, but Kate decided to ignore it.

The children quieted down as soon as they were underway, and Josie started listing all the people who would be there.

"Well, you remember Margie Quinn. She'll be there with her husband, John Keenan. And John Keenan, the tall redheaded one that Nancy used to date. I think he

77

went to La Salle and used to drive up here in that old wreck. Well, Nancy married Bob Clarke, but not before John had met Margie. It's funny—they all live next door to each other now. John is working for IBM, and I think Bob is selling heavy industrial equipment for Deere now."

Kate lost herself in the thumbnail sketches of the people she had grown up with, who she would see at the Feis. She supposed it was Josie's way of getting her away from thoughts of Flynn. She let herself be drawn into the conversation.

"Whatever happened to Karen Whelan? I remember she was so crazy about Terry McSweeny."

"Karen went off to New York. She's a buyer or in the fashion office of Bloomingdale's now. Terry married that obnoxious little blonde, Linda Bolger, and they moved to Texas the last I heard."

"Boy, that's a weird match. Linda, who was always sitting in some corner mewing and complaining, marrying Terry! He couldn't sit still long enough to get to know Linda." Kate laughed.

Josie laughed too. "Can you imagine, Terry dribbling a basketball around Linda, sitting in an armchair complaining about the noise?" she asked.

"Meow, meow, Josie," and they both laughed.

"If the two of you are finished ripping apart your dear old friends, I'd like to announce that we are nearly there," Jim interjected as he turned the car off the highway onto a secondary road. It was jammed with cars lined up to get into the grounds.

"I'll park the bus, and I'll meet you at Mrs. Scanlon's booth."

Kate moaned at the suggestion, but they agreed. The

three boys and their mothers got out. One mother in shorts carrying a huge picnic basket, the other in frills carrying a sack of cameras and film.

Jim watched them cross the field. Alone in the bus he allowed himself the luxury of remembering Kate in high school. He had been crazy about her, but then so had half the boys in their class.

He had started going out with her friend, Josie, so he could be near Kate.

"Ah, but then Josie's calm green eyes with the little gold flecks saw me for what I am and trapped me." He smiled to himself, put the bus in gear, and moved it up the line.

There was a huge tent in the middle of the field where the vendors had set up their tables. Off to the left and nearest to them were rides for the children. A ferris wheel rose above the cluster, and the boys whooped with delight and ran rings around their mothers, begging to go on the rides right away.

"Pipe down, you guys," Kate warned. "After we get a table and eat."

Josie sighed and commented on the heat and the blistering sun.

"Stop for a minute, Josie, and give me the other handle."

The small group made their way slowly, the picnic basket swaying between the two mothers, as the boys ran ahead toward the picnic tables next to the beer and food tent.

Flynn scanned the horizon, his dark eyes slits against the sun. They flew past two women. One was tall with auburn hair, and three boys were prancing and running rings around them.

His eyes snapped back. It was her.

A particularly ancient member of the Order of the Hibernians walked up to him, a large cup of cold, foamy beer in his hand.

"Tommy lad . . . glad to see you and the boys. How's the family? We certainly appreciate you boys takin' time out of your busy schedule to come here and do this for us. It's quite a turnout, don't you think?"

Flynn nodded his head automatically at Jim Burke, and responded, "For sure."

Flynn turned to scan the hillock for her, but she was lost somewhere in the crowd by then.

Beyond the tent and the rides and the tables, a green, gold, and white bedecked bandstand stood, and small groups, some in traditional dress, others in jeans and casual clothes, talked and fidgeted and tested microphones.

The field, where there would be Gaelic football and games later on, was freshly lined, and behind it cars were parking.

Jack Herlihy was passing from group to group, waving hello to friends, stopping to talk to others.

The Feis was getting underway—a gathering in a high field surrounded on all sides by a forest and high green mountains.

"A Feis," Kate thought. "I haven't been to one for years. This is an Irish tradition that has survived famine and war and Americanization."

She stopped, setting down the picnic basket, to take her first picture.

"Lord," Josie groaned. "You're not going to keep doing this, are you? We'll never get to a table."

Small knots of people were gathering over the field. People who knew each other, from neighborhoods and families. People who weren't ready yet to move out and meet new people.

Kate smiled to herself.

That will change. A little more beer, a little more time, and after the games all our differences, political and social, will melt away and we are all just Irish . . . and together.

Kate let her camera hang around her neck and picked up the basket again.

The boys raced ahead and found Jim. He was waving to them from a table already filled with old friends.

Josie waved back to him, and they closed the gap between them.

Black eyes began to scan the crowd from a knot of men in kilts and dark shirts. They moved impatiently in the hot sun, their dark clothes making them hotter than most, the cold beer they downed making them high. Some moved away into the breeze, their pipes wailing, a piercing sound that moved through the crowd, making them restless.

"Well, if it isn't the Cat!" John Keenan lumbered toward Kate and Josie, ready to relieve them of their basket.

"Kate!" her old friend, Margie Keenan, squealed. "Kate, where have you been keepin' yourself? Josie here tells us that you moved back ages ago."

In moments friends had surrounded her, talking and laughing.

And black eyes watched as friends ebbed and flowed around her, noting the little boy who pulled at her arm for attention. Watching as women and men embraced her in turn, smiling and laughing and talking.

A mean, sneaky hand reached into his chest and viciously gripped his heart.

"Dad, Dad, are you all right?" His son, Seamus, had come up beside him, carrying a long, heavy case containing his pipes.

"I'm all right," he answered absently.

"Gee, Dad, for a minute there you went all white. Are you sure you're okay?" Seamus's face reflected a real concern.

"Fine, son, fine. Why don't you go calm your sister down? She looks like she'll die before she ever gets the chance to dance."

"Aw, Dad . . ." It was clear that Seamus didn't want the job of holding his little sister's hand.

"Go on with you, now." Flynn's brows knotted, and his son, seeing he was already in one of his moods, turned and left.

Kate finally had a minute to ready her equipment. When she was finished, she looked around and saw Father O'Connor, the visiting Dominican priest, making his way through the crowd, stopping to talk and to touch, small children and the old, bestowing blessings as his white cassock billowed and snapped in the breeze.

Whirs and clicks. Faces and entreaty. A tilted head. A soft smile.

A wrinkled face and arthritic hands that had held children gently, scrubbed floors vigorously, clasped fervently, snatched at his sleeve.

Whir. Snap. Tears in the old eyes. Promises of intercession.

Two altar boys, their sneakers peeking out from beneath their flapping cassocks and white surplices, were busily spreading snowy white linen over the little table to the right of the larger table that would soon be used as an altar.

Whir. Snap. The wine and the water and the white linen towel for Father O'Connor.

Kate was now totally immersed in her work. Moving through the crowd, away from her son and friends.

Faces, faces—Irish faces. Children, laughing and teasing and gamboling, running, with pleading tears directed at mothers and fathers.

Whir. Snap.

Father O'Connor by the outdoor altar, talking intently with Herlihy. The altar boys handed him his case. He opened it and placed the ciborium between the glass-encased candles, then reached for the chalice and placed it in front. The sun glinted off their surfaces, brilliant and blinding.

Whir. Snap.

The altar boys approached him from behind, vestments in place as Jack Herlihy approached the microphone.

"Ladies, gentlemen, and children, may I have your attention." The crowd of about 6,000 rustled to an expectant quiet.

"It is my pleasure to welcome you here . . . and to introduce Father O'Connor. He is visiting us and has been so kind as to offer his services today.

"For the first time at our Feis a mass of thanksgiving will be offered in Irish."

A murmuring ripple of approval rolled through the crowd.

Whir. Snap.

"Father O'Connor is a Dominican priest who has served as a missionary in Africa and South America, and I think all of us here today will agree that we are very privileged to have him say this mass.

"More so because it is in Irish. We have struggled for generations for the right to speak our native language. Today we are free in this great land, America, to celebrate our mass in our language.

"And let us not forget to exhort the Blessed Mother for her intercession on behalf of our suffering brethren in the captive counties."

Whir. Snap.

Kate could feel the small hairs on the back of her neck rise.

And Father O'Connor began the mass.

Kate's ears were washed by the familiar droning and tidal response, but the language was beautifully different.

Whir. Snap.

There were tears and emotional faces all around her. Husbands wrapped arms around wives' waists. Children stood at the feet of their parents, silent.

Whir. Snap.

The medieval ritual was beckoning to the faithful in their tongue, making their hearts and spirits reach out all the more.

Father O'Connor gave his final blessing and retreated from the altar.

The crowd remained silent for a long time. Then the

sounds of children grew louder and were joined by the rustle of parents responding.

Kate went back to her table.

Kevin ran over to her, gave her an unsolicited hug, and went back to stuffing his face with his Aunt Josie's potato salad.

And black eyes followed Kate's every move.

Josie moved toward her friend, a heavily laden plate in her hand, a serious expression on her face. As she stood side by side with Kate, she handed her the plate, and, leaning close, she whispered.

"He's here, Cat . . . right over there, and he's been watching you."

Kate's heart slowed and seemed to thud to a stop. Plate in hand, she looked up, and black eyes met her gaze.

"Well, well, well . . . and who do we have here but the county's most famous girl photographer."

Kate dropped her plate as Bob Scanlon's tall, gangling frame draped itself over her shoulder.

His sandy-haired head dropped down and planted a kiss on her startled lips before she could stop him.

Kate looked up after Bob had moved back from her, only to see Flynn's back and retreating figure joined by a tall young boy falling in step and talking.

She turned to Bob Scanlon, black hatred choking her, and met his hot, bright blue eyes.

"What are *you* doing here?" she snarled. "I thought you had a newspaper to put to bed."

"Put to bed . . . put to bed. Why, Cat, darlin'," he cooed, affecting a rarely used Irish brogue, "aren't you glad to see me?"

She would have continued had Josie not pulled her away with a laughing excuse.

"Are you crazy, Kate?" she hissed. "Everyone is watching you! Remember that you date the man from time to time. I realize his timing was the absolute worst, but get a grip on yourself."

And black eyes watched as her friend pulled Kate away for a private chat, a serious, intent expression on her face.

Kate thought she would go mad.

The day wore on, and Kate worked, and Flynn watched her.

He watched her smiling and talking with strangers, making them easy and relaxed for her camera.

Whir. Snap.

Suddenly she was talking to his daughter, Maureen, making her smile. Flynn had never seen Maureen apart from him, and he watched as Kate knelt down in the grass in front of her . . . and mothered her.

Maureen was probably having another one of her nervous fits, and Kate was reassuring her, patting her hair into place, straightening her dress.

She could be her own daughter, Flynn thought. Then a sharp pain ripped through him as he saw his shy, lovely Maureen look up at Kate and, overcoming her reticence, pose and dance for Kate's camera.

His littlest. Shy and lost without a mother. The ghost in his house dancing for his Kate.

And as he watched Kate, he caught her eye. This time he nodded to her slowly. She nodded back.

She looks frightened, he realized, *and, so beautiful.*

Then Maureen came prancing and dancing up to Kate, dragging Connor with her, teasing and laughing at her big oaf of a brother, begging Kate to take his picture.

And Connor was standing there, the prankster in the family, awkward and ill at ease.

Will wonders never cease! Flynn mused as Connor shook Kate's hand.

A little boy Flynn took to be her son moved into their group, Kate introduced Maureen to him, and they moved off together, talking animatedly.

"Dad, Dad." Breathless Maureen ran up to him. "Dad, we want to go on the ferris wheel, can I have some more money? Seamus only gave me two dollars, and it's gone already."

Kate's eyes followed the little girl and Kevin as they ran up to a man in kilts. Her eyes traveled up his body until they met Flynn's dark, intense ones.

It was then that the sorrow and sadness inside him welled up. All the bitterness and grief and disappointment of his years rolled over him, wave after wave. He very rarely let the man inside of him out. It was always the father or the husband or the cop . . . never just plain Flynn.

He didn't care if he made a fool of himself. He didn't care if he blew his life into bits. He would have her in his life, one way or the other.

But, you sad fool, he chided himself, *what if she won't talk to you? After all, the way you left her five years ago . . .*

Whir. Snap.

Kate had raised her camera and taken a picture of him as he absent-mindedly caressed Kevin's head and hugged his daughter to his hip, talking to her. She had never seen him smile like that.

It was beautiful.

"Oh yeah, Dad, this is my friend, Kevin Zandt. That's his mother over there taking pictures for the paper. We've been helping her."

Kate watched as Maureen pointed to her, watched as Kevin shook hands with Flynn and then ran off with Maureen toward the ferris wheel.

Her eyes were brimming with tears, and she thought her heart would explode.

He touched me, and now he has touched my son, she thought to herself. *He has children, so he must have a wife somewhere.*

And Flynn watched as she turned from them, her eyes full.

Later, after she had recovered her composure, she cheered Nicky on in the under-fourteen-year-olds' Gaelic football match with Josie and Jim.

"Get in there and get it, Nick!" Jimmy bellowed at his son, "and stop playing against your own, boy!"

Nicky ran for the ball, picked it up, and ran five steps with it. The referee's whistle shrilled.

"Three steps, Nicky, three steps!" Jimmy yelled, and turned to John Keenan. "I can't stand it, let's get another beer."

"Jim, let the boy play the game without directions from you on the side," Josie chided him, and shooed Kevin and Pat back toward the goal.

"Let's watch some of the dancers, kids."

"Aw, Ma . . . I want to stay here with Dad," Patrick complained.

"Let's leave them here with Jimmy," Kate interrupted. "You can help me take some shots, okay, Josie?"

The two women wandered away . . . and black eyes followed them.

And Kate, with Josie's help, chronicled the Irish language contest and took more pictures of people, just being themselves.

"I've been having a nice chat with Mrs. Scanlon, dear, and I'm ready to go now."

Kate's mother walked up to her.

"Mom, what are you doing here? Where's Dad?" Kate was surprised to see her mother at the Feis.

"You know your father never comes to these things, Kate darling. You look like you should put away your cameras and have a little fun. Why don't I take Kevin home with me and put him to bed? He looks like he is ready to drop."

Kate watched her mother and son move off toward the parked cars. They stopped to say hello to the Ryans, who were talking with the Keenans, getting ready to leave.

Oh Mom, if you only knew what was going on here! Kate thought. *You just walked off with my only line of defense, leaving me here alone with him.*

"We're going now, Kate." Josie had walked up to her friend quietly. "Are you sure you want to stay? Karen Whelan said she was staying late and would give you a lift home later."

Calm green eyes looked anxiously into Kate's darker ones. They stood and looked at each other silently for a moment, and then Kate let her breath out.

"No, I'm not sure, Josie. What do you think I should do?" she asked.

After looking at her friend's face, creased with

concern and worry, Josie answered, "I think you should finish it, one way or the other. And if staying will help gain that end, then stay. He's been watching you like a hawk all day. I don't really understand what's going on between you two, but I think you should find out. And remember, if you need me or Jim, you call, any time. Do you hear me?"

Dark eyes watched as the two women hugged and one left. And those same eyes watched as the one he wanted stayed.

Kate had safely tucked her cameras and exposed film in Mrs. Scanlon's car and returned the keys. Mrs. Scanlon started to make a fuss when Kate mentioned that she was staying longer and would ride home with Karen Whelan. The older woman finally capitulated, saying that she would make sure Bob got the film.

The sun was going down, and a cool breeze was blowing across the emptying field. Kate, feeling disappointed and depressed, decided to wander over the fairgrounds. It had been a good Feis, but she needed to get away from the people all around her. She also needed to look for Flynn.

Just one more chance, she prayed silently.

As she walked, she began to feel foolish and overly romantic, and tears welled up in her eyes. She rounded the corner of the deserted bandstand, and the sounds of laughter and song became more distant.

He was standing there, silently, in the shadows. Tall and immense, he loomed over her.

A shuddering excitement passed through her, and all the strength seemed to cbb from her body.

They stood there in the gathering dusk, just staring at each other.

Flynn focused on the tendrils of her shiny auburn hair tumbling down her long, graceful neck. His eyes wandered over her soft, glowing skin and finally came to her eyes, glittering with tears.

The memory of her tall, slender body under his assaulted him, and lust flared through his starved senses. Then, as she shifted her body, she looked awkward and frightened, and he was seized with an unbelievable tenderness for her.

Kate in turn watched as Flynn's emotions played across his face, his brows gathered ominously, and then he reached out his hand for hers. He took it firmly but gently in his and coaxed her toward the dark woods.

Kate felt an unbearable joy as she followed him.

The last fiery rays of the sunset touched them as they crossed the tree line and the dark quiet green of the woods enfolded them.

Kate was momentarily blinded, and she stumbled. Flynn reached out and caught her by the elbow, afraid to take her into his arms. He was afraid that she would run away again, as she had been doing all day.

Kate murmured, "Thank you," and they walked on in silence. They went deeper into the shadows, and her eyes adjusted to the darkness.

As Flynn was trying to think of something to say, Kate was filling with a cold panic.

What if he is taking me here only to tell me in private that he doesn't want to have anything to do with me . . . that he isn't interested. Oh, God, please no!

They stopped and sat down in a small clearing covered with soft moss. The birches and tall oak trees had given way to tall pine and firs that marched up the side of the mountain in front of them.

They sat there in silence for what seemed like an eternity. The cool wind rustled the leaves around them, sighing through the boughs and ruffling Kate's hair.

Chilled by the breeze, Kate shivered, and Flynn turned his head to her and quietly asked her how she had been—his black eyes pleading with her, his shoulders hunched, and his neck bent down.

Her mind screamed, *Inane, stupid, meaningless, all-encompassing question! I have been sick from loving you, longing for you!*

She pushed at the leaves and pine needles with a stick, trying to control her disappointment, her fear and anger, and—last but not least—her tears.

"Fine, Tom, just fine." But the bitterness and anger got the best of her, and because she was ready to sob her guts out, she stood up and stamped away. Furiously she brushed at imagined dead leaves clinging to her ruffled skirt, thinking all the while, *He doesn't want me. He feels awkward.*

Her tears caught the moonlight, blinded her, and then lost her as she walked, then ran into the woods. She was desperately ashamed of the sounds of her grief.

The air tasted of dead leaves, and a damp musk rose from the forest floor.

She didn't care anymore.

Everything broke in her as she ran deeper into the silence. All she wanted to do was hide there under a sagging bough to sit and cry.

Kate couldn't hear anything except the buzzing in her ears; she couldn't see anything, she was so blinded by her tears. She didn't feel the branches whipping her face or the weeds clutching at her ankles.

Drained and gasping for air, Kate stopped running. Her flesh was cold and sweaty, and she was shivering. She wanted to vomit.

Flynn's hands were hot when he wrapped them around hers. He was shaking, and his ragged breathing echoed the pounding of her heart. He turned her around, and his lips trapped hers. They were soft and gentle, yet they seared her with a burning intensity.

Flynn groaned, and, unable to control himself, he pulled her down on top of him. Down onto the soft moss and pine needles under the boughs.

He rolled over on top of her, roughly pinning her arms above her head. His mouth and tongue were moving over her, his body straining, trying to force her into the earth.

Incapable of reason, he had decided that he would have her this one last time. He was sure that she didn't want him and that he would never have the opportunity again.

An animal rage roared up out of Kate, and she lunged at him. She bit him and shook her head from side to side, thrashing, furious to be free. All the hurt and tears and grief of the past years turned to anger.

His arms slid down the side of her head and his thumbs pressed both sides of her face. She hit him hard with a closed fist on the side of his head by his ear.

Tom jerked back into a sitting position, pulling her up with him. Time seemed to stop as they stared at each other, shocked.

Violent tremors shook his body as he tried to control himself. Finally, in a shaking voice, he broke the silence.

"You aren't the only one who's been hurt! You're not the only one who remembers!"

His hands were cruelly crushing her wrists, and Kate whimpered to him that he was hurting her.

His answer was to shake her.

"I was just fine until I met you. I had everything under control. I got along okay on the job. My men respected me. I was heading in the right direction. Then I met you. Loved you, saw you and saw myself, and a voice from the back of my brain screamed at me. Mocked me. The shock of knowing in an instant that I had never, ever loved anyone."

He was shouting at her and shaking her and crying.

"I saw you that night, and in an instant knew I loved a stranger. I wanted to strangle you. I wanted to put my hands around your white neck and snap it."

He stopped shouting at her and shaking her when he realized that she had gone limp in his hands, and, gathering her into his great arms, he finished, "But then your eyes and mouth and tongue and breath stopped me. I wanted to taste you, run my hand around the curve of your face. I felt sick and wild inside, helpless to stop myself. I felt the weight of your breasts against me, and I was scared to death that some day you would turn on me and laugh at me and leave me."

Kate couldn't see anything except the silky black hairs on his chest as he talked on in that intense whisper of his.

Oh, dear God. These are his arms around me. This is real, she cried to herself. *These are his shoulders, and I am resting my body against his, and my cheek is against his throat. I can feel safe and loved again.*

Shyly and slowly, she reached up and put her arms around his neck.

"Flynn," Kate whispered.

He stopped talking, bent his head down, and nuzzled her neck, his black eyes pleading with her.

Vaguely, she could hear Tom saying her name between gulps of air. He drew the tight ball of her body into his lap. His arms cradled her, rocking her, his throat against her right ear. She could hear the sounds of his crying rushing in and out of his lungs.

He eased her down on the soft moss and covered her with his warmth, as the blood of their bodies began a distant but familiar race. They opened to each other, mouths and minds and tears blending, their sighs and whispers mingling.

Everywhere they touched tingled with delight.

Flynn lost himself in her velvety skin, and Kate in his rough hands.

Then he undid the laces of her blouse, and her breasts came free. His hot, wet mouth traced a fiery path across them, and Kate's breath caught as he caressed her nipples with his tongue.

His hands fumbled with the laces on her skirt as he pulled it away from her body.

As he moved over her, Kate groaned and ran her fingers frantically through his hair and down his back. Brushing aside his kilts, Flynn entered her.

The musk of their lovemaking mixed with the musk of the forest and the pungent odor of the crushed pine needles beneath them.

It felt as if they were alone in a primeval forest, one that had never been walked through before. And he was the man, the solitary, passionate man who walked there with her.

Joyfully, she opened herself to him. Each time he went deeper into her, she was sure she would burst and finally they reached a sun-hot clearing in their shadowy forest. Together they reached for the open crystal-blue sky inside each other, and they flowed white hot and merged there.

Each of them was sure, in that moment, that all of their energy and passion and love was the force that had created the universe.

And then their eyes and noses and mouths and breasts and legs and loins touched and opened again to fingers gently probing and stroking every curve and hidden dark place.

Time passed.

And from that deep, quiet place they opened to each other again and again.

The wind blew once more and died completely.

Love and leaves, eyes and tears, their moans and the musk of the earth all mingled. Their cries of anger and then of love had been carried away on the cool wind, up the mountain and then to the far corners of the earth.

Alone and silent with each other, they slept there, nestling and intertwined under a moonlit sky that peeked through the crossed protective arms of the fir tree over them.

The dawn broke on two people clinging to each other, slowly walking across an empty field toward an old white Volkswagen sitting in the distance.

{ Chapter 7 }

"Hello." Eileen's sleepy voice drifted back over the telephone line to Kate.

"Eileen, it's me. I have something so incredible to tell you." Kate's wildly happy voice began to penetrate Eileen's foggy brain.

"Couldn't this wait till this afternoon, Kate? It's only 11:30. I didn't get to bed until four this morning . . . that is, I didn't get to sleep till four."

"No, no, it can't wait. Sit up and take off those ridiculous blinders you wear to bed and listen to me. God, I don't even know where to begin!"

Eileen did as she was told and grumbled at Kate.

"This had better be good. I am a very unhappy dinosaur this morning. What did you do, win the lottery, inherit a million . . ."

"Eileen, shut up!" Kate was hopping up and down on her bed.

"It's Flynn, Eileen. He's back. I spent the night with him last night, and I drove him to work this morning, and I'm meeting him after work in the city today. He says he loves me, and he said he was sorry, and . . ."

"Wait a minute." Eileen sat up straight. "Are you talking about the same Flynn you have been obsessed with for the past five years, the same Flynn whose picture you just sold, the same . . ."

"Yes, yes! Oh, Eileen, I'm so happy I think I am going to explode."

Eileen experienced a creeping feeling of dread as she listened to Kate trill on. She had heard that same voice years ago, and she remembered it in agony.

"Kate." She interrupted her friend's monologue about the mighty Flynn. "Are you sure the guy is for real this time? I understand how you feel, but what he did to you the last time, how he hurt you . . . if he pulls it again, well, I don't think you could take it."

"I know what you're thinking, but it's different this time. We talked about what happened; we're both different people now."

"Have you told Josie about this?" Eileen asked.

"Of course. I talked to her before I called you," Kate laughed. "She wakes up hours before you do. She's on mother time."

Eileen silently vowed to call Josie the minute she hung up with Kate to get the straight story.

"Listen, I know it sounds unbelievable," Kate went on in a calmer voice. "I know the skeptic in you says things like this only happen on soap operas, but this is really happening."

"Okay, I'm all ears. Tell me what happened." Before Eileen settled in for a long conversation, she said, "But first let me get my cigarettes."

"Please, Eileen, just listen and try to be happy for me." Kate waited while Eileen fumbled around for cigarettes on her night table. "Bob Scanlon asked me to cover the Feis—remember, I told you—for the local paper."

"Right. I remember grumbling to you about working for free and no commission for me," Eileen teased.

"Eileen . . ."

"All right, all right, I'm listening."

"Well, anyway, he was there. Josie saw him first. He was . . ." Kate continued outlining the entire day, up until they had finally sought each other out.

"And then we went for a walk in the woods and, er, spent the night there," Kate finished, somewhat embarrassed.

"You're kidding!" Eileen laughed. "You did it in the woods? What if someone had found you? I mean, what if some poor schnook had decided to take a leak in the woods and stumbled upon the two of you going . . ."

"Eileen!" Kate pleaded.

"All right, all right," she chuckled. "But the woods?"

"Don't you have any romance in your soul?" Kate grumbled happily. "I'm so happy, so very happy."

"Sure, I have romance in my soul. But I like a great big king-sized bed, extra firm for extra bounce, champagne in a bucket, paté, soft music, the view of Central Park, and my answering service taking all calls."

"You, on the other hand, like grass and dirty old leaves, with squirrels and chipmunks looking on."

Eileen laughed. "Can you imagine what the squirrels and chipmunks must have thought? Look at those crazy human beings, thundering away in our nice, quiet forest."

"Eileen, you're impossible," Kate said, laughing. "It was beautiful, it was . . . everything. I am so in love with him. I feel so complete. I never thought I would ever feel joy again in my life, and today I'm filled to overflowing with it." Kate finished in the soft voice of a woman deeply in love.

Eileen's eyes filled momentarily. She wondered what it must feel like to experience such ecstasy and joy and love. And for a second she allowed herself to feel intensely jealous of her friend, then replaced it with a genuine feeling of happiness for her.

"Listen, Eileen . . . Are you there, Eileen?"

"Yeah, I'm here," she answered quietly.

"I've got to get off the telephone. Kevin's going to Grandma Zandt's today, and I've got to finish getting him ready. I'll call you later, before I go in to meet Tom, okay?"

"Okay. I'm meeting Ira for brunch, and after they're having a sale at Saks and I'm going to do a little shopping. I should be home around four o'clock."

"Oh, I forgot." Kate stopped Eileen before she hung up. "Did we hear anything from Time-Life Books about my Faces book?"

"No. I put a call in to Don, but he hasn't returned it yet." Eileen sat up and put her feet on the floor. "Listen, I've got to have my coffee. I'll talk to you later . . . and congratulations."

Eileen yawned, stretched her way into her kitchen,

and made coffee and a poached egg in record time. She was too hungry to wait for brunch.

Huh, she thought to herself. *Maybe things will be different this time. In the middle of her dreams-come-true, she remembered to ask about her book. Maybe she's not so out of control, or thrown by Tom Flynn.*

Eileen slipped on her robe and slippers and made her way into her office. Manuscripts and books were on every chair, lining the walls and shelves, crowding in on her as she sat down at her huge library table desk.

She picked up the telephone receiver, dialed, and sipped her second cup of coffee while she waited.

"Hello, Josie, it's me, Eileen."

"I was wondering when you were going to call."

"Well, what do you think? You were there yesterday. Tell me what really happened."

Eileen settled back into the chair and put her feet up on the desk. She sipped her coffee and listened, without interrupting.

"Well, that's just about what Kate said, but you left out the heavy breathing and the ooh's and aah's."

Josie laughed back at Eileen. "Well, Kate was right about one thing. He is a beautiful hunk of a man. Those kilts and the flashing eyes and dark stares . . ."

"Careful, Josie, careful," Eileen teased, "you wouldn't want Jimmy to hear you."

"I wonder if it's true about them not wearing anything under those kilts."

"Josie, for a happily married woman you are mighty curious."

"There's no harm in wondering," Josie defended herself.

"Hah! Listen, gotta go. Ira's going to kill me if I'm late again. My love to Jimmy and the kids. Talk to you later."

"Right. I'll keep you up to date, and you do the same. I'm still not convinced he's for real this time."

"Me neither."

But he was for real this time. He was even more desperate than he was five years ago. He had come to the point where death had a certain clear appeal.

Then she had finally put herself in the right place at the right time, and from the moment he had seen her he had felt the same radiant joy he had all those years ago. His heart and soul leapt out of him at her, and this time he had followed. He started the day in a kind of trance, one moment feeling terrified, the next so happy he could cry.

He had showered and changed at work, thinking how lucky it was that his family virtually ignored him. He had put up with the jokes and remarks about showing up for work in kilts.

He went through the morning roll call without hearing anything and doodled all over the day's rap sheet.

He even asked Tim to drive.

All he could see was her face before him. All he could hear was her voice.

"Tom."

"Yeah." Flynn roused himself and turned his head to his partner.

"Are you going to tell me what's going on, or am I alone on patrol today?"

"I don't know where to begin," Flynn answered.

"Well, why don't you start by explaining to me why

in hell you showed up for work in kilts with a gorgeous redhead driving your deathtrap!"

They both laughed. "She's beautiful, isn't she? Her name is Kate."

"Kate?" McBride turned his head away from the traffic and the street and gave Tom a sharp, questioning look. "Isn't she the one . . ."

"Yup, she's the one, the one and only Kate Mary Gallagher."

"Maybe you'd better start from the beginning. I take it you never went home after the Feis yesterday?"

"You take it right!" Flynn said with emphasis. "And if I could figure out a way to never ever go back to that hell again, I'd move in with her right now!"

Tim drove, and Flynn talked and told him pretty much the same story Kate had told Eileen and Josie. Except he didn't ooh and aah, or breathe heavily, or jump up and down with delight, or hug himself and whirl around with tears in his eyes, only to stop and stand still feeling himself well up with eager tenderness and loving.

He might have if level-headed Tim McBride hadn't brought up the subject of Joan and the kids. It brought him down with a crash, and his face turned to stone.

"Shit, Tom, I'm sorry I brought it up. Fuck! I haven't seen you smile in years. Christ, when am I going to learn to keep my big mouth shut!"

Tim turned in to the park at 79th Street, and they drove through in silence, watching the streets and the people. Sometimes the job drew you out of yourself, onto the sidewalk. You were walking with the people, sitting in the sun on a bench, watching people having petty arguments, watching lovers meet, embrace, and pose for each other. Then begin the ritual of their very unique ways of loving each other.

Some held hands, some held fingers, some clutched each other arm around back, some talked and walked and laughed, and others were shy of each other, and a few could barely disguise their unbridled passions.

Tim glanced over at Tom. He was gone again in his head. McBride guessed his partner's ritual was the unbridled passion version.

He had been Tom Flynn's partner for eight years and had gotten to know him in pieces. Flynn wasn't a talker and seldom divulged information about his personal feelings. But Tim knew one thing.

Flynn's marriage was a disaster.

During that nightmare trip to Florida in the motor home Tim had experienced firsthand the deadening effect Joan Flynn had on her husband.

He shook his head, trying to clear it of the image of Tom and Joan and the embarrassment and pity he had felt for him then. He turned in the safe shadow of the patrol car to see if Tom was still out of it.

Yup, Tim thought to himself. *He doesn't even hear the calls on the radio.*

Flynn was staring off into space, his hat back, his face peaceful, none of the usual deep frown lines creasing his brow, furrowing his cheeks.

Not the way he looked on the trip to Orlando. Tim turned his mind back. At best they were an uneven couple. Joan was rake thin then, with her overbleached hair tightly curled. Tom was tall, dark-haired, and powerfully built, calm and keen minded. And all the while Joan nervously clutched at him with her cadaver hands.

Her hands were bony and worn and always seemed to clutch and snatch. Tim could never imagine them caressing or open and giving.

Tom had tried on that trip, but the lines in his face grew deeper with each mile they covered. Joan babbled nonsense, and Tim's poor Margey listened out of politeness and tried to understand what the woman was saying.

All the while Tom acted like a man with a hot poker stuck up his ass. Gently he tried to help make sense out of Joan's nonstop chatter. He squirmed and fidgeted and spoke in a voice harsh from restraint. Finally on the third night, Joan got drunk and called Margey an Irish cunt. It would have been funny if Joan had been anyone other than who she was, Tim thought.

When she said it, Tom looked like a man turned to stone, getting ready to blow apart. He had got up slowly from his chair and took Joan by the arm, painfully, and in tones he used on the streets with child beaters and murderers, told her to get into the camper and that he would join her shortly.

Tim remembered thinking briefly that his partner looked angry enough to kill.

After the door clicked shut behind Joan, he turned to them slowly like a dead man. He walked over to Margey and Tim, standing in front of them, just a bit too far away, and started to apologize very formally for his wife's behavior.

Margey, bless her, jumped up from her chair, laughing, pulled Tom to a chair, and handed him another iced tea, telling him "not to bother about it, everyone has too much to drink occasionally, we all say stupid things sometimes . . ."

She reached under the table then, took Tim's hand, and squeezed it hard. Then she turned her eyes on him, pleading with him to say something to Tom to ease the tension. But before he could respond, Tom interrupted in a voice so filled with misery that it stunned him.

"I think it would be best if we left." He put up his hand to stop them as they began to protest.

"I'm going to go down to the park office and call and make reservations, and we'll fly back."

Margey interrupted, saying that this wasn't necessary, and Tim was still trying to find his own voice when Tom finished.

"It is necessary. I'm sorry, but I want to leave. I thought it would be a good idea, us coming I mean, but I was wrong. I'm sorry we've, I've, ruined your trip."

Then Tim remembered getting up when Tom started to leave and saying he'd walk him to the office.

He knew Tom Flynn needed to go home so he could escape from this woman, his wife.

A car tore up Madison Avenue and screamed around the corner at 90th Street. Tim reached up and flipped on the siren.

He reached over and poked Tom. "Wake up. I think we have a drunk driver."

Tom sat up straight, refitted his hat, and reached for the radio.

They heard the sound of squealing brakes, the crash, glass breaking, and rounded the corner seconds later.

"Would you look at that," Tom chuckled. "The jerk's gone and parked himself on a fire hydrant."

{ Chapter 8 }

"Jesus," Kate swore out loud, "this thing is a deathtrap. It barely has a clutch."

Kate ground Flynn's old Volkswagen into reverse and tried to parallel park it correctly. She gave up after the third time. She was afraid there would be nothing left of the clutch if she tried it again. She hurriedly gathered her purse and shawl from the passenger seat and pushed open the cranky door with her knee.

It was ten minutes to seven, and she contemplated not putting a quarter into the parking meter.

After all, she reasoned, *he's a cop, he can fix a ticket. No, Kate, not this cop. He's not like that.*

She felt around at the bottom of her purse, found a quarter, and put it in the meter.

She smoothed the skirt of her white silk dress and nervously fluffed up her hair.

Then she wrapped her huge lavender Galway shawl around her bare shoulders and started walking down Columbus Avenue to the Museum Café.

She felt nervous and scared. She was sure she looked all wrong, that he would hate her in the dress she was wearing, that he had changed his mind about her, that he wouldn't even be there. Then she remembered with a smile that he would have to come. She had his car.

When she was a block away she had convinced herself that her hair was a mess and that she was wearing too much makeup.

And then she was at the door. She pulled it open and walked in with as much dignity and calm as she could muster through her nervousness. As she was thanking God that she hadn't dropped her purse, she spotted him at a table in the rear of the restaurant, mutilating the plastic straw from his drink. She had just a brief moment to watch him before he saw her. He looked as nervous as she felt.

He glanced up and spotted her across the crowded restaurant. His whole body seemed to break into a giant sun-filled smile when he saw her. He pushed his chair back noisily and went to her and embraced her.

All her fear and nervousness vanished at his touch and were replaced by wobbly knees and giggles.

"What's so funny?" he whispered in her ear after kissing it.

"This is the first time I have ever seen you in clothes." He pulled back, smiling, and arched his eyebrows quizzically. "I mean, other than kilts."

"And which do you like better?" he asked in a hoarse whisper. She could hear the desire in his voice, and she felt a warmth and yearning seep through her body.

"The kilts," she murmured, brushing his neck with her lips as she spoke.

"Why?" His voice was low, and he drew her to him and held her tighter.

"Oh, just because."

"You are driving me crazy."

Kate could feel his body responding to hers.

"Let's either sit down and have a drink or get the hell out of here."

"Let's leave."

He threaded her arm through his, turned them around in the middle of the crowded restaurant, and they left.

It was beginning to get dark, and a cool breeze was coming up, riffling her hair, cooling her, and moving the impeccable tablecloths in the outdoor cafés. They crossed Columbus Avenue, and Flynn embraced her in the privacy of the dark under the trees. He cradled her in his arms and kissed her longingly. When he released her lips, she breathed a sigh of pure happiness and contentment.

"You look beautiful." His voice was soft and laden with love. He asked her where she had parked the car, and they walked up Columbus Avenue toward it.

An inextinguishable desire was mounting in her, and Kate tried to focus on the city around her. She had never felt this way in her life, reckless and burning to be alone with him again. She wanted to hide away in a cave with him, warm and safe, and never come out.

She tried to focus on the octagonal concrete-block sidewalk, the heavily greened trees surrounding the Museum of Natural History, the museum itself, anything to keep her from losing control of herself.

But as they walked along in companionable silence, her awareness of him overcame her—the feel of his hip moving against her as they walked, the taut muscles of his arm under her fingers, his chest against her forearm, the sound of his breathing, the scent of him, everything.

"I know this really great place," she began hesitantly, the fight for control lost, "where the food is quite good, the ambience wonderful, the dress optional, and it's only forty-five minutes away."

He stopped and bent down and kissed her again.

"I thought you'd never ask."

That first evening together in the city seemed a million days away. They had driven home slowly, all the rush and desperation gone. They had made a hodge-podge dinner of leftovers with wine under candlelight. They talked quietly and held hands, exchanged tendernesses and love. That was the night they pulled away all the layers of the wasted years they had spent apart. Flynn quietly told her why he hadn't come back, his fears and pain.

Kate had cried, and he had held her in his arms and continued, hesitantly, to the hard part.

He told her he had always known she had tried to find him. He told her about the times, and there were many, when she had almost succeeded. He told her how he had felt then, his anguish, his agony and entrapment. She was a mass of hurt and anger and love. Then he begged her, tears spilling down his cheeks, to forgive him. He begged her to understand that he had needed the time they were apart. He had needed the time to grow and change, to understand himself. He had to sort out his life, to come to know what was really important, not the rote existence he had been living.

She forgave him with her whole heart, never questioning him about Joan and his children now. She knew that he loved her, that she would have to let him work it out himself, and that she would accept any decision he made.

She pushed back the dark shadows and howling misgivings that threatened to rush in on them and basked in the glow of his love.

He carried her to bed and made love to her patiently and very tenderly. That night she was very shy and girlish and funny, and she slept curled in his arms.

He had lain awake holding her. Looking at her, he was stunned at how deep his feelings really were.

She whimpered in her sleep, and he dried his eyes and pulled her tighter to him. As he was drifting, right on the edge between sleep and awareness, he heard her whisper, "I love you, Tom Flynn."

"Flynn, do you believe in God?" Kate asked a few days later. She placed her empty wine glass carefully on the table beside their double chaise and rolled back, putting her head on Flynn's shoulder.

"No . . . I don't anymore. Do you?" He reached up and brushed a stray lock of hair from her eyes.

There was a full moon and a cool breeze blowing through the woods behind Kate's house. She shivered, and Flynn pulled her closer to him.

"Do you want me to get us a blanket?"

"No, just stay here and hold me closer," Kate purred.

She snuggled deeper into his arms and sighed with

deep contentment. He smiled down at her upturned face and kissed her on the temple. They lay like that, comfortable and warm, in silence, and thought for a while.

"Yes, I believe in God."

"Really? I wouldn't have thought so."

"I do. But not the Catholic God you don't believe in anymore."

Flynn shifted her out of his arms and stood up.

"I'm going to get another drink. Can I get you one?"

"No thanks. Just come back soon. I'm cold."

"God is God. Are you sure you don't want another drink?"

"Okay, get me another. Flynn, why don't you believe in God anymore?"

He had already made his way across the back patio and into the kitchen. Kate could hear him breaking open another tray of ice to make their drinks.

Why don't I believe, he thought to himself. The scenes of death and degradation he had witnessed over the past seventeen years as a New York City police officer whirred by. His mind went from one painful image to another. The five-year-old child he had found rotting in a refrigerator. The fourteen-year-old girl, a runaway, then a prostitute, then dismembered. The endless line of grandparents abandoned in the Bronx and Brooklyn, found weeks after they had died alone. *That's why I don't believe in God,* he thought to himself. *How could any merciful and all-forgiving God permit those things to happen?*

"Because of all the death and pain and suffering I have seen." Flynn handed Kate her wine and resumed his place in her arms.

"If there really was a God, then he wouldn't allow . . . Look, let's just change the subject, okay, honey?"

Kate took a sip of her chilled white wine and, reaching across his chest, put it down and continued talking.

"You know, Flynn, I first believed in God when I was about twelve. I had just had a terrible fight with Deirdre, and I was really in the wrong. The whole family was angry at me. Even Brian was angry. He called me a little witch. Anyway, I went outside, way in the back to the field behind our house. I think I went there to have a good cry and punish them for not loving me enough to let me be wrong.

"It was very hot, and the Queen Anne's Lace and Golden Rod were in full bloom. The grasshoppers were making a racket. I lay down and looked up at the sky. It was one of those summer skies with absent-minded little clouds floating across a deep, penetrating blue.

"After I had cried about all the injustices being done to me, I stopped to look at the sky. I lay there on my back with my arms out and my palms pressed into the earth. I saw the curve of the earth in that sky.

"It was so immense. After a while it made me feel tiny. I remember thinking that there was plenty of room all over the earth for all the children to lie like that and see the sky and feel small . . . and maybe fall off."

Flynn chuckled and pulled her closer to him, and Kate continued.

"I started to feel very frightened. I felt that the sky and then the clouds and then the air were all pressing down on me, so I rolled over.

"I started to watch the bugs in the grass—ants,

grasshoppers, flies, and lazy bees—and I started to feel immense. My fingers felt thick and heavy. I had become a giant. Then I realized that I could very well be lying on thousands of living creatures too small for me to even see. So I rolled over onto my back. I looked up at the sky, hoping I would feel small again. But I didn't. I just felt like myself. Medium."

Flynn cupped her chin in his hand, moved her face, and kissed her gently on her lips, pulling her even closer, and said, "I love you very much, Kate. Shut up."

But she continued.

"Flynn, I was a part of the sky and the earth and everything around me. And then I felt apart from everything. That feeling that I had that day, being a part of and apart from everything, I have carried in my heart all my life, and, Flynn, I believe that feeling inside of me is what God is. Like Kevin is a part of me and apart from me.

"Not very Catholic. No mean God with lightning bolts sitting up there in the clouds baiting you with promises of salvation or damnation if you don't say you're sorry. A God ever ready to hurl you to hell or raise you to heaven.

"That's not God, honey, that's called pantheism. Your belief that nature is God and God is nature. It's being a part of nature, being at peace with everything around you, and being aware of your place in the scheme of things and living there . . . well, that's wonderful for you."

"Who, may I ask, said that's not God, Father Flynn?"

He rolled over on top of her and buried his face in

her neck, kissed her there, and muttered, "Where's my collar? Where'd I put my collar?"

"Right! The Catholic Church said so! Right?" Laughing, Kate heaved him off of her and sat on his chest.

Flynn was laughing helplessly. "If you had gone to Catholic schools, my little heathen, you would have been taught about the Catholic God you so easily dismiss. You know? Saint Patrick's shamrock, the Trinity, the Father, the Son, and the Holy Spirit. Three people, one God, hmm? You know, the image of the three leaves all coming together in one long stem?"

"That's fine, Flynn, but you say you don't believe in God anymore, so all of this is pointless dialogue. Unless, of course, you've changed your mind in the last few minutes, hmm?"

Suddenly he became very serious, and Kate could feel his body relax under hers.

"It was very comforting when I had those beliefs. Emotionally I guess I'm still attached to them, but intellectually I can't accept them anymore. It's left me feeling very empty at times. An emptiness which I am glad you don't have. I envy you."

Kate embraced him, feeling as if she had hurt him. "I'm sorry," she whispered. "I didn't mean to hurt you. It's just that, well, at the Feis, well somehow if you're not Catholic you're made to feel less Irish, and I feel very Irish. They make me feel like an outsider, and it hurts my feelings and makes me angry, so I pick on any handy Catholic I can find."

Flynn reached up and grabbed her.

"Come here, you little heathen. Father Flynn wants to feast on you now."

"You! I'm serious!"

"Of course you are . . . and so am I."

"Mommy." Tom and Kate heard Kevin's voice calling from inside the house.

"Oops." Tom broke their embrace quickly and guiltily.

"I'd better go see what's the matter." Kate started to get up from the chaise when Kevin suddenly appeared beside them in the moonlight.

He was wearing his Superman pajamas, and his coppery gold hair was rumpled, his face crumbling with tears. He looked at Flynn uncertainly, then went to his mother and curled his sturdy little-boy body into her lap.

"Mommy, I had a bad dream." Flynn watched her enfold Kevin into her body. The warmth and love that encircled her son, as her arms did, was palpable.

"Hush now. You don't have to cry anymore. I'm here." She rocked him gently in her arms, letting him cry, his bare feet sticking out, resting on Tom's chest. His tears gradually subsided, and as she held and rocked him she made a singsong humming noise.

"Tell me what the dream was about so I can make it go away." And she continued to rock and hold him.

Flynn watched them with wonder. Here was this woman he loved, turning into a warm and comforting mother before his eyes. He had seen the little girl in her, the passionate woman in her. She was sometimes shy, very often funny, as well as bright and smart. He knew from the photographs on the walls that she was a brilliant photographer and, from hearing her talk on the telephone, a complete professional. He had already decided she was a good mother, but now he was overwhelmed with the sight of just how good, how good and deeply loving.

"Mommy." Kevin's voice was small and burdened with tears. "Mommy, I dreamed that I woke up and saw you and Tom walking into the woods. I was too afraid of the dark to follow you. I yelled and yelled for you to stop, but you didn't hear me." He started to cry again, and Kate held him tightly and kissed him and asked him if that was all.

"No, Mommy, then Sam came into the house and asked me where you were, and I told him that you went away into the woods with Tom." Kevin's voice rose, and he pulled away from her and looked into her face and finished. "Then Sam got up and went into the woods after you, and he left me all alone too. I was all alone, Mommy. I didn't know what to do, and it was dark, and I couldn't find the telephone, and I was afraid." He started to cry very hard then, and she held him tightly until his sobs subsided.

Flynn was seized with a near uncontrollable desire to scoop both of them up in his arms, to tell them both that no one was going anywhere, that they were safe.

But the image of Maureen loomed up, and his guilt with it. He suddenly wanted to go back to his house and check on all of his children. He needed to know that they were safe and asleep in their beds. He needed to see Maureen tucked in with her teddy bear clasped to her delicate frame.

". . . and you know I would never ever leave you or scare you." Kate's gentle, reassuring voice brought him back to their reality, and he listened. The moonlight was streaming down on them. It was warm and still and green all around.

"I love you with all my heart, and home is where your heart is, and my home is here with you. You are my home, Kevin. It wouldn't matter if we lived in a tepee or an igloo or a mansion, you are my home, I am yours. I would never ever leave you."

Flynn felt a burning and a tearing hurt begin inside him. She was right, and his heart was torn in two.

"I love you, Mommy."

"I love you too, sweetheart. Let's tuck you back in bed before Teddy realizes you're not there."

"Oh, Mommy, Teddy isn't really alive."

"Okay." She smiled down at him and gently brushed back his hair. "But it's very late, and you still have to go back to sleep. Come on. It won't be morning for hours yet." They moved away from Flynn, out of the moonlight and into the dark of the house.

He lay back on the chaise, impatient and hurting. He wondered if Maureen ever had separation dreams, and if she did, if Joan ever held her and comforted her. He realized what he was saying to himself. He should know if she did, he should be there to hold and comfort his children, because he knew Joan never would. Not the way Kate did or the way he could. He felt sick and angry with himself at his neglect.

Then he became aware of Kate standing in the moonlight watching him. Her face was creased with concern. He started to speak, but she held up her hands and stopped him.

"No, let me say it." She paused, looked down at her hands, then back up at him. "I think you should leave and go there . . . to check on your children."

He got up and looked away from her. She stood there with her hands at her sides. He turned to her and gestured helplessly, and she filled his arms with her body and her love.

"Thank you. Thank you for understanding."

She pulled away from him and looked up. A serious expression covered her face.

"Whatever happens, please don't ever say thank you. I don't know what I want you to say instead, but somehow thank you separates us and makes me feel like a stranger to you."

She walked with him to the door, and he turned to her and said, "I love you."

"I know, Tom, I know. Go now before I think of a way to make you stay."

The door clicked shut quietly behind Flynn. Kate heard his feet crunch on the drive as she rested her forehead against the door. She heard the car engine fire, then finally start, and she heard him drive away.

She didn't cry. She didn't do anything. She just went to bed and slept.

{ Chapter 9 }

Kate twirled the telephone cord nervously as she waited for Eileen to answer on the other end. Tom's suit, shirt, and tie were laid out neatly on the bed, his good shoes, socks, shaving cream, razor, and toothbrush packed away in his sport bag.

Kate was a wreck. She paced the rug in her bedroom as far as the telephone cord would allow.

"McKenna Agency." Eileen answered the telephone.

"Hello, Eileen. It's me, Kate."

"Hi. What time can I expect you and Tom?" Eileen's normally cheerful voice stopped Kate's pacing. Except by reading her mind, how could Eileen know how apprehensive she was about tonight?

"Oh, well, I should be there at about 5:30 if that's all right with you."

"Fine. You can shower and change here," Eileen responded.

"Thanks. I was hoping you would offer. I'm dropping Tom's stuff off at the station house . . ."

"Why?" Eileen interrupted. "He can change here too."

"No, Eileen, I think he'd feel more comfortable changing at the station house. He said he would get to your place at around 7:30. Okay?"

Eileen hesitated before she asked her next question.

"That's fine with me, but I have to ask you. Are you sure it's Tom who would feel more comfortable changing at the station house, or is it you?"

Leave it to Eileen to see through all the false barriers and right to the heart of the matter.

"Oh, Eileen, you're right," Kate admitted as she sat down on the edge of her bed. "It's me! What if you don't like him. What if Ira hates him, what if Deirdre calls him a pig. What if he hates you guys? What if . . ."

"Whoa there." Eileen stopped her. "What's the matter with you? This is the man you love. You wouldn't pick someone to love that all of us wouldn't like. Sure, maybe there'll be some uncomfortable moments, and the fact that he's still married is a sore point with me, at least, but, Kate, we care about you and we want to like him."

Kate could feel some of the tension easing, and she thanked Eileen for being so terrific.

"Nonsense. We are all a pretty bright group of people, and we all want to get along, you dumbbell!"

"Dumbbell, am I?" Kate laughed back to Eileen.

"That's right, dumbbell. I don't know how your Tom

can stand being with such a twit. Now cut the crap and I'll see you at 5:30. And Tom is welcome to shower and change here too! See ya." Eileen hung up before Kate could say another word.

Eileen was right. They'd both be more comfortable in her huge apartment. Nervously she put in a call to the station house and in her best professional voice asked the desk sergeant to have Mr. Flynn call Ms. Katherine Gallagher. She gave him her number, adding that it was important but not urgent.

She went back to sewing the little name labels on the clothes Kevin was taking to camp the following Sunday. After she finished his last pair of shorts, she made the beds and advanced on the kitchen. She had just plunged her hands into the hot soapy water when the telephone rang.

She made grumpy noises to herself and, wiping her hands on her jeans, snatched the telephone off the hook.

"Hello."

"Hello yourself." It was Tom. "You sound like you're ready to bite people. What's up, little girl?"

"Oh, Tom," she sighed back. She wanted him now. Right there with her in the kitchen. She missed him, and she wanted his arms around her, the feel of him solid against her.

"I'm sorry, honey, I'm just grouchy this morning."

"No kidding," he teased gently.

"Listen, why don't you meet me at Eileen's. She invited us both to shower and change there."

"Great. That's a lot more appealing than the locker room at the station. I can be there . . . say 6:30. Okay?"

Kate was staring at the soap bubbles in the sink, and as she listened to Tom she started to cry.

"Are you there, honey? Hello."

"I'm here," Kate sniffed back.

"What's wrong, sweetheart? What else is bothering you? Tell me."

"Oh, Tom, I miss you. I want to hold you right now. I want to forget everyone and everything in the world and run away with you." She finished trying to hold back her crying.

"Kate, I love you. Can you hold out a little while longer? I'll try to get to Eileen's earlier, and we can talk, and I can hold you and whisper dirty words in your ear."

"Oh you!" He had her laughing through her tears. "I'll see you later."

"No, listen." He was laughing too. "If it makes you feel that good, I'll call you back later and give you your own personalized obscene telephone call. How about . . . And then my tongue will . . ."

"Tom Flynn, go back to work!" She felt better, and he knew it.

"Listen, little girl, I'll see you later, and I love you."

"I love you too. Stay safe for me."

"I will."

She hung up, pushed her apprehensions out of her mind, and set about making lunch for the boys. Nicky, Pat, and Kevin were out in the woods painting the clubhouse Tom had built for Kevin.

When the tuna salad sandwiches and tall glasses of lemonade were lined up and waiting on the kitchen bar for the boys, she went to the back door and called them in for lunch.

All in all they hadn't done a bad job. There actually was more paint on the clubhouse than on them. They squirted each other with the hose, rinsing the paint off and drying themselves with clean terrycloth rags.

Kate could hear them talking and making plans for their clubhouse, and every now and then she heard Kevin's voice repeating Tom's name.

They had been awkward with each other at first, feeling each other out. Kevin was resentful of the time his mother spent with Flynn, time that previously belonged to him alone. Tom was reluctant to get close to Kevin because it made him feel guilty about his own kids, particularly about Maureen, who was Kevin's age.

But then one night Kevin had mentioned a clubhouse and asked Kate if she would help him build it. She was starting to answer when Tom interrupted, telling Kevin that they would get up together the next day very early, make their own breakfast, and build it together.

"And we'll let your mother sleep late tomorrow, okay?"

Kevin was thrilled, and he said it was okay with him. When the clubhouse was finished, the relationship between Flynn and Kevin had form and structure.

Kate watched the boys cross the patch of back lawn and approach her. They looked tanned and healthy, and Kevin looked the happiest he had ever been.

"And remember, no girls!" Nicky was going over the clubhouse rules when they came in.

"What's this?" Kate said in mock outrage. "No girls in your clubhouse?"

"Aw, Mom, you're not a girl exactly. You can come in."

"I am too a girl," she teased back.

"Aw, Mom, you're a mother. It's different." Kevin quickly changed the subject and asked, "What's for lunch?" They all groaned when she said tuna but filed into the kitchen anyway.

"What time will you and Tom be home, Mom?" Kevin bit into the second half of his sandwich.

"Very late, honey. And no, before you ask me, you can't wait up."

"Who's gonna babysit me?"

"Noreen."

"Can Pat and Nicky spend the night?" Kevin asked the question most mothers dread, and it was followed by a chorus of pleases and unreliable promises of excellent behavior.

"That's up to Josie and Noreen."

"Yay!" All three of them jumped up and down and hugged her, saying thank you, and raced for the telephone.

She knew Josie would say yes and wondered if Noreen was crazy enough to say yes too. She heard three little boys begging on the phone and figured they had passed Josie and were down to the nitty-gritty with Noreen. After a little more begging and several more unreliable promises she heard an outburst of yays and assumed Noreen had capitulated.

Kevin came rushing back into the kitchen and hugged her.

"Thanks, Mom. I promise we'll be good. We're gonna finish painting the clubhouse, okay?" He started to leave after she said yes, then stopped and turned to her.

"Mom."

"Yes, sweetheart."

"Mom, I really like Tom. I hope you marry him." He turned and left quickly to rejoin Nicky and Pat, who were already busy painting.

She stared after him as he ran across the grass into the cooler shadows of the woods.

Oh, merciful Mother, she was scared. *What have I done?* she asked herself. *What if Tom and I don't make it? What if Kevin loses Tom too? What if I lose him?*

She stood there and allowed all her fears and doubts to possess her, and then slowly her love for her son and for Flynn firmly pushed them aside.

What is human life worth if we refuse the courage of our hearts, to love no matter how impossible it seems? I can never lose what I have now. The fight is really his. His love for me, his children, even Kevin, versus his guilt and misplaced sense of duty.

She turned to the sink and finished washing up the pots, then put the rest of the luncheon dishes in the dishwasher and turned it on.

The buzzer sounded in Eileen's apartment, and she hollered, "I'll get it, Kate."

Kate smiled to herself. Normally it would have been, "Kate, will you get the door." She turned and finished hanging Tom's clothes in the guest bedroom closet, and took a few deep breaths to steady her nerves.

"Hey, Kate," Eileen called from the door, "there's a tall, good-lookin' cop at the door. Do you think I should let him in?"

Kate dropped his shoes and rushed down the hall like a teenager. He filled the doorway and was leaning one arm up on the frame casually, hat back, the other hand

on his hip. She stopped dead in her tracks as if she had
been hit in the gut with a baseball bat.

He was standing there, grinning down at Eileen,
oozing more sex appeal and charm than she thought a
man could possibly ooze. Eileen was rocking back and
forth on her stocking feet. *My God*, Kate thought. *She
even has her hands behind her back like Little Bo Peep*.

She stood there watching them flirt with each other
as a burning, consuming jealousy raged through her.

Tom glanced up and caught the look on Kate's face.
As he straightened up and moved toward her, Eileen
turned, confused, and saw Kate nod stiffly, turn on her
heel, and head down the hall back to the guest room. In
the distance Kate could hear them talking. She was
struggling to keep from crying.

"I don't know, Tom. The guest room is down the
hall, first door on the right."

She heard him thank Eileen, walk down the hall, and
open the door.

"Kate?" His voice was innocent and concerned. He
walked over to her and turned her around to face him.

"Kate, what's wrong? Honey, tell me."

"Nothing." She hoped her face was a stony mask. He
took the scarf she was fiddling with out of her hands,
but she continued to look at the floor, refusing to meet
his eyes, afraid that he would see the jealous tears
there.

Holding her by the shoulders, he bent at the knees
and ducked his head sideways, trying to get a look at
her face. She turned her head away from him.

Furious with herself as her tears started to flow in
earnest, she tried to break away from his grip. And
then, to make matters worse, the teenager in her

blurted out, "Maybe you'd rather I stay here and you and Eileen can go out together."

She turned her tear-stained face up to him. He was trying very hard not to smile or laugh at her and to be serious and reassuring.

He lost. A huge grin of delight and amazement split his face, his eyes twinkled mischievously, and he laughed.

"You're jealous! Why, you crazy little girl, you're jealous!"

"I am not." She broke his grip and stamped away from him into the adjoining bathroom.

She slammed the door, turned on the shower, stripped, and got in.

She felt like a fool and continued crying as the hot shower pummeled her face.

She heard the bathroom door open, then close, and the swish of the shower curtain. Then she felt his naked body behind her.

He turned her around gently but firmly and covered her mouth with his. He was still kissing her as he soaped his hands and started to wash her body.

She tried in a weak attempt to squirm away from him. He didn't let go.

Then a familiar hunger built up in her, and he pushed her up against the tiled wall and took her there. She wrapped her legs around his waist and her arms around his neck, and over the sound of the shower she could hear him groan with each thrust. She heard her own voice and then a sobbing cry break free from her throat. She went limp and let her legs slide down his.

He pushed the wet hair out of her eyes and drew her

to him. "I love *you*. I want *you*. I need *you*. I don't love, want, or need any other woman but *you*. You do not have now or ever will have any reason to be jealous of another woman. Understood?"

"Understood," she whispered back. He gave her a firm kiss, handed her the soap and a loofah pad, and told her to wash his back. She did, then he did, and then he washed her hair.

When they got out of the shower, he dried himself off quickly, then he dried her slowly, and never stopped looking into her eyes.

They re-entered the darker guest room. Tom closed the door to the hall and took her again.

Afterward, she lay on top of him, resting, his arms and legs wrapped around her, and wondered to herself if her hunger for him would ever diminish.

She propped herself up on his chest, her damp, tangled hair hiding their faces as she kissed his lips sweetly, then his closed eyes, and whispered to him that she was going to get up and get dressed.

He roused himself from his half sleep and did the same.

"I'm starving," Flynn said. He was standing behind Kate, and in the mirror she watched him finish his tie. She was dressed in heavy green silk, her hair cascading down her back. His suit was light gray, and he wore a blue shirt that accentuated his dark good looks. She stood there transfixed by the image of the two of them in the full-length mirror. She caught his eye, and he smiled at her.

"We sure do make a handsome couple." Tom wrapped his arms around her waist, and they stood there looking at their image.

Kate waited until the tightness in her throat eased off and responded. "We do, don't we," she said to his eyes.

"Don't think about it." He was looking at her image intently. "Don't think about it, and trust me—please trust me. I'll do something about . . ."

Kate turned around in his arms and stopped his lips with hers before he made promises to her that he couldn't keep. She always stopped him. His life was stressful enough, and she was determined never to be yet another source of stress or guilt.

"Hello in there." Eileen's teasing voice made them both smile. "If you two have stopped making up for lost time, I'd like . . ."

Kate walked over and opened the door.

". . . to let you know that Deirdre and Nye are here," Eileen finished, studying Kate.

"You know, Kate, women only look as radiantly beautiful as you do when they are either in love, pregnant, or new brides."

"Thank you, Eileen." Kate made a mock curtsy.

"So which is it with you? I know you're not a new bride—so you're probably pregnant, right?" Eileen gave Kate a poke, called her Cat the Brat, and preceded them down the hall.

Tom put his jacket on and followed the two of them into the living room. They both looked sensational, Kate's red hair on green silk, Eileen's curly black hair topping red silk. Over their heads he saw Kate's sister Deirdre.

These Gallagher women were amazing, nothing but nonstop good-looking women.

Flynn gave Kate's shoulder a reassuring squeeze. She

moved to her sister. They exchanged hugs and greetings before she turned and introduced Deirdre to Flynn.

He did the same thing to Deirdre that he did to Eileen, and Kate was secretly amused as she watched her little sister lose her voice. Deirdre never lost her voice.

Nye stuck out his hand and introduced himself, then reclaimed Deirdre with an arm around her waist.

The buzzer went off again, and Eileen went to get the door. Tom and Nye went to the bar and made drinks for everyone.

"It's probably Ira. Make me a martini, two olives, dry, and Ira will have a scotch."

They could hear the "hello darlings" and "you look delicious" and kissing noises at the door, then a bag rattling and "here's the milk and butter." Then Dr. Ira Gottlieb, author of *Sexual Violence,* entered the large, comfortable living room. He was tall, sandy-haired, and gangly. He always looked rumpled, and he blinked behind his glasses. He was also filthy rich, through Eileen's fine agenting of him, and was as warm, compassionate, and loving as a man could be.

Introductions were made all around. When he came to Flynn he stopped.

"I came here tonight predisposed to dislike you." Kate's ears started buzzing, and she felt panicky. "But, any man who can make Kate as happy as she is right now, I have to like." They shook hands and exchanged relaxed smiles.

Ira put his free arm around Kate's shoulders and held his drink with the other.

"This is one incredible woman you have here, Tom. Take good care of her."

"God, Ira, you've got to be the biggest conversation stopper in the world." Eileen broke the tension and continued, dragging Kate into the kitchen. "Help me get the hors d'oeuvres, Kate."

Talk and easy laughter flowed again as Ira settled in. Kate heard Ira ask Deirdre if it was true that she was an Irish fanatic.

"Here we go, Eileen. Ira's just fired up Deirdre."

"What, Kate?"

"Ira's just asked Deirdre if it's true that she's an Irish fanatic."

"Well, one thing's for sure," Eileen said as she put the last little sandwich on the tray, "this isn't going to be a dull evening."

After finishing their drinks, the three couples wandered out into the night. They decided to walk to dinner. It had rained earlier that evening, cleaning the air and the streets, and now a cool breeze blew through Central Park, rustling the leaves as a man's fingers would thread through his beloved's hair. All over New York lights started to wink on as the sun set.

They walked slowly, talked quietly, and enjoyed each other's presence. By the time they had reached 90th Street it was dark. Kate stopped and looked up at the sky. It was a marvel of black velvet and clear, brilliant stars. She sighed with deep contentment, hugged Tom to her, and whispered, "I love you." He bent down and kissed her on the tip of her nose, and they held each other for a bit.

No one interrupted their moment, each waiting for them to continue their walk, each reacting privately to the sight of Kate and Tom in love.

It was promising to be one of those special summer

nights when lovers do happy things together, make sweet love, and laugh in pleasant disbelief.

It was the kind of night that beckons more regular people into Central Park than muggers, when people crowd the Staten Island ferry and wax philosophical and romantic.

A gentle night for a beautiful city beleaguered with violence and neglect, living in consort with untold wealth.

All the windows of the restaurant were open, and delicious aromas wafted out onto the sidewalk and quickened their pace.

Harry Jones was playing Cole Porter tunes on the piano. He was a handsome man, sort of a cross between Steve Canyon and Richard Widmark, and when he saw them walk in his face broke into one of his famous shining smiles.

Kate and Eileen raised their hands and wiggled their fingers at him, chorusing, "Hiya, Harry."

George, the owner, showed them to a huge table in the corner by the open windows. A round of drinks, compliments of Harry, more Cole Porter and cool calming breezes, and they were relaxed and expansive and ready to dine. The murmur of truly satisfied diners ebbed and flowed around them.

George returned for their order, and after much hemming and hawing and indecision he said, "Since none of you knows what you want, why not let me pick dinner for all of you?"

They all agreed and went back to their conversation. Nye and Deirdre were trying to explain to Ira why they were so involved in Irish politics, and Tom and Eileen were interjecting from time to time to reinforce the points they were making. Kate was cradled in Tom's left arm, her head against his shoulder, and as she listened to them talk she mused to herself.

She was here with family and friends and the man she loved, the man she knew she would love for the rest of her life. She was filled with a deep sense of completeness. All the turbulent desperation in her soul had been replaced, finally, by an overwhelming peace.

"Wake up, dreamy eyes." Tom's arm cozied her. "The food is here."

The pungent aroma of bouillabaisse surrounded her, and all around the table words like "scrumptious," "delicious," "fantastic," came out in sighs between bites. George served them cucumber salad with yogurt, curry, and tumeric dressing and a mysterious cluchen à la George that crumbled the defenses of the most avid dieters. The wine was perfect and unplaceable, and he polished them off with a fresh fruit sorbet, rich thick coffee, and armagnac.

Harry joined them, and their conversation resumed. Kate excused herself and went to the ladies room. The evening was a staggering success. She patted cold water on her flushed face, freshened her makeup, recombed her hair, and left.

As she moved across the room toward their table, she could hear Tom's and Ira's raised voices. It sounded like they were arguing, and, startled out of her wistful mood, she rejoined them quickly.

"It alarms me, Ira, that you seem to be more concerned with the fact that I called her a nigger bitch than with the fact that she dipped her infant son into a pot of boiling water to shut him up!" Tom's body was radiating anger, and Kate ran her hand up and down his back, hoping it would have a calming effect on him.

"Tom, what upsets me is the attitude the police have toward the people they police. The societal impact of using racial epithets from your position of control and power over a downtrodden and impoverished minority only leads to the speculation that you view all minorities as less than equal, with a kind of conspiratorial disdain. Obviously the woman had severe emotional problems that should have been dealt with."

"Ira, the bottom line is still the fact that she boiled her baby boy. There are millions of people with emotional problems, millions of poor people, millions of people who face difficulties and tremendous hardship that do not boil their infant children. Unfortunately, cops never see those people. We only see people in crisis. How, may I ask, would you suggest I vent my rage, my anger, appropriately? My partner and I tried to get this baby to the hospital before he died. He died in my arms in the car. Huge pieces of flesh fell off as I held him. It stuck to my pants, the wet blanket wrapped around him, to my bare arms. He was just a small, brand-new human being, crying out for food and the reassuring body of his mother, and she boiled him to death. It sickens my soul.

"You don't know what a kike bastard is until you see his mother rotting into the floorboards of her apartment, having died of starvation, and him driving up in his Mercedes from Scarsdale to claim whatever pitiful belongings might be of value left in her apartment. Do you know what a rotting human body smells like? A human being that a month earlier ventured out onto the streets after hours of preparation? To bathe and dress and look like there's nothing wrong when you are starving to death, a person that looks to the police officer for protection so she can make it to the store and back to buy cat food and rotting vegetables?"

Ira had turned an uncomfortable shade of white, and Eileen was gripping his hand under the table.

"You don't know what a spic bastard is until you have seen a ten-year-old girl, raped repeatedly by her brother and fifteen of his friends, then cut and mutilated but still alive. How do I approach the child that this has happened to without frightening her? How do I reassure and help her before the ambulance arrives? Where in my heart and my soul can I find a gentleness so profound that I can reach out to her in those moments and make her feel safe at least? Do you know what is in the eyes of a ten-year-old child who has been raped and maimed, Ira?"

Tom's voice was filled with anger and grief, and as he continued Kate moved her body closer to his as if to protect him, and Harry Jones moved close to him on the other side.

"And then there are the mick bastards that beat up their children and the mothers who don't feed them and send them out to the streets to beg.

"In every ethnic group there are the monsters, and if I use racial epithets to try to vent my rage and anger and the mortification of my soul—tough shit! Because I am also the one who knocks on the door in a filthy building in the Bronx and sees a proud, dignified Cuban, hard-working and painfully clean, collapse. These hands, these arms hold him in his grief after I tell him that his son—his hope, his reason for living—has been knifed to death on his way home from his psychology class at Columbia. And my rage gets worse, Ira.

"I am just a man in a blue suit, with a badge and a gun, put out onto the streets to protect, to enforce laws, to help . . . and I am beginning to feel like a human garbage man, helpless to protect, unable to help, and"—Tom spat out a bitter laugh—"stripped of my ability to enforce the law. There are no laws, Ira. There is a war going on out there, and, as it has been said before, cops are a thin blue line of underpaid mercenaries, hired to contain the rage and despair of the poor, so as not to disturb or in any way ruffle the feathers of the disdainful, indifferent rich."

The silence at their table had extended to the tables surrounding them as the "indifferent rich" listened.

"Ira, I'm scared shitless. I love, I have feelings, I have children and Kate who I want to feel clean for, whole for. I look down at my own little Maureen and I see the eyes of Estelle Lopez. I am frightened for Kate when she wanders around this city taking pictures. But I am more alarmed for cops because it has changed us, thrown us out of balance . . ."

Ira interrupted and in a gentle voice finished for Tom, "Because you are afraid that the very violence you abhor is becoming a part of you? And that you are losing your ability to be an open and giving man?"

Tom was nodding yes each time Ira questioned.

"Tom Flynn, if every cop on the streets of New York felt the way you do . . ."

Tom interrupted, saying, "Most do."

"Then I would like to see it."

"Whenever you want to, Ira, you can come out with me and McBride on a night tour."

They reached across the table to each other and shook hands.

"I like you, Tom Flynn."

"You're not so bad yourself, Dr. Gottlieb."

The whole restaurant sighed with relief, and Nye signaled for the check.

George came over to their table and stood before Flynn.

"The dinner is on me, Mr. Flynn. That man in the Bronx was my Uncle Hermes. You are welcome in my restaurant anytime."

"Thank you, George, but the department calls that payola. I thank you for the gesture—the dinner was terrific—but I really want to pay for it."

George shook his head no.

"I don't care what your department calls it, your money is no good here."

George stuck out his hand. "I would also like to shake your hand and tell you that the time you spent talking to my uncle helped him. You may not know it, but I think you must help a lot of people."

They wandered out into the night, savoring the cool, fresh air. Eileen and Ira invited everyone back for a nightcap, but Deirdre and Nye begged off. Deirdre embraced Kate, then Eileen, and then Flynn. She whispered something into his ear, and he smiled.

Eileen and Ira, Tom and Kate were in a mellow mood as they made their way back to Eileen's apartment. They walked and talked quietly, Kate and Eileen talked about her upcoming "Faces" book, and Ira and Tom continued their talk, but in a much more relaxed way.

Ira was really getting into what it's like to be a cop, and Tom was trying to explain. Thoughtfully, almost as if he were talking to himself, Flynn described a cop's feelings of isolation, the imbalance that gradually invaded the way he viewed life, and Kate listened, her conversation with Eileen at an end.

What he was saying and the way he was describing how he felt touched a deep chord within her. She vowed she would make him talk about the job more, make him talk to her, so she could try to soothe him with her love and her understanding.

"Tom, what do you think *is* the problem?" Ira's question was a genuine one. "I mean, what do you think the answer is?"

"It's the same tired old response: education." Tom paused, then went on. "Without going into hours and hours of text and my own experiences, I still think it comes down to education. But not quite. It's more like information, then experience. Successful experiences are the only weapons people have, and the poor are so grossly uninformed and the gap between the harshness of their reality and their real vulnerability in American society is so narrow that it only takes a few disastrous encounters with, say, welfare, the telephone company, Con Ed, or the neighborhood clinic to leave them feeling helpless, then jaded and bitter. All their hopes seem smashed, all their honest effort pointless. They wind up frustrated and angry."

Tom paused again to think. "I know this sounds very simplistic, but I really believe that the solution is that simple and that impossible to implement. The need to know. The need for correct information."

"I'm not sure I understand you." Ira stopped walking, and they stood talking in front of Eileen's building.

"A lot of my job is explaining to people how to go about getting the simplest things done. How to get a driver's license, medical care, the simple who, what, and where of everyday paperwork. They need to know how to get a social security card, where to go and what to bring. Something you and I take for granted seems a monumental achievement for the poorer minorities."

Kate shivered and yawned and, drawing her body into Tom's, said, "Listen, you guys, I'm tired, and I think I want to call it a night."

After goodnights all around, Tom and Kate made their way back to her car.

As they drove out of the city, over the George Washington Bridge, Kate looked back over Tom's shoulder.

"It's like a glittering jewel floating in a black sea." She rested her head on his shoulder and sighed.

"Did you have a good time? Do you like my friends, Tom?"

He had been very quiet and was frowning, lost in his thoughts.

"I liked them fine, Kate. The question is did they like me?" He hesitated, took in a deep breath, and finished.

"Are you ashamed of me, Kate?"

"Am I what?" Kate sat upright in her seat, turned to him, and watched his profile.

"You heard me. Are you ashamed of me?"

"There is nothing about you to be ashamed of. If you are referring to your statements tonight at dinner, well,

I'm more ashamed of myself and my friends for being the sometimes mealy-mouthed ineffectual liberals that we are."

He pulled the car over into the Alpine Lookout, turned it off, and reached for her, crushing her to him.

She was shocked and frightened when she felt his tears on her face.

"I wish I could make the world safe for you and me and our children. If anything were ever to happen to you, if anything ever hurt you . . ." He couldn't finish. She held him tightly and let him cry.

{ *Chapter 10* }

"Hello?" Kate flopped down on her bed and answered the telephone.

"Hi, it's me." Flynn's voice was as cold as stone, and Kate sat bolt upright on her bed, all the warning bells going off in her head at once.

"Hi yourself. What's wrong? You sound terrible."

"One of those fucking FALN pipe bombs went off in Tim's face today."

He could see her running her fingers through her hair as he listened to her sincerely concerned voice respond to him. Joan had never understood his feelings about his job.

"My God, Tom, is he going to be all right? Is there anything you can do? Is there anything I can do? You remember my telling you about my friend Ann, you know, the surgeon . . ."

His heart constricted. All the years with Joan, and all

she ever wanted to know was what time he would be getting home and should she wait dinner. And here was Kate, putting aside their concerns, thinking of his partner.

He wanted to cry, he wanted to be sick, and for the first time in his career he wanted to go home, to Kate, and forget the job and his responsibilities.

"No, Kate. I know she's one of the best, but we're at Bellevue . . ."

Kate interrupted him. "Bellevue, thank God! They have the best nerve specialists in the country. Is the special team working on him?"

He imagined her face, creased with worry as she spoke, concentrating on his every word.

He talked. "It was one of those bombs they make from a pipe and fill with gunpowder and nails. It's the one I told you about that is ignited by a flashbulb. They taped it under a hall light and ran a wire from the socket to the door jamb. So when Timmy opened the door . . . we were responding to a family disturbance call . . . I mean, they set it up that way . . . My God, Kate, the people in the building had to have known and cooperated!

"When he opened up the door he got it in the face and . . . I was still out by the car. Why not me? Why Timmy?" Flynn felt he couldn't go on.

"Tom." Kate's voice was soft and very gentle. "I understand how you must be feeling. Listen, I think you should stay there until he's out of surgery. He won't be so frightened if you're there with him. He trusts you. He would have to be brave for Margey, but he knows you love him. He can be afraid with you, okay?"

The years, the endless years of conversations with Joan descended on him like an oily black cloud. He had never hated her before, but he did now.

"Tom . . . Tom, are you there?" Kate's worried voice cracked through the inky oily sludge around him like sunlight.

"I'm here, Kate, I'm here," he whispered.

"And I'll be here when you're finished there. Remember, I love you, and I'll be waiting."

It was a mob scene in the hall outside the phone booth. Reporters were wandering around, and someone mentioned that the commissioner was on his way uptown and the mayor was on his way downtown.

Kelly from the bomb squad stopped him in the hall, took him by the elbow, and drew him aside.

"I'm sorry about McBride, Tom." He hesitated and then continued. "I've got to know what happened. We're pretty sure you are right about it being an FALN special. Look, I'm sorry, but we've got to talk now."

Flynn had stopped listening to what Kelly was saying when he saw Margey rushing down the corridor. Her hair was a mess, and she wore a sweater that she clutched closed with her left hand.

Her eyes were wild and full of pain. When she saw Flynn she let out an animal-like howl.

"Tom, Tom, Tom . . . is he . . . is he?" She threw herself into his arms and let the last vestiges of her courage fall from her.

Merry Margey, Merry Margey, wherefore art thou, Merry Margey, Flynn thought to himself, and then moved his eyes down to finally meet hers. He had never been able to get used to the look of reproach, masked by fear, pain, and tears, that inevitably surfaced in a cop's wife's eyes. It always shocked and revolted him, and he always let it pass. He had seen much worse in other eyes.

"No, Margey, he's alive . . . but he's been hurt badly." Margey's eyes cleared as Flynn felt tears starting in his. She gripped his forearms viselike as he swallowed and continued.

"It was a pipe bomb, Marge. We were answering a family disturbance call, and Timmy opened the door." Flynn coughed and went on. "It went off in his face."

Margey was sobbing through gritted teeth, tears streaming down her face. All her nightmares came true. She couldn't contain herself any longer and buried her face in Flynn's chest. His arms went around her as her body relaxed, and she sobbed. He continued in a quiet voice as he moved them and sat down on a nearby couch.

"They've been working on him for two and a half hours. They don't really know how badly his eyes have been hurt. He must have seen the flash a split second before the bomb went off. It seems he started to raise his arm and turn his head." Flynn faltered and continued. "He was conscious through the whole thing, Margey. The pain was pretty bad, but"—Flynn pulled her back by the shoulders and made her look at him—"he told me to tell you that he loves you. He said, 'Tell Margey I love her, Tom, tell her I love her.' He kept repeating it all the way on the ride to the hospital."

Margey's sobbing subsided. She blew her nose and sat sideways against Flynn, his arm around her. She was shutting down, looking inside herself quietly for Tim. Gradually her breathing became normal.

They sat there. Kelly from the bomb squad approached Tom again. Satisfied by Margey's assurances that she'd be all right, Flynn finished his interview with Kelly.

The mayor arrived, just after Margey's mother appeared, relieving him as chief emotional supporter. Then the commissioner hurried down the long corridor, and each in turn nodded sympathy at Margey and reassured her, telling her not to worry about a thing. At least the commissioner made a serious effort to get some information on Tim's condition and on how the operation was going. Flynn finished detailing the incident with Kelly and rejoined Margey and her mother. The commissioner shook his hand and slapped him on the back.

Flynn wanted to punch someone.

The reporters and two photographers became animated. Tim was being brought down.

He was as white as the sheet that covered him on the gurney. His whole head was wrapped, his right arm heavily bandaged.

So he had managed it, Flynn thought to himself. He hadn't been able to tell Margey that because there was so much blood everywhere he hadn't been sure just how badly Tim had been hurt.

Mr. García from the little grocery store across the street had brought him towels to help staunch the blood, and the small neighborhood crowd that had gathered was sympathetic and a little helpful. They all knew who had done it, and in a hodge-podge of Colombian to Puerto Rican Spanish had cursed them.

They were the older people in the neighborhood, the people who had come to depend on the police for protection from the younger political and not so political hoods in the neighborhood.

God, there had been so much blood! Head wounds are like that. Tim had lain there, his left leg lolling back and forth, crying and moaning in his pain. He held Tom's hand, sobbing out, "It hurts, Jesus, Mother of God, it hurts."

Tim hadn't said a word about Margey, but Tom knew he loved her and would have said so if the pain hadn't been that bad.

Jesus, the blood! Tom looked down at his pants. His knees were stained even darker where he had knelt in a pool of his partner's blood after he had called in for assistance and an ambulance.

They wheeled Tim by. Margey was attached to his left hand as they rolled him into the special intensive care unit they reserved for cops and other victims of violent crimes. The press followed to the door. The noise in the hall was deafening. They started toward Tom, but the mayor and the commissioner declared they would hold a press conference downstairs in the lobby and steered them away from Flynn. Mercifully they left him alone.

He still wanted to punch someone.

Suddenly his captain was at his elbow. Captain Simpson didn't waste words on false sympathy. He understood what Tom was going through. They sat and talked for a while. The captain didn't try to urge him to do one thing or another. He mentioned that Dihello, who lived near Flynn, would give him a lift home if he wanted. Tom waved the offer away, saying he was going to stay a while. The captain slapped him on the back, stood up, and told him to call in if he wanted anything. Simpson went in to see Margey and check on Tim again, then left.

The corridor was emptying, dark and quiet by then. Tim was still sleeping, and Margey, much recovered, came out to Tom and talked to him in quiet, motherly tones.

She asked after Joan and the kids, then, quickly regretting it, bit her lip, looked up at Tom with gentle eyes, and asked how Kate was.

Flynn loved Margey at that moment. He smiled at her softly, kissed her gently on the lips, and said, "Thank you." She squeezed his hand, got up, and went back to Tim.

No wonder Tim loved her so much. Cops' wives have two nightmares. One Margey had just gone through, that their men would get hurt on the job.

The second is other women. Women loved cops. The uniform, gun, and name tag made them the good guys, the protectors, safe. And Flynn was living the other nightmare.

Tim had told Margey about Tom and Kate, and from the goodness in her loving heart she understood and put aside her own fears.

When Tim had told Tom about his conversation with his wife, he jokingly referred to the rest of the evening. "And I had to make it an extra special night with her." He looked sideways and winked at Tom, who smiled and shook his head in response.

"You know how she is! How a beauty like mine could think I'd go elsewhere, well, women are like that. As if she didn't have enough on her mind."

Flynn looked up. Margey was smiling at him through tear-filled eyes, gesturing for him to come.

"He's awake, Tom, he's asking for you." She took him by the arm and, putting her hand on the small of his back, propelled him toward the bed.

Tim's left eye blinked up at him, and Flynn felt the dread leave him and tears choke him.

Margey and her mother left the room. He took Tim's hand and felt him grip it back. It was a firm grip.

"How you doin'?" was all he could manage to choke out.

Tim gripped the hand he held, his good eye filling with tears. "You're a good man, Tom Flynn," he rasped, "a brother to me. It was a blessing you were there with me, so you could lie so beautifully to my Margey."

Flynn sat down on the chair beside the bed and pulled himself up close to his partner.

A few moments passed before Tim got his breath back and continued. "You know I love you like a brother, Tom, and you, you big jerk, need a good brother."

Flynn put his head down on the white sheet covering Tim and sobbed. Tim's good left hand came to rest on his brother's head.

They stayed like that for a time.

{ *Chapter 11* }

Kate had opened all the windows in the house to the winds gusting in from the northwest. Heavy with the promise of a storm, they cleared the house of the last vestiges of stale summer air.

She had stripped her garden of every available flower in bloom and packed the rooms with their fragrance and colors. Everywhere she went, music and soft Irish laments followed her.

She picked the tomatoes from her garden, thin-skinned and sweet. They were the size of double fists. They went into a salad of fresh basil and bib lettuce. The canteloupe went warm from the sun to the refrigerator for later. Two perfect bottles of High Tor wine, saved for years for a special occasion, were chilled to go with the trout from her father's catch of that day. They were filleted and ready for cooking.

She bathed in the dark, in perfumed water, and thought about her earlier conversation with Flynn.

He had called her that morning from the hospital. It was 5:30. The hushed whispers of the hospital staff surrounded him, and behind those sounds were the rustlings of the very ill waking up to another day of either dying or recovering.

He had stayed in Tim's room all night, dozing and waking. Margey in dim light, her lips close to Tim's, breathed love into his body, her body straining to him, holding his hand between her breasts, her eyes wounded by her own great love for him.

Flynn knew he was intruding, but he watched in fascination. Then the ugly thought came in on him. That could be his Kate, and he could be there, like Tim. He felt panicked and went to call her.

He talked and talked there in the hall. About how he wanted to live now, and he asked Kate if she was afraid.

Kate swirled the water in the bath around her.

Oh yes, she was afraid. Every time he left her sight she willed herself not to think about the danger he was in every minute he was at work. She would touch his body, look into his eyes, experience his kiss before he left for work, and pray each time that there would be another touch, day, kiss . . .

She didn't tell him all this. She answered him saying, "I don't think the powers above would have gone to such great lengths to bring us together again only to rip us apart. Besides, my love will keep you safe."

And in the hall of Bellevue Hospital he sighed to himself at her foolishness, yet hoped she was right.

And he talked on. About Joan and when they were

first married. How he had wanted to have a family of his own, do the right thing, that he hadn't loved Joan when he married her, that he thought she would make a good wife and mother, that she was safe.

Kate had asked him then what he had meant by safe. He said he didn't really know. It was more a feeling than an articulated thought.

Kate knew, but she would wait until he came to it himself. It was sort of the way she had felt about Sam Feeny. Someone you could be married to, not really in love with, safe. They couldn't hurt you or control you or wreck your life, because they didn't have the power of your love to use over you.

She ducked her head into the water, perfuming her hair, and thought about the preparations she had made for this night.

This night was going to be different somehow. She knew it, and she knew he knew it.

The table on the patio was draped in stiff white linen, dressed in the oldest, heaviest silver of her family. The tall, slow-burning candles stood ready, encased in crystal chimneys.

Everything waited for Flynn.

Kate eased herself out of her bath, took an oversized terry towel, and blotted herself dry. In the mirrors of her bedroom she watched as a perfect reflection of herself ran hands over her nakedness. She thought of Flynn and watched in amazement as her flesh tightened in expectation.

She went to a closet, pulled out a white lawn dressing gown, and draped it over herself. It flowed around her, gently caressing her skin with a delicate softness.

* * *

He came into the kitchen as she stood over the sink tearing lettuce. He was wearing khaki shorts and nothing else and kissed her on the back of her neck. She turned her face to him, and he kissed her on her lips, then moved from her and splashed some Jameson's into a glass, fetched his pipes, and went outside to the patio.

The whiskey went down smooth and easy, and he faced the darkening woods and began to pump up the pipes. Then he tuned up by bouncing a few notes off the back wall of the house. His mind was still filled with the hours he had spent with Tim at Bellevue . . . and the hours he had spent thinking about his life and Kate.

She turned off the stereo and went to the back door. The setting sun was splashing bloody color over the landscape, through the woods, and over Flynn. Behind the sound of the drone she could hear the crickets sawing away, then silence, and then a high, thin, piercing wail that stunned her.

Flynn paced and played, baiting the storm, daring it to happen. He made the pipes sob and cry and plead and talk.

Kate listened and watched as the candlelight flickered over his back.

She listened and prayed that at the end of his lament there would be a high sweet note held, and no more.

She prayed that he would end high, long, and clear. He did.

She went to him, and soon their moans were the only sounds in the thick silence around them.

He reached up and under the white lawn gown and caressed her. Then, trembling, he put his hands on her bare shoulders and pushed the dress away from her body. She stood there naked in the moonlight, a white lawn puddle at her feet.

The clouds overhead raced by across the moon, casting light, creating shadow. Flynn walked around her, touching her, looking at her, and touching her again.

She was in an agony of fragmented modesty.

He stopped in front of her, looked at her long and quietly, then said, "You are a very beautiful, lush woman."

He stripped his shorts off and stood naked before her.

She had never really looked at him before, just parts and impressions, never really seeing the standing naked man. Black hair running down his chest into his groin, his flaccid penis, the hair covering his very heavily muscled legs. A little extra flesh at the waist, then an immensely broad back tapering to firm, tight buttocks.

"You have a Rodin body." She smiled at him. "As you know, I love Rodin's sculptures of men."

Her attempt at humor was met with a calm silence from him.

She took a deep, nervous breath. "I have never really looked at a man before, I have no one to compare you to, but I think you are a perfect man."

She looked up into his eyes, silently pleading with him to help her in her embarrassment and nervousness. He waited quietly and calmly for her to finish.

"I always look at you, I always ache for you," she started stammering, and held out her arms for him.

He enfolded her with his body, and she whispered up to him, "It is your warmth, and then there are times when I miss the sound of your laughter so acutely, or the smell and texture of your body, asleep next to mine, that I pretend you are just near, reading in another room, or . . . I just love you, Tom, I just love you, Tom."

Then he continued. "It's your eyes that I can't stop seeing, no matter where I am or who I'm with. When I close my eyes, I see your eyes. Your face is clear, and I want you all the more."

She was shivering in his arms, trying to press herself into him.

"I love you, Kate, I love you more than I love life."

They stood holding each other a while, then re-dressed and ate dinner. Comfortable with each other, they talked about Tim and Margey. The prognosis at the end of the day was good. Kate talked about Kevin. He was having a wonderful time at camp, and he missed her and Tom. Flynn talked about an upcoming job action the PBA was considering. Kate talked about Brian and Betsy. Flynn shook his head and said, "Poor bastard." Kate sighed and said, "I know, but what can he do? What can she do?"

The telephone rang, and Kate got up to answer it. She talked to Josie briefly, and he cleared the table. After everything was put away into the dishwasher and drawers, they went to bed.

She moved into his arms, shivered deliciously, and called him a great big bear of a man.

He growled playfully, kissed her neck, and hugged her tightly. He became silent and still, she expectant, and in a hesitant whisper he said, "I want to make love to you, I want to make love to *all* of you."

She felt her whole body flush. "You do . . ."

"No, I don't," was his answer, "and I want you to let me this time. I mean really let me."

Without another word, he began to move his lips slowly down her body, stopping when he felt her tensing, starting again when she relaxed, all the while whispering to her how much he loved her, telling her how beautiful she was.

"No, stop . . . I can't." Her voice sounded near tears.

"Yes, you can," he answered hoarsely. "You can, and I'm not going to stop until you do."

He reached up and took both her hands in his one, leaving the other free to gently stroke her body as his mouth moved slowly down.

Suddenly her blood turned to fire, and as her body convulsed a cry broke free from her throat. He groaned and moved up on her body quickly, and into her slowly.

And when they were complete with each other he pulled her close to him again and told her she tasted like strawberries.

"No I don't," she sulked.

"Yes you do," he teased back.

"No I don't," she said hopefully.

"You do, and I'm going to do it again," he teased in a chuckling voice.

"No you're not," she said firmly, then added, "at least not now."

His laughter was like thunder, and he gave her a big, wet kiss on the mouth, hugged her to him, and told her to go to sleep.

She murmured "okay" and did. He lay awake,

watching the storm lash the trees and lightning streak across the sky.

Joan forced her way into his thoughts, then Maureen, and Seamus, Connor and Mora. He was going to have to leave them. The pain of possibly losing his children cut him, but the thought of losing Kate was far worse. It was then that he realized he was afraid of her. He had wanted to go home to her last night and forget everything—Tim, the job, everything—and roll himself up into a little-boy ball and sit in her open body with her woman arms around him, her breasts there for his face to burrow into and be at rest. At rest only because he knew he could rise up and be a groaning, stamping, lustful man and enter her body with his.

Sometimes he would actually pull back and watch her face when he was with her. Her eyes, when he was moving in and out of her, always arrested wayward fantasy and brought him to the somehow frightening reality that he was with the woman he loved. He wanted to deny its completeness. It sometimes overwhelmed him, and he felt like he was drowning.

She always looked like she was in pain. The pleasure was so intense. It had alarmed him at first, but when she begged him to go on, he grunted and held himself back and watched her.

The changing moods and vagaries of her femaleness moved across her face and flesh like racing clouds on a high, sound, sunny day. When she came she cried out for him like a child, a whimpering woman who at any other time was possessed of immense strength and good sense.

Kate rolled over and pressed her back into his body,

157

interrupting his thoughts. She pressed her bottom into his groin and used his arm to lever herself into his chest, then sighed in her sleep and relaxed again.

He loved her then the most. He felt his own power, his body, his excitement, and his love. Sometimes he felt he was bringing down this prey. Sometimes he was angry with her because he was in love with her, and he would conquer her, and she would let him, then yawn pink-mouthed, snuggle into his body, sleepy and trusting for him to cherish.

And he did.

He hoped she would never ever know how weak and fluid her loving of him made him feel, how his arms lacked strength, his fingers became awkward and clumsy, tenderness and desire crowding his throat, tears stinging his eyes. He was relieved, still believing that she didn't know how deeply he loved her. Sometimes it drove him mad thinking of her, but the madness was sweet and poignant, and he loved the way it made him feel.

They slept on. The fragments of their everyday adult personalities hovered out in the wastelands, while the fierceness of their innocence, long held in check, had its day.

Ecstasy—they shared ecstasy and love and fear of each other, humor, and sleep.

{ Chapter 12 }

Flynn rolled over and found the bed beside him empty. There was a note propped up on the pillow from Kate telling him that she had gone shopping. He eased himself back into the pillows, put his hands behind his head, and smiled to himself.

"What a woman," he said to the sunlight and the empty bedroom. He replayed all his favorite images of her in his mind. He fell asleep again and dreamed small, happy dreams of the two of them and what it would be like when he finally broke with Joan.

Joan. The very thought of her woke him abruptly, and he swung himself out of bed quickly and hustled himself into the shower, refusing to accept thoughts of her. She was like all the warning music in horror movies, all the bad lighting that portended disaster.

Refreshed from the shower, he dressed in a clean shirt and pants and padded barefoot into the kitchen to make some coffee.

He reached up and took down the coffee canister, and under the lid was a note from Kate:

> Don't drink too much coffee, you know it makes you jumpy.
> I love you very much.
>
> Kate

And when he opened the refrigerator door there was another one:

> Now, not too much overindulging, Thomas Flynn. How about two boiled eggs, whole wheat toast, grapefruit juice . . . and later on you can have me for dessert, hmm?
> I love you madly and I want your body.
>
> The Mystery Woman

When he finished his second cup of coffee, he rinsed his dirty dishes and put them in the dishwasher. The note in there read:

> If you're reading this note you're on your way out. I *love* you, I *need* you, I *want* you forever.
> Keep yourself safe for me and come home soon.
>
> . . . with all my love,
> Kate

He poured himself a third cup of coffee. He drank in the peacefulness surrounding him as he wandered through the early morning quiet of the house.

He wasn't ready to give this up. He wasn't ready to go through the emotional ritual of steeling himself to go back to his house and to Joan.

He wandered into the bedroom. The perfume of her body hung in the air everywhere. The outline of her head, hip, and leg was still discernible in the tossed sheets and covers. It invited him. He turned and walked to the French doors and opened them to the fragrance and sunlight of the morning.

Tall blue delphiniums, red and white Sweet Williams, and pink carnations had replaced the daffodils and tulips. Across the lush green lawn, yellow and purple foxglove rang gracefully over the heads of pink and white phlox. White feverfew, red salvia, and snapdragons completed the design. Then the whole massive far garden was bordered by huge, smoky sprays of delicate white baby's breath.

Her garden amazed him. He stood mesmerized by the play of light across the lawn. The fragrances of the flowers warming in the sun wafted by him. Squirrels sat on their hind legs and nibbled crabapples, ignoring him. Robins and bluejays perched on the bird feeder while chickadees foraged nervously on the ground below in groups twittering and eating.

It was getting late, and Flynn gulped down the rest of his coffee before he finished dressing. As the front door clicked shut behind him he gave silent thanks that the woman who had created this home loved him. He reached into his pants pocket to reassure himself that he had the keys to the front and back doors and felt for his paycheck in his breast pocket.

By the time he had started his car he was already rehearsing his responses to reentering his house, his life. He was trying to shut himself down, deaden his awareness of the beauty around him, so the ugliness of his life with Joan wouldn't intrude on the precious time he had with his children.

He didn't notice Kate's shiny red Porsche round the bend in the road as he made a left onto it, ahead of her.

The wind was whipping her hair, and the car radio was blaring. Kate was singing along with the music at the top of her lungs, intoxicated by the beauty of the day, in love and happy.

The car was stuffed with presents for Flynn. She had started out that morning to buy him a bathrobe, and she had. A thick terrycloth robe in royal blue. Then the memory of his painfully worn socks and frayed gray underwear moved her to a buying frenzy. Tee-shirts, size 44, socks and undershorts, good cotton broadcloth shirts, a beautiful new leather belt, and a pair of trunks. She managed to stop herself when it came to buying shoes.

But the buying fever was still on her so she stopped at Al's Antiques and bought a night table for his side of the bed, and at Christopher's she found a brass reading light with a glass shade. She reasoned to herself that it was time he had a place to stack his books and newspapers and a good light to read them by in bed.

She stopped by the butcher and ordered her meat, including a filet mignon to make Beef Wellington for the next day.

Then, making a major decision, she stopped by

Vanderbilt hardware and bought a strongbox with a combination lock for his gun. He could bolt the box to the far right-hand corner of his side of the closet. His gun usually went under the bed, and it made her nervous. It could go in the box now.

The gun frightened her. The sight of the murky gray metal seemed sinister and evil and deathly cold. She thought about him wearing it, using it, and about another one being used on him. She thought it would be better if the gun were locked away in the dark of the closet, where all dangerous, deadly things should be.

As she came around the bend in the road, she saw him pull out of the driveway and drive away. She down-shifted into second as if to pull into the driveway, then changed her mind and tried to catch up to him.

It was funny the way he drove, leaning over to the left against the door. He explained to her that it was the gun. If you sat up straight the gun was always poking you, and out of habit he drove leaning to the left, the way he drove when he was on duty. He was two lights ahead of her when he pulled onto the Palisades Parkway. She figured she could easily catch him with the Porsche when she got on, and she relaxed.

The lights changed, and she got on the parkway going south. She whipped the car through the gears into fourth. He still wasn't in sight at 70 mph, so she pushed the car up to 80. In the distance she saw him signaling to get off at an exit ahead.

"Where is he going?" she asked herself as she signaled and moved into the right lane to follow him. She was beginning to feel mildly disturbed.

When she pulled off the parkway he was ahead of her

again, and she roared away from the stop sign. Once again he was two lights away from her in the traffic, and she pulled out in the left lane and beeped her horn, hoping it would attract his attention.

It didn't. He pulled away from the light, and she moved back into the right lane. She saw him signal another right, slow down, and turn.

Suddenly she felt frightened. Her palms got sticky and wet. She felt a little sick.

He was going to his house.

She shifted down and signaled a right-hand turn. She couldn't stop herself. It was as if she was on a tow rope and he was dragging her.

She saw his car pull into the driveway of an ordinary green house behind a beige Impala. There was a woman unloading groceries. She saw Maureen hugging him and Connor, Mora and Seamus making their way toward him.

Then she saw Joan take possession of her man—her man! It was simple. She handed him a bag of groceries to take into the house. Such a simple gesture, something that was expected of him as the father and husband and head of the household.

Kate felt her heart convulse, and she shifted up and roared by the scene. She knew she was going to explode and tear in half. She gritted her teeth, tears running, as she drove like a madwoman. She had to get home before she came apart.

Everyone turned when they heard her wind the engine out. Flynn's family saw a woman with long red hair in a shiny red Porsche drive by.

He saw his life drive by.

He had seen her face, contorted with bewilderment and grief, and for one insane moment he almost ran down the road after her, to deny what she had just seen, but just then Maureen interrupted.

"Daddy, wait till you see what Mommy made for lunch." She was jumping up and down with delight and took his hand in her little one and pulled him toward the house.

He staggered then, straightened himself, while in his mind he was frantically trying to think of a way to leave and go after her.

"Dinner'll be ready in ten minutes. Wash up." Joan's flat nasal voice cut into his thoughts. He couldn't leave now. He was trapped.

He helped put the groceries away, barely aware of the conversations going on around him. As usual, Joan had nothing to say to him, except for an occasional direction, like putting the cans of peaches down in the basement.

Joan and Mora had the food on the table and called to him from the kitchen. He couldn't remember when they had eaten at the dining-room table.

He was making a tremendous effort to control himself. Mora and then Connor had been on the telephone, every moment he had been sitting in the living room pretending to read the Sunday paper, all the while writhing with impatience. He promised himself he would leave the house as soon as he finished dinner. He tried not to think about Kate, but the image of her face as she drove by kept coming to him.

He sat down to Joan's usual macaroni and cheese with limp vegetables and tough steak, all served up on her latest collection of Melmac dishes. The smells from the food nearly made him gag, and he forced some macaroni and cheese down. She did make good macaroni and cheese. Mora refilled his glass of milk, and he tried to focus on what his children were saying to him, but he couldn't.

He bit down on a piece of steak, and this time the fat and the gristle really did make him gag. He looked up into Joan's glaring, hostile eyes.

That did it. He downed the rest of his milk and got up. All the talk at the table died. Maureen's head was bent over her plate. He knew she was crying, but he couldn't bear it another minute longer.

"I think I'm going to go out for some fresh air. I need some fresh air." Then he paused. "Maureen, come walk me to the door."

Silently he reached into his breast pocket and handed Joan his paycheck. She took it and turned it over, making sure he had endorsed it.

Maureen slid out of her chair and quietly stood at her father's side. When they reached the front door, Flynn opened it and went down on his knees in front of his little girl. There were tears in his eyes to match the tears in hers. He held her by her slender, delicate arms and talked to her in a breaking voice.

"I know I'm making you sad, and I know your mother says bad things about me." Maureen nodded her head. "But I promise you . . . I love you. You are my colleen awling. I am not a bad man, and I love you . . . and someday, and I promise you it will be soon, things will be better. But no matter what happens now—no matter what—you must promise me that you will never doubt that I love you. Do you promise?"

Maureen nodded again. She looked so miserable. He pulled her to him and held and kissed her.

She pulled away from him a bit and said, "You don't love Mommy anymore, do you?"

"No . . . I don't," he answered in a whisper.

She looked into his intense dark eyes with her calm green ones. "I don't either, Daddy. I only love you and Connor and Seamus . . . not Mora or Mommy."

He was shocked by the intensity in her voice.

"I'm going back in and finish my dinner." She pulled his face down and kissed him. "Don't forget me, Daddy."

The house was dark, and when he tried the front door he realized the bolt was shot, so he made his way to the back and let himself in through the bedroom French doors.

The room was torn apart, the telephone off the hook.

Kate lay face down in a fetal position. Her hair was a tangled mass. She was making painful little animal noises, rocking herself, clutching a pillow and a man's bathrobe with the store tags still on.

There were brand-new jockey shorts, tee-shirts, socks, and dress shirts thrown all over the room. When he turned her over, her face shocked him.

Her eyes were swollen shut, and her lower lip was bleeding. She looked like someone had beaten her up. She was shivering, and there was a faint odor of bile coming from the bathroom.

As gently as he could, he took her, the pillow, and the bathrobe into his arms and rocked her.

He was frightened by the violence of her grief, and when he reached to touch her face he felt her wince. Hot tears forced their way out of his eyes, and as he rocked her he hushed her, saying, "I'm here, I'm here, I love you."

Then deep inside of him he felt something tear, and in the same moment he was overwhelmed with relief. He was there, and he was going to stay there. There was no more Joan, no more marriage. Somehow he would work it out with his children.

Flynn looked down at her swollen face, and when she tried to open her eyes to look at him and couldn't, it cut him deeply. It made him wild inside.

No, he would never leave her, not ever. He vowed he would never let her be hurt this deeply again.

He ran her a bath, soothed her and bathed her, held her and reassured her. He changed the ice on her face three times, straightened the room, and was embarrassed and very touched by all the clothes, particularly the underwear, she had bought for him. He wondered what the strongbox was for, understood that the table and lamp were for him, and put the table on his side of the bed and plugged the lamp in.

He made her a hot buttered whiskey and made her drink it. Then he held her as she slept.

Then he found a note:

> hurt,
>   my eyes hurt.
> I do not see you.
> I am being blinded
>   slowly,

by the sight of the entire world
 going by
without you in it.

It was dated two years back. She had pulled it out of a diary and reread it, while he was forcing himself to eat macaroni and cheese.

{ *Chapter 13* }

The house was like death. The kitchen reeked of Lestoil. Joan knew the smell nauseated him, but she had never found it in her soul to find something else to clean with. He crossed the dark kitchen, opened the refrigerator door, and looked for a beer. He was relieved that everyone was asleep.

"So! You finally decided to grace us with your presence! The stranger to our house and home finally returns." Joan's nasal snarl cut through the uneasy silence of the kitchen.

She made her way to him and yanked him around by his arm. "What's the matter? Did your whore get bored with you tonight and send you home for the droppings, Tom? Did she finally see the fat tired old man we always have here, Tom?"

The cold light from the refrigerator framed his wife. She was fat and puffy. Her overbleached hair was wrapped painfully in rollers all over her head.

She looked like hell.

She pulled her wrapper tight around her. Flynn noted that it was missing all but one button and was none too clean. He looked at her then, really looked at her. She squirmed and retreated under the scrutiny.

"Ain't I as beguilin' as your whore, Tom? Tell me now, is she prettier than I am? Does she do all those disgusting things to you that I won't do, Tom? Well, you're out of luck, boy o'. I've called your mother and told her what's going on, and she wants you to call her tomorrow, and Father McCarthy wants to talk to you too."

She backed away from him. The smirk on her face only made her look more grotesque.

"That's right, do ya hear me, Tom Flynn? I said Father McCarthy wants to talk to you too. And if you're not home every night after work, and on time too, I'll call your captain."

Flynn downed the cold beer and threw the empty can in the garbage.

"I want a divorce." He brushed past her and started up the stairs to his room.

"So you can go to your whore?" Joan snarled at him.

Cold black rage filled him. He answered, "Let me put it another way. I'm going to divorce you, Joan. I'm gonna leave you."

She isn't even smart enough to make me feel bad, he thought to himself.

Joan's crying started softly in the kitchen, and when

he didn't come down the stairs to appease her, her voice changed and started a high keening.

Gradually the lights went on all over the house, and the drawn faces of his children peeked out through the doors.

"So this is when everything falls apart," he whispered to himself.

As he took off his shirt, the low lamplight caught a red and gold glint. A strand of Kate's hair had worked its way into the dark fabric of his shirt. He found her scent on his collar. He rolled his shirt into a ball and held it to his nose, breathing in her scent, letting go of his rage.

He spent the rest of the night packing his belongings and pacing his room. He would stay until morning. He wanted to talk to the kids.

Flynn had his belongings packed and neatly tied. He had found one dusty old suitcase up in the attic. It held most of his clothes. He tied his books in sacks with twine.

Joan had spent the night on the telephone, his children awake in their rooms. He had gone downstairs and told Joan he wanted to use the telephone. She snarled at him that she wasn't going to let him call his whore on her phone. He brought the books to his car. On the third trip Joan, crying and pleading, tried to stop him at the door. She begged him to stay, not to go. She still loved him, and what about the children?

He tried to be nice about it, but she got ugly again, hurling epithets, and they got into a physical tussle at the door, Flynn trying to peel her off him without hurting her, Joan trying to scratch his eyes, and when she bit his hand he slapped her. He regretted it. It had shocked him, the sight of her teeth in the fleshy part of his hand, so he hit her reflexively.

He went to the telephone to call Kate and was talking to her quietly, as much to reassure himself as her, when Joan snatched the receiver out of his hand and started screaming a stream of abuse at Kate. He hung up the phone midstream. He was so angry he could have killed her in that moment. After he grabbed her by the arm as painfully as he could manage, she dropped the phone. He walked her to a chair at the kitchen table and forced her into it.

He was breathing heavily, his lips back against his teeth, his nostrils flared, his eyes on fire.

"If you ever"—his voice was quivering with rage— "do that again, if you ever bother her, if you ever open your mouth with that filth again"—he shook her very hard—"I will permanently shut it." He shook her again. "Do you understand, you horrible hag?" He released her abruptly, and she stumbled and nearly fell off the chair.

Flynn left the room. He was shaken by the violent anger he had for Joan. He wanted to hurt her, really hurt her. His hate suddenly didn't seem enough.

He called Tim McBride from the telephone in Joan's room. He needed to talk to someone about how he was feeling. Tim would understand. Kate would be alarmed, and she just might do something stupid, like drive over and fall into this snakepit.

Tim was still on sick leave, but he was doing very well. He answered the telephone on the third ring.

"Yeah." His voice was sleepy, and Flynn could hear Margey asking who it was in the background.

173

"Tim." Flynn took a deep breath before he continued. "It's me, Tom. I'm sorry to wake you, but I . . ."

Tim interrupted him. "What's wrong? What's happened? You sound like hell."

"I'm leaving Joan. I—we just had a scene in the kitchen, and I need to talk to you. I'm so fucking angry, I'm afraid I might hurt her."

"Talk, partner . . . Margey, would you make me a cup of tea? I'm here, Tom. What finally happened?"

Tom talked, Tim listened, and the sun came up.

He told Tim the whole story. How he had met Kate. The years in between, which he had spent denying what had happened, denying his feelings for her. How he had tried to love Joan, or at least stay married to her. How his pain had finally been overcome by his need. He talked about his guilt about leaving Joan, not caring about her. Then his anxiety about leaving his kids in her hands.

Then he told Tim how he felt about Kate. How he had come to feel about himself. How he wanted to live for the first time in years.

"That does it." Tim stopped him there.

"What?" Tom was confused.

"I'm coming over."

"What are you, crazy? You're not well enough!"

"I'm well enough to see you safely through that front door, Tom Flynn. You don't know what's in store for you when you finally try to walk through that front door."

"What do you mean?" Tom sounded anxious.

"Just this, that for the past few months you've been a changed man. I've gotten to know you better in those months than in all the years you've been my partner. And Kate is the reason you've turned into . . . well, you're even a better cop. And I'm gonna make sure you stay this way."

"Okay, I could use the moral support . . . moral . . . funny." Flynn laughed a bitter laugh.

"Just promise me you'll stay upstairs till I get there."

"Okay."

Tom went back to his room and slept until ten. He awoke to the sound of his daughter Mora knocking on the door, telling him that Mr. McBride was downstairs asking for him. He roused himself and opened the door. Mora was dressed. She looked like she had been crying.

"Thank you, Mora." He reached out to touch her, and she drew back. *Getting more like her mother every day,* he thought to himself.

"Tell Tim I'll be right down," he said.

He went to the bathroom, brushed his teeth, and washed the fatigue out of his face and off his neck. He went back to his room, got his suitcase and his last stack of books, and made his way down the stairs.

There was a hum of adult voices coming from the kitchen. Tim sat alone in the living room. He signaled to Tom to be quiet, stood up, and joined him by the stairs, taking the suitcase.

Just then Father McCarthy spotted him through the kitchen door.

"Tom, Tom Flynn, would you please join us in the kitchen?" He was a young priest who was trying to muster as much intimidation and authority as he could in his voice. Father McCarthy silently wished that old

Father Murphy were here instead of vacationing in Bermuda.

"I'll take the suitcase out to the car, Tom, and I'll be right back." Tim's voice had more authority and reassurance than the priest's. Father McCarthy was filled with bitter resentment.

The priest wondered how he could possibly deal with a man who was used to power and authority, much less two of them. Why was old Murphy always away on vacation? He was more concerned with his tan and the new wallpaper in his bedroom than with his vocation.

Reluctantly, Tom entered the kitchen and was staggered by the sight of his own mother holding his whining wife. Maureen sat at the table, and Connor and Seamus flanked their grandmother.

"Thomas Flynn, I want to talk to you." The sound of his mother's angry voice did not have the effect on him she wanted it to.

They had miscalculated. The shock of his mother's disloyalty to him, the betrayal to him, hardened his heart.

And she knew it.

"Now, Mrs. Flynn," the priest started in with soothing tones.

"No, don't interrupt her," Tom spat out. His voice was cold and calm. "Let's hear what Tom Flynn's loving mother has to say to her son."

Tim had rejoined him by the door and was gripping Tom's upper arm with his left hand. He was blinking at the harsh light with his good eye, the patch still in place over the right one.

"Father McCarthy, is it?" The priest nodded his

head affirmatively, and Tim continued. "Maybe this discussion should take place at some other time, when everyone's a little calmer."

Tom almost laughed. Tim was using his best cop voice. The one they both used on family disturbance calls. Tim would sound like this even if there were blood and weapons and sixty people drawn up and ready for battle.

Unfortunately, it didn't have the calming effect on Joan that it was having on the priest and Tom's mother. She jumped up, losing all her self-control, and attacked him, screaming. "What's her name? What's the whore's name?"

His son Seamus, who had stood by his mother's side just as woodenly as Connor and Mora, suddenly spoke.

"I know who she is, Ma. I know who she is and where she lives and what she does."

"Tell me, Seamus, tell your mother so I can go there and kill her!" Joan ran to him and clung to his shirt.

Flynn looked up and met his son's eyes. The hatred he saw there stunned him and decided him.

"That's a nice piece of work, Seamus. Then you'll know where to reach me." His voice was hard and quiet. "Let's get out of here, Tim." They both turned and headed for the front door.

Somehow Maureen had slipped out of the kitchen and was waiting for him outside. She was crying, and she reached for him blindly.

"Daddy, please don't go." Flynn dropped to his knees, and she leapt into his arms, sobbing.

"Daddy, take me with you, please don't leave me."

He held her fragile little body in his arms and felt her

fine brown hair cling to his tear-stained cheek. She was trembling and crying and begging him to take her with him.

He pulled her away from him. He was sick inside, but decided.

"I have to go. I have to. I can't take you with me right now, but I will try to." He started to cry, and he felt her little-girl hands on his cheeks. "Remember, I love you. Promise me that you'll always believe I love you."

She had become quiet and serious. Her tears had stopped. "I promise, Daddy, but promise me, Daddy, promise you won't forget me."

He hugged her to him and whispered, "I swear on my immortal soul I won't forget you. We'll be together soon."

He stood up and went to his car. She stood in the doorway, her hands behind her back, and watched him drive away.

It nearly killed him.

No one else joined her to see him leave.

Tim followed him to Kate's. She was standing at the open door before he got out of the car.

He was afraid to look at her, afraid of what he might see in her face. Absurdly he felt like a bad little boy, and he felt like giggling gleefully.

Tim helped him with the books, and when they passed through the front door Tim smiled and said a big hello to Kate. Tom looked into her eyes and saw sadness and concern.

He didn't want her to touch him or kiss him or say

anything endearing, and somehow she was smart enough to know it.

He couldn't bring himself to put his things in the bedroom yet, so he plunked everything down in the hallway.

"Listen." Her voice was soft and calm. "I've made both of you something to eat. It's on the stove. There's milk, beer, soda, whatever, in the refrigerator." She paused and looked from Tom to Tim.

"Margey called and asked me to drive over and pick her up as soon as you got here. She wants to drive you home, Tim. She figured you'd be pretty tired by now."

Kate looked back to Flynn. His face was relaxing. He looked less angry.

It must have been a nightmare, she thought to herself.

She had her keys and her purse in her hand and was on the way out before Flynn could think of something to say to stop her, so instead he said, "Let's eat. I'm starved."

They made their way to the kitchen. Tim did look exhausted, and Flynn seemed empty and drained.

He served up the veal and wild rice. There was a salad in the refrigerator. Tim started eating before he sat down. When he did sit, he looked up at Tom with a twinkle in his good eye.

"Do you always eat this good?" he asked in a teasing voice.

"Yeah—veal, wild rice, salad," Flynn said between chews.

"All this and that too?" Tim teased back.

"Yeah, and that too." A smile forced its way to his mouth. A chuckle followed.

"You wouldn't believe . . ." he started to say.

"Oh yes I would. You are a lucky son of a bitch, Thomas Flynn." Tim threw his head back and roared with laughter.

Tom laughed with him, the tension draining completely from his body.

Kate made record time driving to the McBrides' house. Margey was waiting for Kate when she arrived, and after locking the door, Margey slipped into the shiny red Porsche.

"Kate?" Margey said her name like a question.

"Yes, Margey?"

"Um, could I, I mean would you let me . . ."

"You want to drive the Porsche?"

"Yeah, desperately. Would you mind?"

Kate was already opening her door, laughing that she didn't mind at all.

As they drove away from the McBrides' house, Kate eased back into the leather seat. It was one of the few times she was a passenger in her own car. When Tom drove they were always talking, and she never really had the opportunity to enjoy the sensation. She closed her eyes and relaxed, and Margey drove on, downshifting as she took a sharp corner.

"Nice, Margey. I didn't know you could drive like this." Kate chuckled.

"Do you mind if we drive for a while?"

"No. As a matter of fact, I feel a little funny about going back to the house right away." Kate sighed a heavy sigh and wondered to herself why she felt afraid.

"I know. I feel funny about it myself. I would rather leave Tim to handle Tom right now." Margey took a deep breath and continued nervously.

"It's funny, and I don't mean this as a reflection on you, but I feel kind of sad for Joan today." Margey wanted to talk about Joan. She wanted to tell Kate about her.

Margey down-shifted and made a left-hand turn onto the parkway going north. They drove in silence for a while. Margey's comment had, at first, made Kate angry. Now she was feeling a great sadness welling up inside her.

In a voice edged with tears, Kate asked Margey to tell her about Joan. "I don't mean what I want to hear. Tell me about her when she was young, when she and Tom first met. You knew her then, didn't you?"

"Yes, I knew her then." Margey edged the car up to 70 mph and continued. They passed Exit 13, the traffic thinned out, and the scenery changed to mountains, massive rocks, and an occasional chalet in the distance.

"She was one of those girls who tried too hard, cared too much, cheered too loudly at the basketball games. Tom used to kid her about that a lot. He said that was how he first noticed her, her cheering, that is. She was never much to look at, you know, brown hair, brown eyes, medium height. Yeah, medium all around."

Margey fell silent. She wasn't sure she should be telling Kate about Joan. She had conflicting feelings of guilt and betrayal.

"Margey, I'm not asking you to tell me about her because I feel like a smug, victorious bitch. I'm not even sure why I want to know." Kate stopped and thought a minute, then continued. "I can promise you, though, that it is not out of meanness that I want to know. I think it's because Tom could never give me an unbiased picture of Joan, and I want one."

"Kate, I feel a little like I am betraying her," Margey answered. "I know she doesn't really know about you. Maybe you have no right to know about her."

"Let me tell you a story, and then you can decide," Kate answered. "One night Tom was really angry and going on and on about Joan this and Joan that. At one point he started to make fun of her. He said she waddled like a duck and farted like a skunk."

"You're kidding!" Margey interrupted her. "That doesn't sound like Tom."

"No," Kate said, "it doesn't, and it isn't. I told him then that one of the things that hurt me the most when Felipe left me and went to live with Berthe was that I was sure that they would lie in bed at night, and after they made love Felipe would tell her all those intimate funny things about me that only he knew, that they would lie there and laugh at me and then make love again."

"Oh, Kate, I'm sorry," Margey interjected.

"No, let me finish, Margey." Kate took a deep breath and went on.

"I told him that the only way I could feel okay about the situation was if he never betrayed her to me. I told him that I didn't want to know what she looked like, didn't want to know her secrets, didn't want her personality entering into our relationship anywhere."

"So why do you want me to tell you about Joan?" Margey asked.

"Because you can't tell me any of her intimate secrets. Because you can tell me about a woman I'm going to have to deal with very shortly. Because when she finds out where Tom is living, she will then find out about me. Margey, you're the only person I know who knows her, and you are honest enough to tell me the truth, even if I don't want to hear it."

Margey answered Kate by beginning her story immediately.

"Joan never had a chance with Tom. When she was eleven her father died and her mother was left with four little girls, a half-paid-for house, and very little money. Her mother went to work downtown, way down on Wall Street. She supported the girls in a style she thought the neighbors would approve of. Sad. They only made fun of her behind her back. They said she was putting on airs, and all the while she thought she was being perceived as the valiant widow. Anyway, she dressed the girls in the latest teen fashions, stayed up all night sewing them what she couldn't afford to buy. Why, Joan had more felt poodle skirts than I did.

"I guess Mrs. Connelly's crushed dreams were passed on to her daughters, magnified a hundred times from years of 7 A.M. masses praying for her daughters on her knees."

Margey stopped her monologue at the Seven Lakes Drive circle. After she negotiated the turn, and got on the parkway going south, she started talking again.

"She never married or dated even. I guess she gave all her love and energy to them. Anyway, Joan was the youngest, and all her sisters were married by the time she entered high school. She never dated any big shots, just nice guys, regular guys, that her mother never approved of. You see, all of her sisters had married well, and Mrs. Connelly had big plans for Joan. But Joan was dating this fella, Archie Lyons. They were pretty serious until her mother found out that Archie's father had done time. She broke it up. I guess Archie was Joan's last chance for happiness. He really loved her, the real Joan, not Mrs. Connelly's version of what Joan should be.

"Then Tom came along one day after a game. He was a big letter man then. He asked Joan out, and she thought she had died, gone to heaven, and come back again. Mrs. Connelly was beside herself with joy that Tom Flynn had asked her baby out. She proceeded to pour on the clothes, approval, and invitations to dinner . . . and was she ever a good cook.

"Tom was very popular with the girls. Very tall, even then, dark, and sort of shy. He says he asked Joan out because he understood the desperation behind her overeager behavior. Tom once told Tim that he had gotten tired of most of the girls and that Joan seemed like a worthwhile project."

"Must have been during the 'maybe I'll be a priest to please my mother' stage," Kate interjected.

They both laughed, and Margey added, "And after they discover sex they decide to go into the Department instead.

"Well, Joan was very worshipful, and Mrs. Connelly doted on Tom. It was senior year, and Tom asked Joan to marry him. He told Tim he asked her because it was time to get married, she was there, and she put very few demands on him. He tested for the force the same time Tim did, and they both got on. They got married, and Joan got pregnant."

"What did you and Tim do?" Kate asked.

"We fooled around a lot," Margey answered, glancing at Kate. "Then I got pregnant, and Tim threatened to tell my father if I didn't elope with him. We eloped, and I finished school after all the kids were born. It was very important to me then, and I guess I'll go back to nursing when the kids leave."

"I didn't know you were a nurse," Kate said.

"Oh yeah, and a good one too. Anyway, in about her fifth month Joan changed. She must have realized that she wasn't Mommy's little girl-toy anymore and could be Mrs. Flynn."

Margey hesitated and chose her words very carefully. "I guess she turned first on her mother and then on Tom."

"What do you mean, turned?" Kate asked.

"I mean she went from a sweet, shy, and trusting maiden to a demanding, carping bitch. She tried to get Tom to satisfy all the dreams her mother had filled her with. Tom tried for a while, then gave up and left her to herself."

By the time Kate and Margey got to the house, both Tom and Tim were half smashed. They had made quite a dent in the bottle of Jameson's.

Margey made a half-hearted attempt to be angry with Tim, then gave in to their prevailing merriment and poured herself a drink. She eased herself into Tim's arms and watched Tom and Kate clinging to each other. Clinging was the word for what they were doing. *For dear life,* she thought to herself.

They talked about kids and work and helped Tom move his stuff out of the hall and into the bedroom.

It was getting dark when Margey announced it was time to leave. Tim mumbled something about a party, and Margey mumbled back.

"Sorry," Tim laughed. "I guess we ought to leave you two alone together."

{ Chapter 14 }

It was a sticky green day. The scent from the roses in the garden hung in the oppressively humid air. Grass cuttings stuck to his legs. As he mowed the lawn sweat ran down his scalp, neck, and face. His palms slid on the mower handle. His tee-shirt and shorts were soaked and clung to his skin.

"Cold beer, a cold shower, and I'll turn the air conditioning on to Antarctic," he said to himself.

He focused carefully as he cut the grass by the edge of the garden. The last time he had done it, he hadn't paid enough attention and mowed down a precious dahlia. Kate had caught him trying to stick it back into the ground. He had looked up at her so guiltily that she couldn't stay angry with him. He smiled as he finished mowing the edge. He liked it when she laughed that way. She even snorted. He prayed that Kate wouldn't come home from the supermarket before he finished and had escaped to the cool of the house. The last thing he wanted to do was haul in grocery bags. Kevin was inside watching cartoons. He'd break the kid's arm if he made a fuss about watching the Yankee game. "Naw, I wouldn't do that," he said to himself. "I'll just give him a beer and introduce him to the fine American art of sitting around on a hot summer afternoon in air-conditioned comfort, watching a ball game and getting plowed." He was laughing to himself as he put the lawn mower away. "Made it," he said to himself.

Tom thought about Kevin and how different he was from any child he had ever been around. Kevin seemed so much more aware of events and the way people related to each other than his kids did. Perhaps a lot of that was his own fault. He had raised his four children —with the possible exception of Maureen—in a traditional way. He had never paid too much attention to what they had to say about anything outside immediate family problems. When he came home from work he was always tired, and the tensions of the job were not easily washed away. Joan viewed the children as four problems to be solved, and her conversations with Tom about them always focused on what they did wrong rather than what they did right.

He had first noticed the marked difference when Kevin came home from camp two weeks earlier. Two things happened immediately. First, Kevin was genuinely happy to see him. He got a kiss just like a father would. It made him feel good. Second, and more important, was the conversation between Kate and Kevin about camp that went on for hours.

Kevin came in, and the first thing Kate didn't do was

demand that he put his stuff away. Instead, the conversation that had been obviously going on in the car continued right on into the kitchen. They talked through hamburgers, French fries, and soda, and finally finished as Kate and Kevin together put all his stuff away. He had kind of followed them around, listening to Kevin tell Kate about all his friends at camp, about how he would manage to see them through the school year, and then, when they were unpacking his belongings, showing her each and every summer souvenir. Like the lopsided ashtray. Kevin had explained exactly how he had made it, step by agonizing step, and Flynn wondered how Kate managed to keep her patience. He realized that she wasn't particularly interested in how he had made the ashtray, but that he had made it for her, that he wanted to share everything about his life with her.

Kevin trusted his mother, her love of him, and her interest in him absolutely.

Tom had wondered in the beginning how a little boy, who had endured so much hurt, could be so securely happy. It was her attitude and her effort and love as a mother that had accomplished that.

There was something else, too, something almost awe-inspiring about Kevin. Conceptually, he was far beyond his eight years, and Kate had the wisdom to encourage Kevin's imagination.

A couple of mornings after Kevin had returned from camp, Tom had slept late. He had come down the hall to the kitchen when he heard Kate and Kevin talking. He stood outside the door and listened to a conversation about God.

"Mommy, do you think people made God or God made people?" Kevin asked.

"I don't know, Kevin. What do you think?" Kate responded.

Flynn saw Kate stop buttering the toast and give her son her complete attention. Her eyes were riveted on the little boy as he answered.

"I've been thinking about this a long time, Mommy. I think God put people on the earth so there would be someone here to know there was God. But people might have made God for when they've had their feelings hurt. See, that way God could make them feel better when they wanted him to."

Flynn saw Kate's eyes go soft with pride and wistfulness. She resumed buttering the toast. "You know, Kevin, I think you're on to something. I can't give you a better answer than that."

Never, thought Tom Flynn, had he had a conversation with his children about that kind of subject, not even with Maureen.

It was quiet in the kitchen for a while, and then Kevin began to talk about a rope swing he wanted to hang from the mimosa tree, and Flynn walked into the room.

He guessed that was the day he had really started to love the boy.

Tom slid open the French doors and entered the cool bedroom.

He could hear Superman and the Super Friends waging a war against an evil genius from a distant planet in Kevin's room. He went to the bathroom, stripped off his sweat-soaked clothes, and stepped into the icy shower. He let his mind go back to that incredible morning.

"Good morning, everyone. What kind of a rope swing do you want, Kevin?" Tom sat down on the stool next to Kevin as Kate handed him a glass of freshly squeezed orange juice.

"Good morning, Tom. The kind with knots in it. You know, that I can wrap my legs around and hold on to and swing like Tarzan."

"You can forget the mimosa tree right now," Kate quipped.

"Aw, Ma . . ."

"Now, Kevin, your mother's right. It's an ornamental tree, and the branches just aren't strong enough. How about that big old maple behind the garage?"

Tom warmed to the subject. He explained to Kevin that it was a really good place to have a rope swing—no flowers, and crab grass abounded—and he looked at Kate, who smiled back at him, and finished, "And we can even get a load of sand for you to jump into off the swing."

"Oh, Ma, can I, please?"

She smiled indulgently at both of them, said yes, turned, and flipped his eggs over easy.

He stepped out of the shower and dried himself off hastily.

He drew on a clean pair of shorts and a shirt, and thought he'd better get the beer out of the basement and into the refrigerator before Kate came home with the groceries. He wanted to get Kevin and the TV in place in the family room before Jim Ryan came over with Nicky and Pat and before Tim arrived with the sandwiches. The game started at two o'clock, and he wanted to have everything finished so they wouldn't be interrupted.

"Hello. Is anyone here?" He poked his head out of the bedroom at the sound of Kate's voice and saw her struggling down the hall, both arms loaded with grocery bags.

"Here, let me take those." Flynn relieved her of both bags and followed her to the kitchen.

"There are plenty more in the car, dear, and, by the way, I got three six-packs of cold beer."

"You're a good woman, you are, you know that, Katherine Gallagher?" He took her face in his hands and gave her a big, playful kiss on the mouth.

"I put the car in the garage. Jesus, is it hot out there."

He had never seen a Porsche so filled with food. He counted them. Eleven bags of groceries. She must have bought out the store.

He carried them in, two at a time. Five minutes later the bags were all in, and Kate was putting away a mountain of food. Kevin had already come in and snuck off with a Nestle's Crunch bar. Meat, there was so much meat, and no chuck, no plain ground beef, and no macaroni and cheese.

"I bought a filet mignon." He stared agog. He'd never seen eight pounds of the most expensive beef in the world in one piece. "I think I'll make a Beef Wellington for tomorrow night's dinner."

There were no canned peaches either. The fresh fruit went into a sink of freezing cold water along with fresh vegetables. He started examining the cans on the countertop in front of him.

The labels all seemed to be in French or Norwegian. He picked up a little can that said $7.95.

"What the hell is this? Seven ninety-five? What costs seven ninety-five that comes in such a little can?"

She answered him from the sink without turning around. "Snails, honey, snails."

"You bought a can of slugs for seven ninety-five?" His voice was edged with disbelief.

"Not slugs, dear. Snails. Better known as escargot. After they're cooked in a taste-tempting sauce of butter, garlic, and fresh parsley and then stuffed into these . . ." She reached up and got a cylinder full of what looked like sea shells from the cabinet over the island counter he had been sitting at. He stood up and took them from her.

"Sea shells? You cook slugs in good butter, garlic, and parsley and stuff them into sea shells?" He was trying hard not to laugh. By the expression on Kate's face he could tell he really had her going.

"Look, darlin'. There are a couple of big rocks in the backyard. I'll be headin' out that way, and I'll bring ya in a little sackful." She made a face, and he came around the counter, gave her a hug, and whispered into her ear, "You're crazy. You're really crazy. You know that, don't you?" They broke their embrace, and he asked, "How much did all of this cost, anyway?"

"Two hundred and thirty-nine dollars."

"Two hundred and thirty-nine dollars! Holy Mother of God! We've got to have a talk about money, honey."

"Hello! Anyone home?" Jim Ryan's cheerful voice was followed by Nicky and Pat running down the hall to Kevin's room.

Jim Ryan entered the kitchen, finding Tom and Kate

in a loose embrace. "Don't you two ever stop? Where's the beer, my man?" Jim headed toward the refrigerator. "The game's getting ready to start. Where's Tim?"

"Makin' yourself at home as usual, Jimmy," Kate said laughingly, "and still not having a shave. I don't know how Josie puts up with you."

"She loves it, Kate. I scratch her back with my face every Saturday morning." Laughing, Tom and Jim headed to Kevin's room to get the TV away from the boys. It was going to be difficult. Godzilla and Mothra were doing battle.

Before moving in on the kids, Jim and Tom stood and watched the movie. "Say, Tom, how can you tell Godzilla is in the bathtub with you?" Jim asked.

"All right. I give up. How?"

"You can smell Cleveland on his breath." Jim finished his joke the way he always did, whooping at his own wit.

"All right, you guys," Tom said. "Game time." All three boys protested vehemently. "Please, just ten more minutes," Kevin appealed to Tom. "Godzilla is getting ready to breathe fire on Mothra and kill him."

"How do you know?" Tom asked, smiling at Kevin. Kevin knew he'd been had.

"Because I've already seen the movie six times," Kevin answered in a resigned voice. He got up and turned the TV off. "What are we supposed to do now?"

Tom took a mental survey. There were miniature pinball games, every board game known to man, a modest kid's stereo, a mountain of sporting equipment, and a ten-by-twenty swimming pool he himself had installed in the backyard by the maple tree. Flynn put his hands on his hips, cocked his eyebrow, made a sweeping gesture around the room, and said, "Well, you guys could die of boredom in here or go outside and drown yourselves in the pool. But if you're really good, I'll give you a beer and let you watch the ball game."

Nicky, Pat, and Kevin laughed. "Yeah, right, Tom." During this exchange Jim Ryan had been watching with growing interest the ease with which Tom handled Kevin. He really was acting like a father, and short of calling Tom "Dad," Kevin acted like his son.

Fathers and sons, sons and fathers, Jim recited to himself. *The kid's really looking good.* "Hey, sport, don't swim in your clothes." Jim stopped Pat as he started to run out of the room. "If I bring you home with wet clothes, your mother will kill you and me too."

"Uncle Jim." Kevin crossed the room and opened a dresser drawer. It was crammed with neatly stacked clothes. "I can lend Nicky and Pat extra swimming suits. I have lots."

Tom was startled. Kevin had enough of everything for three little boys. *I'm really going to have to talk to Kate about money,* he said to himself.

Tom lugged the TV down the hall to the family room, and they attached it to the cable. More money. He had to admit you got better reception on cable.

Jim sat down cross-legged on the floor in front of the TV and turned to channel 2, just in time to see Godzilla toast Mothra like a giant marshmallow.

"For Christ's sake, what are you doing?" Flynn asked. "The game's getting ready to start."

"Well, I didn't want to miss the good part," Jim answered, looking like a kid his sons' age, engrossed in the science fiction thriller. He reached up and switched to the game. The familiar tenor of Robert Merrill singing the national anthem was just ending, and Kate brought in the beer. Tim was behind her with a bag full of subs, the patch over his eye flipped up.

"I don't suppose you want to drink this beer out of glasses." Kate set down a tray with two six-packs of ice-cold beer on the old coffee table, unfolded a double brown supermarket bag, and set it on the floor. She smiled. "And to think I was getting ready to make cute little finger sandwiches for you." Before she left the room, she gave Tom another kiss and Tim a kiss hello. She asked after Margey and left.

"Holy cow! It's been a long time since the Yankees played in a laugher." Phil Rizzuto's voice filled the room. The Yankees were ahead, 5 to 0, and there wasn't a lot of high drama left by the end of the sixth inning. "Shut up, Rizzuto," Tim growled at the TV set. "I love it when the Yankees beat the shit out of someone." He downed the last of the beer. Tom got up. "Well, guys, you want to crack another keg?"

Jim asked, "You got some potato chips?"

Tom, remembering the eleven bags of groceries, said, "I'm sure I can find something somewhere."

He picked up the paper bag, now filled with empty beer cans, and walked down the hall to the kitchen. He could hear the boys splashing and yelling in the pool.

He entered the kitchen. "Kate, do we have any chips? Jimmy wants some potato chips." Kate looked up at him from behind the counter. She was dressed in an old pair of navy blue jogging pants and one of his old shirts. The sleeves were rolled up, and she had her hair in pigtails. There was flour on the end of her nose. Her hands were covered with the dough she was kneading for the Beef Wellington.

"Gee, honey, I don't know. But there's some fresh fruit in the icebox. You could have some of those stone wheat crackers, you know, those little round ones with sesame seeds on them."

Flynn stared at her in disbelief. She had just spent two hundred and thirty-nine dollars on groceries, and there weren't any potato chips. "Wait!" Kate said, lifting a dough-encrusted index finger. "You know that tin box in Kevin's room? It's under the bed. The one where he stashes his Nestle's Crunch bars. He's either got potato chips or Fritos in there."

What could he say? She was so cute, standing there behind the counter, looking like a little girl playing Mommy and baking things. All she had told him to do was go into a kid's room and conduct a treasure hunt for a 69¢ bag of potato chips.

Dave Winfield had just finished hitting another home run. Tom put the beer on the table and tossed Jimmy a bag of Fritos. Kevin apparently liked Fritos more than potato chips. It was the bottom of the eighth. The Yankees were creaming Kansas City, and the three men were feeling no pain.

"Jim, how long have you known Kate?" Tom asked.

"Oh, I don't know, about twenty years. Why?"

"Did she always spend money like it was going out of style?"

"Yeah."

Fat lot of help you're gonna be, Flynn thought to himself. Tim shot Tom a questioning look, and Jimmy didn't miss it.

"Well, wait a minute." Jim turned his attention away

from the game. "It all depends on how you look at it. The Judge, Kate's father, always had money. I mean, not a lot of money, but more than most of us. And Kate always could spend more."

Sensing that this wasn't what Tom wanted to hear, Jim continued. "When she was married to that creep, Felipe, she was pretty frugal, for her. I mean, she clipped coupons and bought clothes on sale with the best of them. I guess after the divorce she did go a little crazy. I mean, buying that old Porsche wasn't the smartest thing for a struggling single parent to do." Tom was listening intently. What had been casual conversation suddenly seemed serious to Jim.

He continued. "You have to understand, Tom, that the divorce really shook her up. And that stupid Porsche, particularly after she got it repainted and practically replaced every working engine part, made her happy. She knew it was a dumb thing to do. It was like a big red statement. She was gonna show him . . . Felipe, that is . . . that she didn't give a damn, and she drove around in that shiny sports car to prove it.

"This house, on the other hand, was a very smart buy, all things considered."

"Do you know what she spent on groceries today?" Jim shook his head no, and Tom continued. "Two hundred and thirty-nine dollars. That's what she spent."

Tim looked up from where he was lying on the couch.

Jim Ryan was beginning to get very edgy and alarmed for Kate.

"Don't get me wrong, Jim. Kate is a wonderful woman, but she can't keep spending money like this.

Between us, we don't have that much together. A big chunk of my pay has to go to Joan and the kids. I don't have a lot left over to contribute to this household. I don't really know how much money she has. I mean, do you know what she's making all of us for dinner tomorrow night?"

Jimmy shifted in his chair. It sounded like trouble in Paradise to him. "Beef Wellington, escargot, two kinds of wine, and a fresh fruit compote," Tom said without waiting for a response.

"What's a fresh fruit compote?" Tim asked. Flynn started to explain, and Tim was amazed that the man, one, had pronounced the word and, two, knew what it was.

"Look, Tom. I think you should talk to Kate about this. I know that the house is paid for and Felipe left her a sizable insurance policy. She is beginning to earn money as a photographer."

Jim reached out from the chair with an open right hand, and leaning over, an intent, sincere expression on his face, continued. "She's a reasonable woman, Tom. You can work it out with her.

"Maybe her biggest fault is that she loves and gives too much." Tom smiled and nodded.

"You're right, Jim, I will." *But how do I do that?* he added silently. *How can I talk to her about the way she spends money when I'm not contributing much to the household expenses?* He suspected that he was barely covering the expenses he incurred by living with her. His money had been going to Joan and to the kids and his lawyer. Jesus, he hated the guy. It seemed he was fouling up the process of the divorce just to tack more money onto the bill.

But you get what you pay for, and Tom couldn't pay for a lawyer like Brian, Kate's brother. And he wasn't about to ask for charity legal services. He didn't mind doing a favor now and then for someone, but he couldn't bear to ask for one.

His father was right. "Pride goeth before a fall." He'd rather fall and get up than feel like half a man.

He forced his mind back to Tim and Jim and the conversation they were having.

"Kate." Tom put his book down.

"Umm," Kate responded. She was working at her light table. She was looking at some black-and-white negatives she had developed after dinner, framing with a grease pencil what she would develop later.

"Kate, can we talk? I want to talk to you." She was totally absorbed in her work. Her hair fell in her face, and periodically she would impatiently push it back behind her ears.

"Sure, honey. Just let me finish these last two. I need a break anyway." She turned and smiled at him.

She had been aware that something was bothering him all day. She put the glass down. *I'm going to find out now,* she thought to herself.

"Kate, I think we should have a talk about money."

"Money?" She was incredulous. Money was the last subject she expected to be discussing with him tonight. His divorce, their children, collectively and separately, his job, her job, and the upcoming shoot in Bermuda that she was sure he didn't want her to go on.

"What about money, Tom? We don't have any money problems."

"Kate, I don't know that we don't. I don't mean to

criticize, but, sweetheart, you spend money like you're making it in the basement." He smiled at her, as engaging a smile as he could muster behind his genuine anxiety.

While he smiled, he watched her get her back up.

Mistake. Money was not a subject she talked about lightly.

"Kate. Look, maybe I phrased it incorrectly. I'm worried about how we are going to get through this mess. And I want to know about your finances and see how they mesh with mine so we can, er, make a budget." He finished lamely.

Kate got down from the stool at the light table and joined him on the sofa. She nestled into his arm and sat silently for a while. So did he.

"Talking about money always makes me angry and defensive." She started taking a deep breath. "Please hear me out because I really have a lot to say on the subject."

Flynn put the marker in his book, set it on the table, leaned back, and held her in his arms as she talked.

"When Felipe died everyone had a lot to say to me about how I should, or should not, spend the money. It was Betsy, only Betsy, who supported me whole-heartedly in what I wanted to do. What I was trying to do. I will admit, but only now, that buying the Porsche was a mistake. It cost me thousands of dollars to get it into the shape it's in now, and I don't know if the money is recoupable. The house, after a lot of argument from my dad, I finally got, but I'm getting ahead of myself. That was during the divorce."

She stopped talking and was obviously very upset. He sat and held her, not talking, realizing that this was going to be one of those catharsis conversations. She continued.

"I guess what I am trying to say is that everyone is always trying to tell me what to do with my money, and I'm sick of it. The mistakes I've made, and there have been many, are mine to make . . . or were. And when the subject of money comes up I feel ashamed of what I've done, because my father and Brian have never let up on the subject, and I'm not used to talking to someone who only wants to help."

She was crying, and it made him afraid. He didn't know why.

"When Felipe died the mortgage on the house was paid off. He had death insurance on it. So I only have to pay the taxes, which are $1,800. His insurance policy was for $125,000."

Flynn was shocked.

"And of course half of that was left to Kevin for his education and support. The other $62,000 or so was left to me. I spent quite a lot of money on the studio, as well as remodeling the house. I have $39,000 left. Kevin's $62,000 is invested in CDs. I can cash them in any time I want to, but I would rather not."

Flynn sat and listened to her talk guiltily about sums of money that he would never be able to save, much less invest. Granted, his pay had reached $35,000 per year, but still . . .

"So you see, for the first two years I earned nothing and lived off the money we got from the insurance company. Last year I earned about $12,000. This year I have already made $28,000."

He felt like a fool and just a little sick to his stomach. She was probably even going to out-earn him soon. She was, by his standards, a wealthy woman—by the standards of the group of people she came from, only comfortable. She was in great shape. She could afford her lifestyle, afford him in it even, and certainly tomorrow night's dinner.

Money—his lack and her abundance of it—bothered him. He realized he'd probably be the brunt of rich-widow jokes for a while, and that bothered him too.

{ *Chapter 15* }

Everything was tense, but kissy and huggy at the door. Tim, Margey, Eileen, and Ira had purposely arrived early and were in their corner, ready to work the family crowd over. Jim and Josie had arrived with Brian and Betsy. Tom was busy getting everyone drinks. Kate was forcing her diet-bound friends to eat her hors d'oeuvres.

The Judge and Mrs. Gallagher arrived, and Kevin stampeded down the front hall with Nicky and Pat in tow. He gave each grandparent a messy kiss and asked the Judge for the video game cartridge he had been promised. After hugs and grandparent mischief it appeared from Nora Gallagher's shoulder bag. The boys raced off to play it.

Kate and Tom brought up the rear. Tim and Ira had Brian buttonholed on the patio and were racing through the law, fishing, football, and golf. Jim was refreshing drinks, and Josie took up the hors d'oeuvres and passed them around.

The Judge reacted as privately as he could. He wasn't prepared to see his favorite child looking as tanned and radiant as she did. Nor was he prepared for the tall no-nonsense man who had an arm around her waist. He didn't want to, but he liked him instantly, and Kate knew her father well enough to know he did. She rewarded him with a dazzling smile. The Judge bent slightly at the waist and offered his hand to Tom. Tom, he was pleased to note, responded in the same old-school way as he took his hand.

"Glad to meet you, sir."

"Pleased to meet you, Tom. And please, Tom, no sir. Everyone calls me Judge."

There was laughter all around over the standard family joke. Kate gave her father a big hug, and Mrs. Gallagher, standing slightly behind him, smiled and winked at Tom.

"I believe we've met before, Mr. Flynn."

"Indeed we have, Mrs. Gallagher, and please, it's Tom."

"And please call me Nora, Tom."

The tension level dropped perceptibly and the crowd got expansive. Jimmy handed the Judge a drink as Josie and Eileen kissed hello. Nora Gallagher patted Eileen's shiny black hair and commented for the thousandth time on its shine and beauty. Bussing Josie and patting her cheek, Nora remarked how well she was looking. Jim handed her her fruit juice and vodka, they kissed and hugged, and she mentioned his nice close shave.

The tension all but vanished, and as everyone laughed Nora took Tom's arm.

"It's not very often I get to take the arm and attention of a tall, handsome man I'm not related to. So, since you're not yet my son-in-law, I'm makin' off with you."

They moved through the house to the patio. Nora Gallagher called back to her daughter in the kitchen, "Kate, darling, the flowers are breathtaking."

Kate had placed cut flowers all over the house. She, Tom, and Kevin had worked feverishly all morning making the house both spotless and beautiful. Around noon Nicky and Pat arrived to swim out back with Kevin. She had admonished them sternly about messing up anything at all in the house. Tom realized then that this was more than just a family Sunday dinner. This was to be his official inspection.

Brian and Betsy were alone on the patio, silent and stiff as Tom and Nora moved through the shadows into the dying rays of the day's sun. Tom could feel her grip tighten slightly on his arm.

"Well, there you are, you two." She smiled brightly at her son and daughter-in-law. Instinct told Tom her cheerful greeting was forced. He guessed why but didn't want to concern himself with thoughts of Brian's difficulties.

The evening was pleasantly cool and breezy. He and Kate had opened all the doors, front and back, and the moist air from the woods mingled sensuously with the scrumptious odors from the kitchen. The easy chairs started to fill up with people in relaxed conversation. The evening promised to be a success.

Kate was in the kitchen sipping wine when Tom came in and hugged and kissed her. Most of the crowd had ebbed through her kitchen, making hungry noises, and flowed out onto the patio.

"So," he teased, "when do I get the slugs in butter and garlic?"

"Oh you." She playfully struggled in his arms and then relaxed there. "Everything's going to be okay."

They held their embrace.

"There they go again!" Eileen's voice reached them from the doorway. They turned to find Josie and Eileen standing, arms crossed, watching.

"It's not safe leaving you alone for a minute." Arms relinquished arms, and Tom kissed Kate's nose and left carrying another tray of snacks.

The three women bustled around the kitchen. Eileen did most of the talking; Josie listened quietly. She thought to herself that this was the first time in recent memory that Kate had seemed both relaxed and happy. An unbidden, unhappy question surfaced among her thoughtful observations.

How could such wild, hot passion cool and forge such comfortable strong bonds between two people who under any other circumstances would have pretended they knew better? Josie ended her musing with a small silent prayer. *Dear God, please let them be one of your happier miracles.*

Then aloud she said, "So Kate, where's this Beef Wellington? I can smell it, but I can't see it."

Beaming, Kate opened the oven door and slid out the golden-brown masterpiece.

"Filet mignon, paté, and a crust extraordinaire, mes amis. You may applaud now."

"I'm starving," Eileen groaned. "When do we eat?"

"As soon as I finish feeding the boys, toss the salad, and heat up the slugs."

"Slugs . . ." Eileen was interrupted by Betsy and Nora.

"Dear, is there anything we can do?" The pair crowded into the warming kitchen. Eileen left saying she'd entertain the men. After Josie greeted Betsy, she left to get the boys ready for dinner.

"Yes, Mom. Could you cook the hamburgers for the kids? The fries are about done. Hi, Bets."

Kate moved around her mother and kissed her sister-in-law hello. *She looks terrible,* Kate thought to herself. *I've never seen her so drawn and unhappy.*

She turned to her mother and hugged her.

"I love you, Mom. Thank you for being so wonderful." Betsy stood silently by watching the exchange of love and friendship. She wasn't jealous of her mother-in-law's love for Kate. Betsy knew Nora loved her too. Nor was she upset by Kate's other friendships. Kate was her very close friend too. She just stood there filled with misery, her chest tight with anxiety as she fought back tears that had been aching to be shed for months. She was jealous of how happily in love Kate was, jealous because her religious principles were such that she couldn't be Brian's wife anymore. She missed him, she missed his touch, the sound of his even breathing when he slept. He didn't try to make love to her anymore. Now she was afraid there would be another woman soon. Another woman Brian would divorce her for, just like Tom was divorcing his Catholic wife for Kate. Suddenly she hated all those Irish intellectual Gallaghers who made no pretense about their contempt for the Church and its rules. If only she had something to protect her from losing Brian.

As Betsy stood lost in her unhappy thoughts, neither Kate nor Nora missed the tide of misery washing across her face. Nora went to her and held her silently. It almost broke Betsy's reserve, but instead she sniffed and straightened her shoulders and asked Kate if she could help.

Kevin, Nicky, and Pat were practically out on their feet when they trooped into the kitchen to eat. They had been swimming all afternoon, using the rope swing Tom had made for Kevin to splash down into the pool. They were polishing off their second helping of French fries and grumbling about having to take showers and get into their pajamas right away. They gave in immediately when Josie, in to ask if she could help, threatened them with no movie. She promptly hustled them off, pajamas and towels in hand. The bunk and guest beds were all made up, and the television was switched to the cable station's movie. They were asleep by the time Kate had put the finishing touches on the salad and had the escargot hot and ready to be served. She made a quick dash to the dining room to inspect the table.

Perfect.

The flowers were all low enough for even the shortest dinner guest to see over. The crystal and silverware gleamed. The linen cloth and napkins were snowy white. Absently she moved around the table, adjusting a plate here, a knife there.

She and Felipe had had many dinner parties. This one was different. Tom never filled her with a sense of possible failing. Felipe always did. He inspected the stemware and silver, and on the rare occasions he found a smudge or a spot he made a noise in his throat that conveyed disgust. Tom, on the other hand, knew about dining and tables and comfort. He appreciated her efforts. He liked to entertain, not impress.

"Are you ready, honey?" Tom had come up behind her, another glass of chilled white wine in his hand for her.

"I'm as ready as I'll ever be. Sweetheart, will you ask Eileen to help me serve and ask everyone else to come in and sit?"

Tom gave Kate a quick kiss and went out onto the patio. He and Tim and the Judge had been talking about the Miranda law. Ira and Brian had been peripherally adding to the conversation. Everyone sounded a little high but happy. Dinner was about a half-hour overdue.

Kate went back into the kitchen and wrapped the three hot loaves of fresh bread she had made. Eileen waltzed in, a nice buzz on.

"Hello, hello, hello. What can I schlepp to the table for you? Ummm . . . hot bread." She tore off a little piece from the sourdough loaf. "Tom is out there impressing the pants off the Judge. I got the impression your father expected him to be a dumb flatfoot."

Eileen moved on to the waiting salad, drained her drink, and crunched away on a fresh carrot stick.

"Yum, this is some meal. Anyway, when Tom started using Aristotle and Plato to introduce his point of view, your father seemed to forget himself."

"What do you mean, 'forget himself'? Kate asked in a mildly alarmed voice.

"Nothing to get excited about," Eileen answered. "Only that your father is talking to him like a colleague, and you know what that means."

"Right," Kate answered. "Brian's going to be pissed. Eileen, stop eating the salad and put the bread on the table."

She returned to the kitchen humming "That Old Black Magic" and carried two of the three salads to the table. Kate could hear Josie putting everyone where she wanted them. Her father at one end, her mother beside him to his left. Tom at the other end, Kate to his left. Brian facing Tim, Betsy facing Margey, Josie and Eileen across from each other, Jim and Ira holding the fort.

Eileen sailed into the kitchen again, picked up the other salad, and commented on the interesting seating arrangement. Kate could hear Tom uncorking the champagne in the dining room. She opened the oven. The new potatoes were perfect, browned in butter, covered with fresh parsley. The baby carrots were an ideal sweet orange. Eileen said so when she popped one into her mouth. The main course stayed warm in the oven. Eileen brought in the cold consommé, laced with sherry, while Kate arranged the escargot neatly on their plates. She served some to everyone but her father and brother, who steadfastly refused to eat them. Tom promised he would. Eileen breezed in with the last salad, sat down, and said, "Ira, pass me everything. I'm starving."

Kate slipped into her chair and starting her escargot, nodded thank you to the compliments aimed her way between bites and sips. She felt Tom slip his hand down her thigh. She turned her head to him.

"Honey, these slugs are great." He popped the last one complete with dipped bread into his mouth. He returned to his conversation and absently stroked her thigh. Kate felt like a naughty little girl and decided she had had too much to drink.

After the first course was hungrily consumed, Kate and Betsy got up and started to clear the table. On her second trip to the kitchen, Kate picked up the telephone on the second ring.

"I'd like to speak to Tom Flynn." It was Joan. Kate knew it in an instant.

"Who's calling, please?" Kate answered as calmly as she could. All the food she had just eaten threatened to come up.

"Mrs. Tom Flynn, if you please. Is this the fuckin' whore he's livin' with?"

So much for the sick feeling. Bless you, you snarling old hag, Kate thought to herself. Bless you for making me lose my temper.

"Yes, this is the fucking whore Tom Flynn lives with. He is currently occupied, and even if he weren't, I'm sure he wouldn't want to come to the telephone."

"Look, you snotty whore, put my husband on the telephone. I want to talk to him."

"Joan, get this, and get it good." Kate could hear Betsy softly whistling her surprise behind her. It gave her more pluck.

"I tend not to talk to foul-mouthed old hags such as yourself. Furthermore, I suggest you look up a synonym for the word *whore* before you convince me that you really are the ineffectual, retarded person Tom is always joking about. Furthermore, if you show up here I will, and you can count on it like the sun coming up in

the morning, have you arrested. Furthermore . . ."
Joan had hung up.

Kate leaned against the wall, the receiver in her
hand. She was trembling and weak in the knees. Betsy
pulled out a chair for her at the counter and hung up
the phone. Kate's cheeks were flaming, her hands
trembling.

"I suppose it had to happen sometime. I just wonder
how she got our number. I had it changed and un-
listed."

Betsy got a cool cloth from the guest bathroom and
handed it to Kate to press to her forehead and cheeks.
The two women sat in silence for a bit.

"That wasn't a very smart thing to do, Kate." Betsy
was getting ready to advise her when Kate interrupted
tightly.

"I know, I know, but the strain of this situation is
getting unendurable. I just want it to be over. I can
barely handle the idea of him visiting that woman who
calls him husband." Kate said this with her face in her
hands and turned angry eyes to Betsy and finished.

"He is *my* husband. I have more than made my bed,
and I damn well want to sleep in it. He is mine, don't
you understand?"

"It's okay," Betsy soothed her, concerned that
Kate's angry voice would penetrate the animated conversations in the dining room. Eileen was obviously
high and entertaining people with funny, gossipy little
stories about her famous clients.

"Kate, I'm only concerned that you made the woman
more angry than she already is, and there is nothing
worse than a Catholic wife filled with self-righteous
rage."

"Right, Betsy, you're certainly the expert on that subject." Betsy jumped up as if she had been struck. Kate regretted her words before they were out and tried to stop her from leaving the kitchen.

"Betsy, I didn't mean it. Please, Betsy, understand, I've been under a terrible strain."

But Betsy wouldn't listen and wrenched free of Kate's hands. *Shit, what have I done now?* Kate thought. *This whole day started out so well. I have a sinking feeling it's going to end badly.*

"Kate, your father's so charming, and I love your mother too." Kate looked up to see Margey standing in the doorway. "What's the matter?"

"Oh, Margey, I just had a fight on the telephone with Joan." Kate was fighting hard not to cry.

"Oh God. What did the bitch want?"

"She called me a whore and then asked to speak to her husband, and I just blew. I'm so scared, Margey." Kate had started to cry, and Margey was by her side.

"Listen, Kate, that woman is no good, and Tom knows it. He has never been happier in his life. He is divorcing her so he can marry you. You guys are going to have a good life. So cut the tears, get the beef, and I'll bring out the potatoes and carrots. Now."

"I also hurt Betsy's feelings, I don't know what's happening to me, I . . ." Kate was taking the dinner out of the oven when Margey answered.

"Look, Kate, Betsy will get over it. Tonight is more important to you and Tom. He is getting on with your family. Don't spoil it by forcing him to be concerned about you. Tell him later. But not now."

They arranged the dinner and started toward the table. Margey stopped.

"Kate." She was thoughtful and obviously had something to say. "If you want to be a cop's wife, right now is a good time to start. We all have to hold back a lot of emotion most other wives can give free rein to. Tonight, remember, tonight is more important in the long run than upsetting Tom and having him come to your rescue. I don't mean to sound harsh, but if I do it is because I love Tom and you have made him happy. Please don't spoil it for him."

Kate was a little stung by the comment but recognized the wisdom of it. She smiled weakly at Margey, and they entered the dining room together.

"Betsy."

Kate wasn't looking forward to apologizing to her sister-in-law for the crack she had made the night before. Confrontations scared her. Nor was she looking forward to the distressing revelations sure to follow the acceptance of her apology.

Kate called Betsy's name again and knocked harder on the back door. The kitchen, through the screening, was immaculate as usual. The house beyond was deathly quiet. Relieved, Kate turned and started to walk to her car.

"I'm coming, Kate, just give me a minute." She could hear Betsy moving toward her through the shadowy depths of the big house.

Kate was feeling queasy and guilty and wasn't ready for the sight of her normally self-composed sister-in-law. Betsy was a tall, long-haired blonde with a defined, fine-skinned face. This morning she was, quite simply, a mess. Her hair was dirty and pinned haphazardly to the back of her head. She wore an old blue work shirt and jeans that had obviously been slept in. Her face was the worst. Her eyes were swollen and bloodshot, and she was covered with an oily sheen of perspiration.

"Come in, Kate." Betsy unlocked the door and immediately turned to the sink, coffee pot in hand. Her voice was low and thick, her attitude torpid. The house and Betsy were filled with a depressing stillness.

Kate was shocked.

"Betsy . . ." She started to stammer out an apology.

Betsy interrupted. "Would you like some coffee? I'll make some."

She filled the pot with cold water and the basket with coffee.

"It certainly is hot today. I never was able to bear the heat. I've been feeling dizzy and sleepy lately, so I nap a lot. The kids spend most of the day at the playground so I can rest. That was a lovely dinner party you and Tom had last night. I, er, we really enjoyed it. Tom is nice. He and the Judge certainly seemed to get on well. Brian said he liked him too."

Kate sat quietly at the kitchen table, listening to Betsy's near hysterical monologue. She was trying to think of a way to get through her reserve when Betsy stopped talking and turned around.

"What are you doing here, Kate?" Betsy's face was hard, her eyes full of anger and tears. "Did you come to continue your dialogue about my self-righteous Catholic housewife self, or have you thought of an even better way to hurt me?"

She stopped and stared at Kate, bitterness and hostility etched absurdly in a face shiny with tears.

"Bets." Kate hesitated, then began again. Her nervousness had turned to pity. She tried to keep it out of her voice. "Bets, I came to apologize for the crack I made last night. I didn't mean it. I was upset and hurt. I've been under tremendous pressure lately, and sometimes I lash out and say cruel things to people I love that I don't mean."

Kate met her eyes and was relieved to see the anger had faded, replaced by simple misery.

Kate got up, turned the fire off under the coffee, and moved next to her by the sink. Their backs were to the kitchen window, and she took Betsy's hand, which was given reluctantly. Kate didn't want to look at Betsy when she talked. Her grief made it difficult to concentrate.

"Brian told me about the vasectomy. He has told me that you two don't make love anymore. He says your marriage is falling apart." Kate felt Betsy grip her hand as her body convulsed and a sob escaped from her.

"But even more important, he has told me endlessly how much he loves you. How not being your husband is driving him crazy. That the reason he did it was because the doctor said it would be dangerous for you to have another child."

Kate cupped Betsy's hand with both of hers and turned to the window and Betsy. "Now. Do I have that part straight?"

Betsy nodded yes.

"What I don't know is what you feel, and it's obvious you're feeling a lot, and none of it good. I love Brian, and he's miserable. I love you, and you're miserable. So I thought since both of you love me, I'd butt in and see if I could help, maybe, okay?" Betsy pulled free

216

and put both hands to her face as if she was trying to hide the pitiful sounds coming from her.

The site of her affected Kate so deeply that she started crying herself and embraced her clumsily, whispering "Sssh" and "It's all right."

A cloud moved across the face of the sun, momentarily throwing the kitchen into darkness. Betsy's crying broke through the stillness in the house, and Kate wondered absently if it was going to rain. As she held Betsy, she reflected on how delicate she was, small fine bones, too thin. Maybe Brian was right. She didn't want Betsy to die either. Through the sounds of her grief Kate could hear the cars in the street, children arguing and laughing, even a bluejay's raucous call as it flew by.

A determined calm had replaced her nervousness and pity. She led Betsy to a chair, got her a tissue and a cold wet washcloth.

"Blow your nose, Bets. We're going to find a solution to this. You both love each other too much for it to go on."

Betsy looked up at Kate, her swollen blue eyes full of hope, her face terribly sad.

"Come on, blow that nose. Try to stop the tears before you fry your baby blues. And here." Kate handed her the cold cloth. "Put this on your eyes, and shut up and listen. You want that coffee now?"

"Yes, please."

Kate got up and turned on the fire under the pot and started to pace and talk. Betsy sat with her elbows on the table and her face pressed to the cloth.

Kate talked, a good deal about the way she felt about Tom, knowing that Betsy felt that way about Brian.

They drank the coffee.

Later Betsy took a shower and Kate made eight huge sandwiches. Her niece and nephew came in, without their usual noise and hullaballoo. They said hi and asked quietly for lunch. She kissed them and ruffled their hair, asked about camp. They both answered dully, and Kate realized how much this situation had upset them. She chided herself for not trying to help sooner.

Halfway through their tall glasses of milk, Betsy reappeared in the kitchen. She was all fresh and powdery and clean. Her hair was neatly twisted to the back of her head. She wore clean white shorts, a bright pink blouse, and a small smile.

The kids got noisy and relaxed and devoured their sandwiches. When they finished they put their dishes in the sink, kissed their mother goodbye, and went out to play again.

Kate and Betsy dove into the food, cracked a bag of potato chips, and opened two beers.

"Kate." Betsy's voice was higher and stronger now.

"Ummm," Kate answered through a mouthful of ham and cheese.

"I know you don't believe what I believe. Even most Catholics think I'm a bit much, you know, fish on Friday, etc. But that's how I was raised. It's how I feel spiritually."

Kate put down her sandwich and dabbed away the mustard from the corner of her mouth.

"Betsy, you don't have to convince me how sincerely devout you are. In fact, you're the only Catholic woman I know I'll listen to about Catholicism. You already know how I feel about lip-service practitioners of any religion. There are few Jews and even fewer Christians I have any respect for."

"True, all too true. It's a horrible thing when people hide behind what they preach rather than practicing it."

Betsy toyed with a bit of cheese on her plate. Kate finished her sandwich and beer in silence.

"I never asked Brian." Betsy began talking again, almost as if to herself. "I never asked him to practice the way I do. I married him fully aware that he was in large part contemptuous of the Church. Intellectually I sometimes find it very hard to disagree with him on the subject. But to me it is a matter of faith, and that is a matter of emotion, and intellect and emotion are very rarely in agreement with one another."

She paused, sipped her beer, and sat back. Kate sat absolutely still. Betsy rarely opened up this much. Her face was bare, the war between her faith and her love for Brian plainly visible.

"You see, Kate, it's two issues. The first one is faith. I simply cannot have sex for pleasure." Gesturing, she continued.

"Pleasure . . . the pleasure is the love I have inside of me for Brian, knowing that each time we make love, his love for me and my love for him, blessed by God in our union, might just be represented by a child."

Betsy leaned forward, took Kate's hands, and gripped them.

"Our children are, to me, God's approval of the total union of our love. I have never asked Brian to practice a religion he views intellectually. It's a matter of faith, not intellect, and you can't force faith, any more than you can force love."

Kate thought Betsy's beliefs were just this side of the

219

Dark Ages, but Betsy had more than proved her devotion as well as never forcing her beliefs on anyone. She was an extraordinary woman. She worked for the socially less prestigious Red Cross, was one of the founders of the Ladies Ecumenical Society in the county, and after a great soul-searching she had joined Catholic women for Pro Choice. Pro Choice cost her many friends and nearly her mother-in-law. She answered Nora's angry accusations firmly and finally. She explained that while she truly believed abortion was taking a life, she couldn't prove it, nor had God come down to prove it. It was every woman's constitutional right to do with her own body what she would, so she had joined the group, and if Nora didn't like it, and if Brian and the Judge thought it would cause trouble at the firm, tough shit! She finished them off by saying that the long arm of the federal government shouldn't be allowed to reach in and stamp "Government Property" on any woman's womb.

Kate admired her very much. Betsy was a credit to her sex. But that pleasure thing—Kate began to wonder if Betsy really ever had pleasure. So she asked.

"Betsy, this is strictly none of my business, but are you saying that Brian, I mean that you never have any physical pleasure from sex, I mean, you know, orgasms?"

Betsy had been watching her impassively as she stammered out the question. Then her face broke into a huge grin, and she started to laugh.

What a relief, Kate thought to herself.

"Kate." She was trying to talk through her giggles. It was a wonderful sight to see, after so much grief, Betsy laughing and twinkling as usual.

"Yes, Kate, I—we—do, lots, most times, all the time. The answer is definitely yes."

Betsy laughed a little more and fell silent.

"I guess that's one of the things that makes it so awful. I miss Brian very much."

Kate felt embarrassed and squirmed in her chair. Betsy, not sensing it, went on.

"So I went my way, and Brian accepted that and was content to have me do so until now. I think he is having an affair with someone."

Kate reacted quickly to that one. She wasn't absolutely sure he wasn't, but she knew Brian loved his wife almost to the point of embarrassment.

"Forget it, Bets. Brian's not getting it on with anyone."

"Did you ask him?"

Kate lied and said she had and that Brian had emphatically denied that possibility. She hoped she was right, and if she was wrong she would string her brother up.

"I know he loves me, Kate, but that's not what's wrong. He doesn't respect me or my beliefs, or at least my right to have those beliefs and live by them. When he went out and secretly had that vasectomy a year ago . . ."

Oh no, Kate thought to herself. *He lied to her about that. She doesn't know that this has been going on for three years now.*

". . . and continued to make love to me under false pretenses while all the while I was loving him in the same way, well it made a lie of our marriage. How could he have so little respect for me?"

Kate started to interrupt, and Betsy stopped her.

"Oh, believe me, I know why he says he did it. Yes, the doctor did say it was dangerous to have more children, but he did not have the right to do it secretly, knowing how I feel and believe. It's my right and my right alone to make that decision. Not his. I have respected him and his beliefs even though I disagree with them. The children go to public school and get their religious training at church and from me. But Kate, when he married me he knew and he agreed to accept my beliefs as part of me. Our agreement is the foundation of our marriage, and by getting a vasectomy he broke it and our marriage with it."

She had started to cry again, and Kate stopped her.

Betsy, in the agreed-to terms of their marriage, was right. Brian was wrong. He broke one of the codicils of their marriage. In the terms of the world, she didn't know, but what was at stake was their marriage, one that he professed he wanted very much, so Brian was wrong.

"Bets, I want you to calm down and blow your nose. Brian won't be coming home for dinner tonight. He's going to have dinner with us."

"Oh, Kate, you can't help, no one can. What's done is done."

"So, how'd it go with her? Did you have it out with her?" Tom's voice flowed in over the wire and all over her. She was so secure with the way they loved each other. Their intimacy was so complete; he was her best friend, her lover, her mate.

"No, not out with her, more in with her. After a lot of tears and conversation I'm afraid I agree with her.

I'm going to have it out with Brian. Do you mind if we have him over for dinner tonight?"

"No, honey, I don't mind. But will he mind having me there?"

"If he does, tough."

Kate reiterated as much of the long conversation as she could. Tom listened quietly without comment.

"Well, what do you think?"

"Personally, I think Brian is really right. But, as you say, in the terms of their marriage he's wrong. I happen to disagree vehemently with Betsy. Catholicism has ruined and maimed a lot of good people trapped in very bad marriages. But if Brian accepted her beliefs and behavior as part of their marriage contract and now has abrogated them, well, he has broken a very fundamental agreement in their marriage, and that makes him wrong, poor bastard."

"Tom, I love you, you're wonderful."

"You think so? I'll be home around 6:30, woman, and see to it you're barefoot and eager."

Laughing, she responded to his broguish humor. "I'll be waiting a good hot meal for yourself. It'll give you that extra bit o' energy that always gives me that extra bit o' thrill."

They laughed together, exchanged I love you's and kisses, and hung up. Kate picked up the receiver again and dialed her brother's line.

"Gallagher, O'Neil, McCarthy, and Gallagher."

"Hi, Midge, it's Kate. Is Brian in?"

"Hi yourself. What have you been up to? I hear you're getting married."

"Midge, Midge." Kate didn't know what to say to

this, and lately she had been asked by many of her parents' friends. "You'll be one of the first to know if I take the plunge again. But he's very nice and very handsome and very tall and very smart . . ."

". . . and very rich?" Midge finished with a laughing question.

"No, Midge, but four out of five ain't bad."

"Irish?"

"Yes."

"Well, it's about time. That's half the battle."

"Midge!"

"I'll ring Brian for you now."

Kate fidgeted with the telephone cord and silently rehearsed what she would say to her brother. She opted for emotional extortion.

"Brian Gallagher."

"Hi Bri, it's Kate."

"Hi Cat. Dinner was great last night. I, we, had a swell time. Listen, I'm busy, can I call . . ."

"Brian, no. I can't imagine how either of you could have had a swell time. I spent the day talking with Betsy."

"Oh?" His voice was a curious mixture of fear and hope.

"Yes, I did. I also told her that you wouldn't be coming home for dinner tonight, that you would be having dinner with me. Brian, we need to have a very long talk."

"About what?" Brian snapped back at her.

"Do you want Betsy back or not? I have the solution, or what I think is the solution."

"What time?"

"Six."

"What's for dinner?"

"Fish."

"Ugh."

"Brian." Kate's voice admonished him.

"Okay, okay, I'll see you then."

There was a click and a buzz, and Kate stood with the receiver in her hand, wondering how she was going to persuade her brother to put himself in the hospital and have his vasectomy undone.

{ *Chapter 16* }

The days passed and turned into weeks, and Tom and Kate seemed to settle in with each other comfortably. Tom visited his children twice a week and talked to his lawyer on the days he didn't.

Kate never asked about his conversations or the confrontations with Joan—confrontations he always had when he went to visit. She realized that Joan was threatening to deny him all rights to his children. Kate had asked Brian's advice about what she could do. She knew Tom would be angry if he knew she had talked to Brian. She couldn't help it.

She was frightened, and she needed to know what was going on. Brian was helpful. He explained that the laws had changed so much that in reality Joan couldn't keep Tom from his children. He added that she could screw him financially, but since Tom was willing to give

Joan just about everything she asked for, there really wasn't much to worry about.

Still, Kate worried. Tom was changing. She wondered if their day-to-day normalcy could hold up under the assault of his children's guilt-producing anger and hurt.

Maureen wasn't doing very well. Tom thought it was because she was the one who spent the most time with Joan and was getting the brunt of her rage and fear.

And Joan was afraid. She was afraid of what the neighbors were saying, afraid that Tom would leave her destitute, afraid that she was really losing her man.

She was losing her man, all right, and the neighbors never shut up about them, but Tom had no intention of leaving her destitute.

She was going to get the house. He agreed to pay the remaining two years on the mortgage as well as alimony and child support. He was not, however, going to continue paying her support when Connor and Mora moved out. He had even suggested paying for her tuition if she agreed to go to school and train for a job. When Joan's lawyer told her Tom's suggestion, she turned into a wild woman. It was hell that night, so bad that Seamus took Maureen and left the house.

After wandering around a while, he decided that this was his father's problem. He called a friend who could drive at night and showed up at Kate's door with Maureen at 9:30 P.M. Tom wasn't there at the time, and Kate and Kevin were confronted by an enraged Seamus and a traumatized Maureen.

Kate hustled them into the house and fed them. Kevin tried to get Seamus to talk to him. He did get Maureen to watch TV with him in his room. After they finished their meal, Seamus asked if he could wait for his father, and when Kate assented he went outside to the front steps to wait for him.

Their pain shocked Kate, and after she cleaned up the kitchen she checked on Maureen, who had fallen asleep, and joined Seamus on the front steps. The night was clear and warm, and they sat together in an uncomfortable silence.

After about fifteen minutes he started to talk, and Kate listened in shocked silence as the boy detailed what had been going on.

Kate didn't know how to relate to Joan's behavior. Apparently, after Tom left she turned into a monster. She slapped Maureen around, screamed at the children, and punished them severely for even the most minor infraction of the rules.

Rules she had made after Tom left. They all had to be in by 9 P.M. Maureen had to be in bed by 8 P.M. She was apparently trying to win Tom back, and when her efforts to be charming or sweet failed, and they did every time, she turned into a maniac.

When the children, pushed to the limit, threatened to tell their father what was going on, she threatened them back. She promised them that if they complained to him she would make sure they never saw him again. The threat of losing him totally, hurt Maureen the most and then Seamus. Connor and Mora were almost of age and didn't take her seriously. They just busied themselves in their young lives and talked to their friends.

As Seamus talked to her, Kate wondered what to say to Tom. He truly thought things were going well at home, and this was going to blow his mind.

Seamus interrupted her unhappy musings when he turned his angry eyes to her and asked in a harsh voice if she was satisfied with what she had done.

She was almost afraid to answer him. His anger and hurt and Maureen's condition scared her. It was obvious that Tom hadn't exaggerated when he told her about Joan and his rotten life. But how could she explain anything to this hurt, angry young man? It would sound like empty, cowardly excuses to him.

She decided not to try, but instead she told him about herself and Kevin. She told him everything she thought he would understand. About her marriage to Felipe in minor detail, about when she met Tom and how they had met again years later. She told him as much about his father's pain as she gauged he would understand and tried to explain why he had left them.

Seamus listened, realizing dismally that what she was telling him was the truth. He understood why his father had left. Acutely. He wanted to run away and hide for the same reasons.

The more Kate talked, the more Seamus liked her. He asked her about her work, and she was relieved to change the subject to something other than pain. Apparently Seamus was very interested in photography, and Kate wound up promising him that she would teach him how to use the developer and enlarger if he wanted her to.

"I'll even make you my helper," she added with a smile. "That is, if you really promise to work hard."

By the time Tom pulled into the driveway they had been friends for about an hour.

The sight of his son sitting on the front steps with

Kate threw him into a panic. When Seamus saw his father he forgot to be upset and walked over to his car eagerly.

Tom got out with a deep frown on his face, and Seamus remembered then why he was there.

"What's wrong, Seamus?" Tom asked in a mildly panicked voice. "What's happened? Is your sister all right? Was there an accident?"

"No, Dad, no. Maureen is asleep inside." Seamus felt strange. He didn't want to talk about it anymore. He just wanted to sit quietly and talk to his dad and Kate and go to bed.

"There was some trouble at the house tonight, Dad." Seamus was looking down at his feet as he continued talking to his frightened father. "I thought I ought to bring Maureen over here."

Kate interrupted him midsentence. "Seamus, why don't you go inside and fix yourself and your dad some iced tea?" She had seen his dilemma and had decided that she should be the one to talk to Tom. "Go on, Seamus. I'll explain what happened to your dad."

Tom stood and stared at her while Seamus retreated to the kitchen.

"Tom," Kate began. "Apparently things at your house haven't been what they appear to be."

"What do you mean? What happened that would make Seamus run away and bring Maureen here?" Tom was really frightened and stunned. He was also vaguely aware of a new feeling. Embarrassment. He was mildly embarrassed that his son had "caught" him at his "girlfriend's" house. It was weird.

Kate started to walk slowly toward the house, explaining in brief what had been going on, saving the bit about Maureen for last.

"When her lawyer mentioned that you would pay for her tuition she went wild. She thinks it's my idea. Unfortunately Maureen thought it was a good idea and asked her mother when she was going to go back to school. She said something like, 'Wouldn't it be nice, Mommy, you and me in school together.' That's when Joan went wild. She must have thought Maureen was mocking her so she slapped her around quite a bit."

"Where's Maureen?" Tom's face was rock hard.

"She's asleep in Kevin's room." Kate hesitated, then added, "Honey, she has a bad bruise on her cheek. I don't know if she got it from Joan or from an accident. She wouldn't talk at all. Not even to Kevin. She just wanted to eat and watch TV and wait for you."

He stopped just outside the front door under the light, and Kate thought, *So this is what an angry Irish cop looks like.*

"I'm going to check on her, and then I'll talk to Seamus."

Kate nodded.

"He can sleep in the guest room. I'll have to call Joan and tell her where they are."

Kate groaned inwardly.

"Tom, that's going to go over like a lead balloon."

"She's lucky I'm not there. I think if I could get my hands on her right now I would beat her to death."

They entered the house together. Tom made his way quickly to Kevin's room. Kate joined a worried Seamus in the kitchen.

"Everything will be all right." She squeezed his arm

reassuringly. "Don't worry. Your father's not angry with you, he's just concerned. He loves you both very much. You did the right thing by coming here."

Seamus stood very quietly and listened.

He watched her face when she talked. He liked the concern and sympathy he saw there. He liked her very much. He wanted to cry.

"Look, why don't I show you the guest room, and I'll get you a pair of your father's pajamas. Take your tea and his. You can change and get ready for bed. You must be exhausted. He has to call your mother to let her know you're okay." Seamus was following her down the hall as she talked. When she mentioned his mother he stopped.

"He has to call her? Why?" Seamus's voice stopped her. There was real fear in it.

"Why does he have to do that? She'll make him bring us home. Then, after he leaves . . ."

Kate reached out for him, interrupting him.

"Don't worry. No one is bringing you back there tonight. And furthermore, when you do go back, your dad will see to it that she never ever does this again. I don't want you to worry. You can stay here as long as you like."

She walked him down the hall the rest of the way. She showed him where the little bathroom was and put fresh towels in it. She told him to take a shower.

"It will relax you," she said. "It will help you sleep."

Tom was in the kitchen on the telephone with Joan. Kate listened by the doorway, not wanting to interrupt him. He sounded like an animal. His voice was a low, threatening growl. He had his back to her, and as she listened to him talk she became just a little frightened.

232

The violence that he talked about on the streets was there in his voice as he talked to Joan.

She turned and walked away. She checked on Kevin and Maureen. They were both fast asleep. The bruise on Maureen's cheek was indeed ugly.

Suddenly they were surrounded by ugliness.

It was two in the morning before Tom joined her in bed. He looked like someone had drained the blood out of his body. She had tried to go to sleep but couldn't. She waited for him, reading.

"Well?" was all she asked when he sagged to the bed. He lay back, his hands crossed under his head, and stared at the ceiling. It was a long time before he answered her. When he did it stopped her heart.

"I have to go back." He was talking to the ceiling. "I can't leave them alone there with her."

"You have to do what?" Kate sat up straight. "You can't be serious."

"Kate." He was serious and at the same time hoping she would say something, anything, that would provide him with an alternative.

"I can't leave them there with her. They are my children, and I love them. She is hurting them, and I can't allow that."

Kate answered him immediately.

"Then they can live here, Tom. The whole bunch of them." Her voice was full of panic. She couldn't believe what she was hearing. She started to cry and shake. She felt sick.

Tom turned and looked at her. Tears were streaming down her face. Her eyes were wide with disbelief. He reached up, and she fell into his arms. He let out a gasp of pain.

"You're right. I can't leave you. I can't leave them. I don't know what to do." They held each other tightly and rocked. Kate's whole body was flooded with relief. Tom gripped her, trembling, and kept repeating, "What am I going to do? What am I going to do?"

They slept like that, and in the morning Kate got up and made a big breakfast for everyone. Tom sequestered himself in the bedroom and talked to his lawyer.

Maureen went outside with Kevin for a swim. She still wasn't willing to speak to anyone but her father. He had talked to her a little bit before breakfast. He was planning to talk to both of them after he spoke to the lawyer.

Seamus followed Kate around the house like a lost puppy. He helped her with the dishes and put away the food. They hadn't eaten much. He talked to her some more about photography.

When Tom emerged from the bedroom he found them in the kitchen. He forced a smile and suggested that Seamus join Kevin and Maureen in the pool. He embraced his son briefly and explained that he had to talk to Kate privately for a little while.

Seamus assured him that it was fine and went outside.

Gloom settled in the kitchen, and Tom started to talk.

"He says I have to bring them back. He said there are certain legal questions that could even involve you in a kidnapping charge if she wanted to be nasty."

Kate was sure that Joan would be nasty if she could gain by it.

"Joan could at that point make sure I don't see the children." He was talking softly. "He said he would call her lawyer and explain that I will press charges against her for child abuse if her behavior continues."

Tom went on to explain the trouble Joan would be in if she repeated her performance. Then he explained his awful position.

"So you see I have to bring them back." His shoulders were slumped, his hands out and open in a pleading gesture. Kate had been sitting quietly listening to him. A new fear slowly invaded her. She pushed it back, went to him, and held him in silence.

"It will work itself out, Tom," she whispered in his ear. "You will see in time it will work itself out. We just have to get through this, all of us, as best we can."

They stayed like that, and both of them listened to the children outside. They were actually all laughing and splashing around in the pool. The nightmare of last night seemed far away. They broke their embrace simultaneously. Tom cupped her cheek with his hand and kissed her softly.

"I have to go out and talk to them now."

She watched him through the window. Kevin came into the house. His feelings were clearly hurt when Tom told him that he had to talk to Seamus and Maureen alone. Kate tried to explain to Kevin what was happening to his two new friends, while Tom was breaking the bad news to his children.

Kate heard Maureen scream, and she ran to the window to see what was wrong. Maureen was striking her father and screaming, "No, no, I won't. I hate her. I won't. Yes she will, Daddy, she will hit me again, and again and again. And you won't be there to stop her."

Kate moved away from the window and away from the desperate tableau on the back lawn. Kate knew that

Tom could make sure that Joan never struck Maureen again. But could he make sure that the psychological abuse would stop? In her heart Kate knew that he couldn't, that the only way was to have them with her and Tom, and arranging that was going to be difficult, if not impossible.

She decided to take Kevin out for the day, leaving the three of them alone. Kevin was still hurt, and the events of the day and, probably in the future, would have to be explained more thoroughly to him.

She went to the patio door off the dining room and called to Tom. After she explained what she was going to do, where she could be reached later, she and Kevin left.

Tom and Seamus and Maureen reentered the house after Kate and Kevin left. Tom felt like a stranger in the house with his children. They ran from room to room examining everything. Seamus was particularly fond of Kevin's sporting equipment. Most of his was very old and worn out. He tried not to show his jealousy, but he couldn't help himself.

Seamus loved to play tennis, and Kevin had two barely used rackets and a plentiful supply of unopened cans of tennis balls.

"Boy, Dad, we never had this at home. Kevin has everything he wants, Dad. I mean, look at this stuff."

Tom was standing in the doorway to Kevin's room, watching his son admire the equipment, pained because he alone could never provide him with a tenth of it.

"Yes, I know," Tom answered him from the door. "I think when Kevin's father, Felipe, died, Kate tried to compensate by providing him with anything a boy could want and need. I guess she was hoping it would help ease the pain of losing his father."

Seamus turned to his father, and before he said it Tom knew what was coming.

"We lost our father, too, Dad." Seamus paused and then continued. "I would still rather have you than all the toys and stuff that Kevin has."

Tom didn't say anything. He didn't know what to say.

"It's not fair," Seamus continued. "Kevin has all of this, a mother like Kate, and now he has my father too."

"Come on, Seamus." Tom gestured for his son to come with him. "Let's go and find Maureen. And you haven't lost me, Seamus. If I can arrange it, you will have gained Kate and Kevin."

They found Maureen in Kate's room. She had pulled several of Kate's dresses out to look at. Her face was covered with Kate's makeup, and she reeked of Kate's perfume.

Oh no, Tom thought to himself. Then aloud he said, "Maureen, what have you done? What a mess you are!"

"Oh, Daddy, she has so many beautiful things." Maureen scampered away from him and opened all the closet doors. Indeed. Silks and wool bouclés, a fur coat, and satin and velvet dresses, pants, gowns, and blouses hung neatly in her closets. Her shoes neatly adorned the racks on the floor.

The three Flynns stood there. They were all thinking the same thing. Joan's small closet was jammed with cheap clothes, often put away unwashed, the shoes in a jumble on the floor.

The wealth, order, and thought that went into being Kate Gallagher Zandt was apparent in every inch of her home.

"Daddy." Maureen broke their silence. "Daddy, are we poor?"

"No," Tom answered absently.

"Daddy, if we're not poor, is Kate rich?" Maureen continued.

The question stirred him, and he thought about his answer.

"She isn't as rich as she looks." He paused, thought some more, and finished. "She's careful with her things, cautious about what she buys." He moved toward his bathrobe hanging in the closet and felt the material between his fingers.

"I think she just insists on quality in everything." Tom stood and stared at the bathrobe like he had never seen it before. He was right. She insisted on quality in everything, in people, in her work, in the food she served, even in the flowers she grew.

He wondered what she saw in him.

{ *Chapter 17* }

"I understand how she feels. I went through it myself."
Kate looked up at Flynn from her work.

"No, you can't possibly." Tom put his book down
and sighed. "You can't possibly because you are beautiful, young, and have tremendous advantages. Like
your family. You also had the best education money
can buy."

Kate interrupted him. "Wait a minute. That very
good education was obtained in part by my winning a
scholarship. Joan had the same chance to further
herself that I did. She didn't choose to take advantage."

"Kate, Joan's background wouldn't let her take
advantage. For Christ's sake, her mother was a domes-
tic. Your mother is married to a judge. Joan's father
walked out on her and her five brothers and sisters

when she was nine." Tom was beginning to get angry with Kate. Angry with her because she wasn't being as understanding as he wanted her to be.

"Tom! You came from the same background! My grandparents knew your grandparents in the Bronx. We all come from the same people. Joan is afraid of losing her meal ticket, not of losing you."

A silence hung in the air between them, neither one wanting to break it by saying the wrong thing. Kate regretted saying that Flynn was only a meal ticket to Joan. Flynn regretted bringing up the subject in the first place. How could he expect Kate to be sympathetic to Joan? All Kate knew of her was the screaming bitch on the other end of the telephone.

And, oh God, there had been so many calls lately. Kate resumed her work at her light table, and Tom picked up his book. But he couldn't read. The last visit with Joan and the kids hadn't been as awful as usual. That was because of Joan.

She was genuinely terrified that he wasn't going to support her and the children. He had steeled himself and went last Thursday during the day. When he got there the house was in an uproar. He could hear her screaming from upstairs that she'd be late for her interview.

Joan had a job interview. It nearly floored him. In all their years together she had never thought to ease his burden by getting a job.

She descended the stairs dressed in a bright orange dress. It was a little too tight and clashed with her hair, but she did look presentable. In a voice that mimicked real dignity, she announced that she had an interview with a local doctor for a receptionist's job.

"And I can't stop to talk to you now, Tom," she added in what she imagined were haughty tones. "The doctor is waitin' to see me."

She had presented a sad picture, a ridiculous picture, but she did get the job. In spite of himself he had to admire her. She had never worked a day in her life, and she had pulled herself together enough to go out and land a job at her age.

While Flynn sat musing behind his book, Kate bent over her negatives and tried to concentrate. As she moved her glass from frame to frame, she thought about what was happening to them.

For something that had started off as well as it had, their relationship was turning into a bad dream. He had warned her that she probably wouldn't like him, that he had developed some very bad habits while he had been married to Joan. He said he would probably bring them with him and ruin them.

Kate had, at the time, kissed him and hugged him and told him she loved him bad habits and all. She didn't believe what he was saying was possible.

But he had been right, and it was ruining them. He was moody and critical, and he had started to close himself off from her. At first she believed him when he said he felt guilty. Later it became clear to her.

It was as if he believed that no two people could marry and be happy and stay and grow in their love. Somehow he had come to believe that marriage was a place for duty and pain and forbearance, not love and intimacy and joy. He let their day-to-dayness over-whelm him and his love for her. He focused on it mentally and started to compare her to Joan.

Kate wasn't giving up, but she didn't know how to

prove him wrong. She had become both an observer and a participant. As an observer he resented her and what he perceived as her self-righteous smugness. He was tired of apologizing, and when she said she was tired of hearing him apologize, he didn't believe her.

When she was a participant she was wild. All her normally good judgment and calm went out the window, and her voice would become shrewish and whining and panicky. When she heard herself she would shut her mouth and refuse to talk.

The arguments about money were getting worse. It was because it was her money. He didn't approve of the way she spent it. When he said so she got angry. She had to admit to herself that him telling her what to do with what belonged to her pissed her off.

She had earned it after all.

They spent the rest of the evening in silence, Flynn either reading or lost in confused thought, Kate bent over her light table reexamining negatives she normally would have discarded after a one-time appraisal.

Around eleven Kate stretched and announced she was going to check on Kevin and go to bed. Tom nodded from behind his book.

Kate shivered as she slipped between the cold sheets. She lay awake, tossing and punching her pillow. When Tom came to bed she pretended to be asleep. She needn't have bothered. He made no move toward her. She lay awake, miserable, wondering what she could do to stop what was happening to them. Then the tears came, and she tried to muffle her sobs in the pillow.

Tom had been lying awake all the while too. When she started to cry he rolled over and took her into his arms.

"There was a time when you wanted to make love to me all the time," she sobbed through her tears. "You looked into my eyes, kissed my mouth with yours, and you were there with me. Now sometimes I feel like you are using my body, perhaps even to make love to yourself, or satisfy some fantasy you've always had, but you don't look into my eyes anymore. My excitement doesn't excite you anymore. It's as if there is no room for my love or desire because you have lost your love and desire for me."

Tom held her tightly while she cried and tried to find the words to answer her unhappy accusations. He couldn't because lately his behavior and feelings had changed. She was, in part, right.

It was awful. Sometimes her body was just a body to him, and when they made love his mind roamed over the hundreds of women who were available to him. Women, he understood them now. His new understanding had come from knowing and loving Kate.

Kate slept. Freudian dreams plagued her every night. Her dilemma was clear; the way out of it seemed impossible. She was forever running down a dark tunnel chasing him, as he in turn ran ahead of her toward a light that decreased in size as they drew near. At the end of the dream he always made it through the small hole at the end of the tunnel, but she didn't. She was left in the darkness. Sometimes Kevin was in the tunnel with her, crying for her; sometimes she was alone.

She realized that the more she satisfied Tom's needs, the more she loved and gave to him, the more it strengthened him. He held himself in higher esteem, felt better about himself as a man. All this did was contribute to his growing sense that he should be contributing this new person to his children. Kate didn't know what to do. She couldn't stop loving him. The more she gave, the more he took, the more she realized it gave him courage to go back and live a life for his children. Even if it meant he had to do it with Joan. She had already given him what he needed to survive.

She knew she could survive anything with him but seriously doubted she could survive anything without him. She tossed and moaned in her sleep. Her intellect answered her heart. It told her to let him go. Let him go so he could find out that once you have loved, and been loved in return, you cannot live successfully for very long without it.

She had a surrealistic fantasy image of how she had changed his life, how her love for him had changed him.

It was as if she had wandered his way one day and, passing him, noticed a knife handle in his back. Saying, "Oh, what's this?" she pulled it out to show him. Once the always present, unknown pain was gone he could breathe deeply, laugh painlessly, and hold the paring knife in his hand. She fantasized that he held the knife in his hand and wondered how he could have lived all those years with it between his shoulder blades.

But now the fantasy was changing. He knew happiness. He had given and received love. He had shared laughter and hope with her and an intimacy he had never believed possible. But now it was as if he didn't feel right without the old familiar pain. And soon he was going to reinsert the knife in his back, voluntarily.

Kate didn't know if it could ever come out again. Only Flynn could do that a second time, voluntarily.

"If I acted one-tenth the way Joan acts, would you have anything to do with me?"

Kate was sitting up in the bed after her restless night. Her hair was all tousled, her eyes puffy, her lips swollen and pouty. He wanted to bruise her mouth even more with his. He wanted to bury his hands in her tangled hair and mess it up more. He wondered absently what it would be like when he lost his desire altogether. He wanted her so urgently in that moment.

"No," he answered in a thick, quiet voice.

"Yet you say I am a million times the woman she is. Why then would you even consider going back to her?"

"Because I place you in the category that I place myself in. We are better, stronger, brighter people. We have greater obligations because we perceive more responsibility."

"That's bullshit!" Kate hopped up and down on the bed, thumping her fists on the mattress. Her full, round breasts bobbed up and down, and he felt himself engorge. He watched her nipples harden under the fabric of her nightgown.

Kate continued in a husky lower voice.

"She's not your child. She's not your responsibility."

Flynn reached up and cupped his hand behind the back of her neck and pulled her firmly down to his mouth, quieting her. He laid her back on the sheets, pulled the gown off over her head, and spent the rest of the night rediscovering the body and the woman he had been ignoring for the past two weeks.

{ *Chapter 18* }

"Joan, Joan, always Joan. Why does she get to use your children like weapons? Why is it okay for her to use Seamus and Maureen without conscience or morality to manipulate you into going home? Why are you the only one who is expected to maintain standards of duty, responsibility, and impartiality when it comes to your children? Why do you let her act like a greedy evil child who plays on your sense of right and wrong, your love for the children?"

"Kate, please, you don't understand. She's like a child. She doesn't know any better."

Kate had lost all control.

"Fuck that. She's no child. She's a grown woman. You just can't stand not playing big daddy anymore. Maybe what you're really afraid of is that she can get along without you. That they all can. Maybe it's you

246

who are still innocent. Don't you know that this miserable harridan has played you like a comfy family fiddle for years? She knows you very well. She knows that you don't know her. She has no morals when it comes to getting her way. She will stress and hurt those children until you do what she wants you to do. And you, my poor stupid darling, will do anything to make their hurt less. Anything because you know the very worst hurt in the world is the one you did not cause. Pain you cannot stop because the person causing it doesn't know or care. It is the time when parents go down on their knees to God and beg. We promise anything, will do anything, to stop their hurt.

"Usually we wind up in agony, still experiencing our children's anguish. But added to this is the new pain we have inflicted on ourselves that makes us even less suitable to teach and guide and soothe our children. They discover in time that they and they alone can stop or allow their pain. We discover that we have lost everything needlessly. They leave us, we become bitter about their lack of loyalty or appreciation, and we grow older and die alone."

Tom knew intellectually that everything she was saying was right. He just didn't know it in his gut. He sat and watched her. He watched her intelligence and her beauty and her strength, and he knew that he loved her more than he ever did before.

He also knew that eventually, because what she was saying was right, he would break and run back to his duty and his pain, because he could not bear his children's hurt any longer. He knew that even if he couldn't help them, he was even willing to be there minute by minute to try to siphon some of it off.

He vowed as she argued on that for the time left to them he would be as loving as he possibly could be. He vowed that he would make the time they had left together last him the rest of his life. There would be no one after her. No one could fill his mind, heart, or loins with the longing she did.

It was madness. She was going off on a shoot the next day. A long-standing assignment in Bermuda. He was wild and jealous and very unhappy that she was going. Yet at the same time he was seriously considering going back to a wife he didn't love, a wife he found repulsive, in order to save his children. He was considering leaving all his hopes and dreams. Madness.

They stopped their arguments when Kevin came into the room. He was getting tense. He could tell that something was very wrong between his mother and Tom. He didn't know what it was exactly, but he sensed it had something to do with Seamus and Maureen.

He remembered that night vividly. He had tried hard to make Maureen feel better when she was watching TV with him. But Maureen claimed that she wasn't upset at all and demanded silence.

He had tried from time to time to talk to Tom. He had tried to tell him how he had felt when his daddy died and how he felt now. Somehow Tom didn't understand what he was trying to do, so he gave up.

"Kev." Tom was calling to him. "Kev, you want to go for a swim? I'll teach you the breast stroke."

Kevin raced into the room, excited.

"You bet I do, Tom!"

"Well, go and get your suit on and I'll meet you at the pool."

Kate, relieved at the break in the tension, announced

she was going to the supermarket and would be back soon.

Kevin and Tom spent the next two hours cavorting in the water, and from time to time Kate would watch from the window. They were like father and son, and she was afraid for her child. She was afraid for herself. What if he didn't love them enough to stick it out? What if he left them?

"What to do?" she muttered to herself. "What am I going to do?"

Kevin went next door after their swim to play with a new child in the neighborhood. Kate went off to the vegetable garden to work on the late tomatoes. Tom joined her a few minutes later.

"Oh, God, you're being selfish! You'd rather your children grow up as guilt-ridden as you are than allow them to be angry with you."

Kate couldn't stop herself. She had kept her thoughts to herself for so long that they burst the dam of her sensible restraint and poured out.

"What the hell are you talking about?" Tom was genuinely puzzled.

"What I am talking about is all our histories. Just suppose for a minute that your father had left your mother."

Kate's mind was working in tenth gear. She knew exactly where she wanted to lead him. She just didn't know if Tom was willing to be honest with himself so she could.

"Okay, suppose my father had left my mother. What has that got to do with me?"

"Would you have been very angry with him? How would you have felt if, after leaving you alone with your mother, he then went out and found a woman that he liked and loved? A woman that made him very happy. Would you have felt that he didn't need you? That maybe it wasn't your responsibility alone to make him happy?"

Tom thought about her questions. He admitted that it would have made him very angry. He allowed that a new mother would have made him feel less needed. And he added, "Yes, I would have been pissed off as hell if he had left me alone with my mother."

Kate paused, hoping she would be able to make her point rather than driving him away from her. "Isn't it true that to this day you are still mourning your father? That you still miss him? That you feel that you left so many things unsaid? That you wish you could have done something to make his life better, happier, longer?"

Tom had focused intensely on what she was saying. Everything she was saying was a truth he held in his heart. "Yes."

"Why do you feel that way? You are now a grown man with children. Would it make you feel good if your children felt that way about you? Would you be happy if your children grew up feeling, shall we say guilty, because they couldn't do enough, say enough to make you happy? Would you be comforted by knowing that after you die they will mourn you for the rest of their lives?"

Kate watched as Tom considered her questions and questions of his own rippled across his face. She waited, hopeful that he would see for himself what she could see, that when he came to the answer it would flick a switch somewhere deep inside him.

The silence in the air deepened around them. Kate could hear the cars rushing by on the parkway in the distance.

"Why do I feel guilty? I see what you are getting at. I feel that way because I know my father stayed married to her because of me. In spite of the fact that he didn't love and maybe even like her, he stayed for me. And yes, if he had left I would have been angry and hurt. But I would still have loved him, yes, and liked him. And yes, you're right, I probably wouldn't still be mourning him."

They had been working side by side in the vegetable garden they had planted together earlier in the season. The tomatoes were huge and just beginning to turn. The basil and marigolds released their odors, keeping pests out of the garden and mingling with the scent of the ripening tomatoes.

They worked side by side in silence. The sun started to go down. As if on a signal they both stopped and moved together to put the tools away. Kate picked some lettuce and one small ripe tomato for a salad.

He watched her from the shed. He liked this woman he loved, he really did. He liked the fact that she planted seeds in the ground and grew flowers to be admired and food to be eaten. He decided that he liked her because she was a very real person. She never wavered in her convictions, never compromised what she really believed in or the people she loved.

Like the harrowing night Brian had come over to dinner. After arguments and accusations that he heard from the privacy of the bedroom, Brian had agreed to have his vasectomy undone. He probably didn't agree with Kate, but he, like Flynn, could never doubt her sincerity or her love. The poor bastard probably thought the odds were in his favor. Unfortunately, Betsy got pregnant again.

He finished with the tools, and as he entered the house he admitted that he didn't really want his children growing up with the same burden of guilt he had. He just didn't know if he could withstand their anger. But he decided to try.

{ *Chapter 19* }

It was the perfect day. The hot yellow of the sun streaked across the unblemished morning sky. It made the placid surface of the bay sparkle. Embraced by the sand cliffs and salt-dusted scrub pine beaches, Gardner's Bay sprawled across the horizon. A lone sailboat, a puff of stark white against the primary blue, glided by in silence.

From their vantage point on the bluff, Flynn could see Shelter Island as promised the night before. Tom and Kate had arrived about 2:30 A.M., and Shirley Cahill had greeted them in a Halston with drinks in hand. The party going on around them was noisy with bright people peppering their conversations with spicy tidbits of gossip. Tom and Kate were exhausted and trying to figure out how to beat a retreat to their room when Eileen and Ira spied them and whisked them away.

As they drew away from the sound of the alcohol-fired wit and intellect, the wealthy silence wrapped itself around them. They had a quick impressive tour of the Cahill house on the way to their room.

Eileen and Ira left them alone as soon as it was polite, but before leaving Eileen pointed out the window and deck and promised them a staggering view of the bay in the morning. Kate had already collapsed on the king-sized bed. Ira showed Tom the black-tiled bathroom and the endless closets artfully hidden behind a wall of rollout drawers.

The Cahill house was amazing.

Murray Cahill was a television producer and a close friend of Eileen's. Shirley Cahill was a fan of Kate's work, and when she discovered Eileen was her agent she insisted on inviting Kate and Tom and "that darling Ira" to one of the famous Cahill weekends.

The house was burrowed into the sandy bluff above the bay. It was a sprawling, comfortable series of attached weathered wooden boxes, all glass facing the water and the western sky.

The Cahills had added on to the original house as their family's wealth and influence grew. Now the family had grown up and departed for their own married lives, returning graciously to present Murray and Shirley with the newest pink little Cahill grandchild. The older couple entertained extensively, and an invitation to one of their weekends meant three things.

One of them was that you were sure to be written up in *Women's Wear Daily*'s "EyeOn" and the *New York Post* as having been there.

The second was that you were a real talent and a real person. A Cahill invitation singled you out as both. A weekend with Murray and Shirley made you glad that such compassionate and lovely people were filthy rich. It restored your faith in the rightness of things.

The third was simply that you had an extravagantly good time.

Murray and Shirley were in their early sixties and had a reputation as a couple of creative genius, hospitality, and honesty. Some said it was because Murray was a half-and-half—Irish and Jewish. Some said it was because Shirley mothered everyone. She had mothered the three boys to their mutual satisfaction and couldn't stop her leanings. So she soothed and listened, approved of and questioned those who came into her ken. She had made the private decision based on her intolerance of boredom that intense, creative people, rife with all that sensitivity and intellect, needed her ministrations the most.

A breeze disturbed the surface of the bay, carrying with it the sun-warmed odor of the salt and the sap of the scrub pine.

It moved through Tom's hair, riffling it, breaking his reverie. The drapes behind him in the window billowed silently, and he reentered the cool darkness of the bedroom. The air was still and redolent with the scent of Kate's body. She slept soundly, unaffected by the unease of his mind.

Unbidden, the memory of his mother perspiring in the small, tasteless bungalow of their Rockaway Beach summer retreat rushed in on him. She had been so proud of that shack and seemed not to mind its violently contradicting wallpapers, colors, and smells.

She was Bronx Irish and, like those Brooklyn Irish, she had her place at the beach.

It didn't matter that she sweated over cabbage, pork butt, and potatoes, a family of eight, and never swam in the ocean. She took the breeze in the evening on the indifferent arm of his father and congratulated herself on having "arrived."

Her arrival was on what Flynn saw as the aging flesh but time-suppled muscle of his father's back.

His father had been a native Irishman. The man had worked his way through the Second World War to support his mother and six children. He had been an activist in the Seinn Fein and an unpopular union organizer on any Atlantic shore. He had tested for the New York Police Department, more than made the grade, gave more than any man should have had to give to tempering the grief and the rage of the poor.

He loved his father. He was the only human being he had experienced the way one experiences a tornado, a caressing lament and a grief cry. Only until Kate.

His father was all that a man should be to his son. Thoughtful but then ultimately offended by the Bronx Irish virginity he had married in hopes of romantic Irish dreams.

In the beginning Tom's mother had been a tall, busty blonde with big blue eyes in need of a way out. He had been her way out, so she married him.

How could such a man, so alive, so quivering with the expectation of life, marry such a pretender? Tom asked himself in the quiet of the morning.

He turned in the silence of the room and looked at Kate's body. He had his own romantic Irish dreams, and she was an Irish woman of intellect and copper.

Yes, a Gormlé, an Irish queen who had strapped her body to the high king of Ireland, Brian Boru, and back to back they drove the Viking invader into the Irish sea—her sword gory, her body splattered with blood, her back still protecting his.

Flynn looked down at her. She was a placid tender mother, a consummate inflamed lover, and he understood himself through his father's disappointment.

Kate belonged to the romantic heroics of his father. But then his father didn't belong to Flynn's time. Tom's soul and sensitivity crowded in on him.

His guilt shortened his breath, and he thought of how he had abridged all that his father suffered. He was not willing to suffer the obtuseness and singular dehumanizing effect that some Catholic women had on their men.

He imagined he could feel his brain stirring within the marrow of his skull. Kate had made him feel the blood rush through his veins. He had felt his own engorgement, his pride and power as a man. He wondered what there was after it.

Then the memory of the fine brown hair clinging to the tears on his face and the fragile beauty of his little daughter Maureen came to him. She had so much courage. It was that same Bronx Irish hope of leaving that hot, desperate vapidness behind that identified her as a child of his and his father's heart.

She wasn't blond.

She wasn't blue-eyed.

She was Celtic Irish and fighting her way out of a different ghetto. She was the Irish lament. She was his daughter.

She would never see her grandmother sweating. She

would only see Joan, a malignant, hysterical result of the brutality of New York's "Irish Need Not Apply." Tom was suddenly afraid for her.

He turned to his Kate.

Her flesh and her hair had been burnished copper by the sun, her body innocently sprinkled with freckles. Her laughter and wholesomeness and her sense of womanliness arrested him, and he thought as he looked at her, "What am I doing here? I feel like I just got off the boat."

She reached up for him from the coolness of the bed, tractable, credulous. The gesture allayed his guilt, and with relief he took his body and entered her with a completeness that always puzzled him.

She was always eager, always compliant to his desire. The suppleness of her flesh under his hands always made him think about his hand that held a gun, that touched the victims of heinous crimes, that gestured false compliance to foolish con artists, that then touched her flesh.

It always made him feel clean.

Then he thought about his children. He was proud of Seamus, who was both a good student and more American than Irish. Connor and Mora seemed to be an extension of a past the Irish didn't create but were always trying to escape.

Then there was the perverting insecurity about Kate and her new star status.

He always saw her as a normal woman in the garden, cooking, with their friends. He wasn't prepared for this. When she was working in her darkroom she was always alone. He hadn't been aware of how successful she had become. Not until now.

He worried about other men. Slick, successful men with money and intellect to engage and entertain her effortlessly. He worried about men who had status.

Status and his lack of it. After all, what did he do? He hung around with junkies and victims and poor people and other cops. When she was working Kate hung around with the great and the near great. *Shit,* he said to himself, *she even gets seated at Elaine's.*

He walked over to the drapes and pulled them open. Sunlight poured into the bedroom.

And now he was here with her and those people. Even the comforting presence of Eileen and Ira didn't mitigate his unease. At the party last night the conversations that ebbed and flowed around him were about people and places and achievements the people he policed viewed as imaginary. The disparity between the groups stunned him.

"And where have you been?" Kate smiled up at him from the bed. She held out her arms and wiggled her fingers at him to come. He did. She nuzzled into his arms, pressing her naked body up against him hard.

"Is the view as fabulous as Eileen promised?" Kate whispered into his neck. Tom held her in silence and listened to her breathe. Absently he kissed her hair and, tightening his arms, drew her in even closer to him. After a while he answered.

"I've been thinking about my mother and father. About how different they are from me, from us, from your parents. About Maureen . . . oh, I don't know."

The sadness in his voice alarmed her. Something inside her sensed that he was turning away, and she tried to bring him back. In a forced, cheerful voice she answered him.

"Such heavy thoughts so early in the morning, Tom?" She pulled away from him and sat cross-legged on the bed in front of him. Her hair fell over her naked breasts, and she tried to get him to smile. In her best charming little-girl voice she said, "I think you should consider a career as a writer. Eugene O'Neill, it has been said, didn't have a heavy thought until after his first whiskey and cigarette in the morning."

She smiled a teasing smile and made a funny face. "Consider how rich and famous your heavy thinking could make you."

He reached out his hand while she was teasing him and started playing with her pubic hair with his index finger. Then, probing deeper, he found the clitoris and lazily played with it. He was watching her out of the corner of his eye. She stopped talking. Her body flushed, and when she met his eyes hers were on fire. Her nipples were hard. He had been reclining on his side and listening to her. He felt his own desire sharpen.

She bent down and took him into her mouth.

He watched her lips move on him, her tongue teasing him. He reached down with both hands and pulled the hair away from her face so he could watch her. His blood was at a near boiling point. He pulled her body up onto his and, rolling her over onto her back, took her in a near frenzy.

She was very hot and sweaty and cried out his name when she came.

He watched her face, her mouth open, her eyes wild. She tossed her head from side to side, and he felt her fingers knead his back. Then he forgot her as his own agonizing pleasure took over.

They lay apart from each other, cooled by the breeze coming in off the bay. She took his hand and held it to her belly, stroking the fine, silky black hair on the back of it.

"Do you know how much I love you?" she whispered.

And in a miserably sad voice, he answered, "No."

"Will you please, please let me try and show you?"

He could hear the tears in her voice, and he could feel his heart harden toward her. He was hurt and angry, and he didn't know why, so instead he answered, "I'm starving. Let's get up and go downstairs and have breakfast."

He bolted to the bathroom, leaving her lying there confused and hurt. He loved her without shame or pride or reason. He was becoming sick with himself.

Tom turned on the shower and adjusted it to a needle-fine intensity. As he stood under the hot, stinging water he let his tears come and mingle with the punishing spray.

He had to get through this weekend. He could hear the party starting downstairs. Bloody Marys, food, and conversation. Her friends and admirers. Only Ira and Eileen were there for him. He didn't like feeling shy; he wouldn't admit he was afraid.

Kate awoke with a start. The clock by the bed said it was two o'clock in the afternoon. Tom was still asleep. She lay back on the pillow, remembering yesterday. Every time she replayed the picture of Marcy Brandon hanging on Tom's arm, on his every word, it revolted her.

He looked glorious. A dark man in dark clothes always does, Kate thought to herself.

She rolled over. Tom's long black eyelashes were bleached at the tips and pressed into the hollows of his eyes just above the cheekbones. Last night he was dressed in a white oxford shirt open at the neck and a very dark navy suit. He wore them and a smile with casual ease. Both fit him perfectly. His deeply tanned hand held a third Jameson's and soda, his black eyes smoldered from his bronzed face, and when he flashed a smile at that bitch Marcy, she came along like a dog that had just been whistled for. Kate was reflecting on all of this and that at the time she had wanted to vomit. Jealousy wasn't something she felt or handled frequently or well. Marcy Brandon was a notorious man-izer, and she didn't care what relationship she defaced. When she saw what she liked, she went after it like an animal.

And she liked Tom.

She ignored Kate, whose jealous rage eroded her good judgment. Tom all the while was playing the innocent. After all, he was just a cop who had never had the undivided attentions of a movie star. Tom thought he was making a good job of the pretense. Kate reacted the way she always chided her friends for in similar situations. She grabbed the next man who flashed her a smile.

Unfortunately, it was the other bitch at the party, Franklin Jones. He was New York's most acidly articulate literary critic. Frank wasn't tactful or circumspect about how his robust articulate attentions affected the men who came with the ladies he decided to charm and conquer. Tom was livid.

Kate rolled away from the sleeping Flynn and clutched her pillow to her face.

Franklin had taken advantage of the situation to its fullest. After a few preliminary gestures calculated to incense, he had raised his voice, sure that it would carry across the room, and asked her if her slumming days were over. He polished his attack by adding that perhaps he should consider himself her intellectual reprieve.

Tom reacted, and the night progressed from a controlled bad dream and wound up on the beach as a careening nightmare. Their immaturity increased with the alcohol level in their boiling blood. Tom hadn't stayed to see Kate's reaction to Franklin's comment. He wheeled Marcy around and made for the door and the beach. Kate didn't even want to contemplate what happened between the two of them before she hit the beach.

Naturally, Marcy found out that Tom played the bagpipes. Naturally, he got them from the car. Naturally, he agreed to play for her. There had been a small group on the beach. It got larger the more he played. They had sat transfixed at first; the skirling and keening music mixed well with the sand, sea, and moonlight. Tom played simple pieces at first and warmed to the attention he was getting from the crowd of highly creative overachievers. His mistake came when he tried to play the "Fox Chase." He found it technically difficult to play when he was sober, and on war pipes instead of his Uillean pipes it was doubly difficult. What came out was a disjointed squeaking sound, and gradually he lost his audience. They resumed quiet conversations or simply drifted down the beach. Naturally,

Franklin, who had abandoned Kate by then, made another nasty crack. Tom dropped the pipes on the tide mark in the sand and stalked off down the beach. After Kate retrieved the pipes and cleaned them off as best she could, it was too late to catch up with him in the dark. She walked down the beach but couldn't find him. For a while she thought Marcy had gone with him, but when she reentered the living room she saw the "big star" in the corner trying to put the make on Franklin.

Her anxiety level dropped, and after wishing Ira and Eileen a quiet goodnight she went to bed.

She knew what he had been thinking, but he was wrong. There was no way to convince him that no one had been laughing at him. No one other than Franklin had been making snide, cutting remarks. He just didn't understand. These people were used to talent, used to drama. The only comments that had been made were how well he played and how eerily romantic the cry from the pipes seemed against the backdrop of sea and stars.

"Let's get the hell out of here." Tom's voice cut through her silent thoughts. She started to answer, but he was already up and moving, throwing his clothes into his suitcase, tossing hers at her. Kate was beginning to get angry.

"If you don't mind, I'd like to pack my own clothes and have a little breakfast. Maybe we could at least stop long enough to thank Murray and Shirley for having us."

She looked up at him, and he shot her a dark, angry look. He was sweating already. All he wanted to do was run away. Tom was afraid to ask where his pipes were.

After his lonely walk down the beach he had come back to find them and all the people gone.

"Oh, by the way." Kate's voice was tense and hurt. "I put your pipes in the car. And no, before you ask, they didn't get wet. I brushed the sand off them the best I could."

Tom snapped his suitcase shut. "Thank you. I'll be back for your suitcase. We can have breakfast on the road. Why don't you go and thank the Cahills? I'll wait for you in the car."

Kate was staggered.

"Aren't you even going to thank Murray and Shirley? I mean, just because you're angry with me is no reason to take it out on them."

He answered in a nasty snarl. "Pardon me, Little Miss Manners. Us poor dumb cops don't always have social graces. I'll thank them on my way out to the car."

Kate showered and dressed quickly, and while she was brushing her teeth Tom came in and took her bag. Frightened and angry, she made her way down the stairs. Shirley was in the kitchen, and when she looked up and saw Kate her face creased with concern.

"Good morning, Kate dear."

"Good morning, Shirley." Embarrassed, Kate continued. "I, um, don't know how to thank you for having us. I mean, I hate to party and run, but there is an emergency at home."

Shirley moved to Kate and embraced her. In a mothering voice she said, "You don't have to lie, dear. Tom was in and just made an equally polite lie about your mother being sick. Look, dear, all married couples"—Kate inwardly winced at the word *married*—"have serious arguments from time to time. But I know

your husband loves you, and I know you love him."
She brushed the hair back from Kate's tense face.

Kate smiled weakly and, clearing her throat, thanked
Shirley again for inviting them both. The older woman
gave her hand a reassuring squeeze and let her go.

When they got onto the expressway, Kate was relieved to see that there was no traffic. Tom had been
driving in silence, and the vibrations from the car were
making her sleepy.

His anger permeated the air in the car. She was
hungry, and she wanted to stop for something to eat,
but she was afraid to start him off again. She couldn't
think of anything to say to allay his mood, so she
consoled herself that he was doing 75 mph in the
Porsche and that they would be home soon.

She woke up from a dream at the toll booth on the
Throgs Neck Bridge. Tom's face was a hard mask, so
she yielded to her drowsiness and went back to her
sweet dream. They were in the woods at the Feis again.
He was holding her again for the first time and telling
her all the things she had never believed she would hear
from him. She was feeling him need her and love her.
She felt the moss beneath her and saw the pine boughs
cross over them. She saw the moonlight peeking
through the branches. In her dream she heard the wind
rustle the leaves around, and she heard his voice again,
glutted with love, saying her name over and over.

Tom's hand shook her awake, and she emerged from
the dream with a sweet, warm smile on her mouth and
tenderness spilling from her eyes.

"I'm sorry. I must have slept."

Her gentle voice nearly stopped him.

"Yes, you did. Help me bring the bags into the house." His voice was flat and empty.

The dream had betrayed her, and the reality of where she was and what had happened rushed in. They sat in the shadow of the car staring at each other. They both began to cry. Kate breathed in the fatal stillness.

"Tom."

"I'm not coming in."

He opened the car door and got out.

It had started to rain heavily. Kate followed him down the path as he carried her bag to the front door. He opened it with the keys, turned, and handed them to her.

Blindly, her heart exploding, her breath failing her, she reached out and put her hands on his shoulders. Dimly she heard him tell her that someday she would thank him. Slowly, the pain tearing her in half, Kate slid her hands down Tom's body, clutching desperately. Sobbing, she went to her knees at his feet.

"Tom, Tom, if you go I will die."

He stood there, the tears coursing down his face. Kate crouched, pressed her clasped hands into her gut, and rocked. Finally she put her forehead on his feet.

"I am begging you. Don't, don't go. Don't throw what we have away. I love you with all my being. I will always love you. You are wrong."

He moved his feet from under her forehead, turned in the rain, and walked away like a doomed man.

{ *Chapter 20* }

Lately he had begun to feel like the empty house he sometimes felt he was hiding in. Just as vacant as the blank, dusty windows that reflected the street activity when the children were in school and Joan was thankfully gone to work. He and Tim were working nights for a while, and the loneliness was deep. Flynn sat at his window sometimes and watched the cars and people and colors, while inside the air was dry and still. Dead.

There was no noise, no cooking smells, no human laughter or tears or mood variations. There were no sounds of love or lust, no anger, no crooning to babies, just fatal stillness.

Tom and the vacant house, eagerly searching the crowd on the street, looking for Seamus and Maureen, who dutifully entered every day after school. They filled the immense emptiness with their love and laughter, complaints and questions.

His beautiful youngest children.

He was beginning to worry that they would come to know how empty and vacant and lonely he was. He was beginning to worry that he would frighten them. And they, out of their loving, would try to fill the void and instead only open themselves up so much that they would feel his pain.

He had tried to read. He couldn't find anything to hold his interest. He had tried to go Christmas shopping, but when he got to the stores nothing seemed right for anyone.

He never bought anything.

He had started to watch game shows during the day. Sometimes he didn't even do that; he sat and thought and stared out his window. Sometimes he slept the day away. When he came home from work his children talked to him in his room. He only left it to eat or to perform a chore Joan wanted him to do.

Sometimes Tim McBride would drive over and drag him out of the house for a game of handball. Then they would go back to Tim's house, and, bless her, Margey would try to get Tom to talk.

He couldn't, he just couldn't. The pain was too great, he missed Kate too much. He felt the whole thing was his fault, that he had messed up everyone's lives, that he deserved all the pain he was suffering.

He reasoned with himself that he had tried to make a commitment, and had, but he had a previous commitment to his children, particularly to Seamus and Maureen. He couldn't keep both, so he honored the one to his children.

Connor and Mora had faired okay without him, but Seamus and Maureen had taken the full brunt of Joan's rage. He had had to step back in between Joan and the children to protect them.

Joan hadn't wanted them when they were born, even less after he had left. They were his children, just as much as Connor and Mora seemed to be Joan's.

But, oh, how he missed Kate.

His pain over losing her was as great as his love for her. Sometimes he thought he would go mad. The sick feeling inside never left him. Not even Seamus's and Maureen's joy upon his return home could wash away the sick feeling. It seemed to him that she was never out of his mind. He always wondered how she was doing. Sometimes after he got off a late tour he would drive by the house, park in the shadow of the trees by the side of the road, and watch it. The house that held the woman he loved, and the whole of his laughter, all of his dreams, all his happy plans for the future.

He felt he had no future now. His future was death, nothing more, just getting through the rest of his life until it was over.

When he was on duty he scanned the streets hoping to see her red head bent over her camera. He listened for the sound of her voice in crowds. He searched parking lots for her shiny red Porsche.

Tim would sit quietly beside him in the patrol car. He always knew when Tom was searching, but he never said a word to his partner about the ever-lengthening silences.

Lately he and Margey had insisted that Tom and Seamus and Maureen stop by the house. They were becoming Wednesday night regulars. Joan played bingo, and Connor and Mora were always out with new love interests.

Tom seemed to relax a little bit, and it gave the children a chance to be alone with their father in a friendly atmosphere. It also gave Seamus a chance to talk to Margey McBride about his worries about his father. She listened and advised, reassured and worried herself in private with Tim.

And sometimes Margey called Kate.

They would start to talk about light subjects, and then Margey would try to bring up Flynn. Kate would either harden up or break down sobbing. Either way Margey was at a loss. Kate and Tom—neither one would let her tell the other about each other's lives.

And there was so much to tell. Time passed, and Margey and Tim worried. Jim and Josie worried. Eileen and Ira worried. Tom and Kate remained silent.

The Christmas vacation had started, and all the children were out of school. Maureen sat at the breakfast table babbling happily about Sister Mary Louise and the first prize in the reading contest she had won at school. She was polishing off the oatmeal her father had made and was eyeing the powdery surface of the sliding hill next to the house. The other neighborhood children had already been around and had asked permission of either Tom or the less receptive Joan to sled in their yard.

Maureen was reluctant to leave her father, though.

"Don't be sad, Daddy, I'll always love you."

Maureen took her father's whiskery face in her small hands and kissed him.

"Go outside and enjoy yourself, little one," Flynn responded softly to his favorite's tenderness.

" 'Bye Da . . ." was all he heard as she flew out the door, slamming it. He settled back into his thoughts again until Joan came into the kitchen and asked him when he was planning to chop more wood for the fireplace.

"I'll do it right now." He got up and fetched his coat and was out the door before she could think to add "your fireplace, anyway."

Joan had turned into a smug tigress when Flynn came home.

Seamus was a constant loving shadow. Flynn knew his son was afraid for him, but he didn't know what to say to dispel the fear. He was too deeply depressed and preoccupied to realize that his silences were deafening. Seamus was convinced that his father was going to die on the job. The only thing that calmed his fear was the fact that Tim McBride was his father's partner and would try to make sure it didn't happen. Flynn didn't realize that the things he did normally, like driving and reading, he did badly or not at all anymore.

Seamus was just waking up when he saw his father go outdoors with an axe in his hand. He dressed quickly and joined him by the woodpile.

"Hey, Dad, here, let me do that." Seamus reached for the axe in his father's hand.

Flynn turned at the sound of his voice. He hadn't heard him come up behind him. He had been standing staring at the wood and the snow, thinking about blood and death and Kate. He had been wondering what she was doing that very minute. He was wondering if Kevin was outside in the snow or inside watching cartoons.

He shook himself.

"No thanks, Seamus, I'll do it. You should go and get some breakfast."

"Oh, I'm not hungry, Dad. Listen, Dad, let's take a walk, and I'll chop the wood for you later."

"No. Don't you have some friends you'd rather be spending the day with?"

Flynn watched his son's face as his mind worked, trying to formulate an answer that would be neither worried nor believable.

"No, Dad, I'd rather be with you." Seamus had decided to give up the fight he was trying to wage, hiding his fear from his father. He decided to try honesty.

"I love you, Dad, and I think you're going to get hurt, and I want to protect you. I'm afraid you're going to die, and I'm scared. I think you should go back to her. You were happy when you were with her."

The tears running down his father's face stopped him. The anguish that filled his father's dark, hollow eyes filled him with dread.

He started again. "Dad, she is a very beautiful woman. I know she loves you very much. You see, Dad, I went to see her, and . . ."

The axe had fallen from Flynn's hand. Seamus heard his father breathing hoarsely and, struggling with the hardness in his throat, he continued. "She said she loves you. She said that it was up to you. That you had to decide to come back on your own, that she couldn't ask you, but that you had to decide. I love you, Dad, and I want you to be happy. You were happy when you were with her. You were different. I like you that way."

Flynn had put his face in his hands and was sobbing

quietly. Seamus, in a panic that his mother or the neighbors would see, guided him around to the back of the woodpile. He tried to hold the massive man in his young man's arms while he cried.

All around the neighborhood Christmas lights winked at Seamus. He held his father, rubbing his back the way his father had when he was a little boy. He was scared, but he held him and patted him and said over and over, "Dad, I love you. It will be all right. I love you, Dad."

He never thought to get a priest or his mother or his grandmother. The only person he thought to get was that beautiful woman his father loved, that he liked, that lived in a house filled with the sound of music and laughter and the delicious odors of cooking food. A woman who surrounded herself with brilliantly colored flowers and an aura of well-being and love.

He just didn't know how to do it.

Whatever brought his father home, Seamus thought, wasn't good enough. Whatever kept him with Kate was good and was what his father needed now more than anything.

Oh God, he prayed silently. *Please help my father help himself. Maybe his leaving wasn't right, but this can't be right either. Please, God, help my dad.*

Help came in the form of Joan. It was a terrible scene.

Joan, wondering what was happening with the wood, came out and found them, Seamus holding his father while he cried.

"What's this now? Standing in the snow sniveling about your whore, Tom?" she snarled.

Seamus struck out blindly, wanting only to stop his

mother from saying anything more. Instead he caught her on the jaw, knocking her to the ground.

"So now my son wants the whore too!" She screamed up at them from the ground.

The sight of her screaming in the snow, filth pouring from her mouth, combined with the sight of horror and shock on his son's face and woke him up from his depression.

He turned to Seamus and told him to get Maureen. He instructed them both to pack their belongings.

"I want you to pack your things, then I want you to help Maureen to pack hers. I am going to take both of you, and we are going to leave here. I'll find us a place of our own."

Tom Flynn reached down and jerked Joan up from the snow, brushed her off, and told her to shut up just as she was about to start a new tirade.

He strode purposefully into the house and called the McBrides. No, they said, they didn't mind if three Flynns camped out at their house during Christmastime. After all, what is the spirit of Christmas about anyway?

Margey was jubilant. Tim was relieved. Flynn felt almost human for the first time since he had left Kate in the rain.

Seamus and Maureen were cheerfully installed in the McBrides' guest room. Maureen was downstairs baking Christmas cookies with Mrs. McBride. He and his dad had been out looking for a place all day. They had a deposit on a two-bedroom apartment. Seamus thanked God for this gift. Then he asked for just one more, just a little bit more from God.

* * *

"No thanks, Bob. No, really, I don't need anything. Well, my mother is still talking to me, and Betsy and Deirdre stop by. Yes, Kevin and I are fine. I promise if I need anything I'll call you."

Kate cradled the telephone and went back to decorating the tree. It wasn't as big as she would have preferred, but it was all she could manage under the circumstances.

"Mommy, Mommy, can I go over to Nicky's? Aunt Josie called and said you probably want me out of your hair. Can I, Mom, can I?"

Kevin had raced in from the back of the house and stood expectantly, a pleading, clowning look on his face.

"Is your Aunt Josie still on the telephone?"

"Yes, Mom."

"Josie?"

"Hi, Cat, how's everything?"

"Fine, Josie, fine. Listen, are you sure that you want Kevin to come over? I know how busy you get the day before Christmas Eve dinner."

"It's no trouble, no trouble at all. Besides, an extra one always keeps them busy and out of my hair."

"Okay. I could use a little peace and quiet. I haven't hit the darkroom for over two weeks, and I could use the time."

"It's settled then. Jim said he'd be over in about twenty minutes. He's going to pick Kevin up on the way to the store. A few of the lights are out on the tree. Is there anything you need?"

"No, Josie. Deirdre has turned into a tigress. She shows up here every three days and fills my shopping order and tells the Judge off at the same time."

276

Josie laughed and rang off.

Long blue shadows had already started their crawl across the snow when Jim pulled into the drive and honked for Kevin.

Kate walked her son to the door and part way into the drive. Jim waved hello to her from the van.

"Listen, they say it's going to snow again tonight. I'll be over in the morning with the jeep and plow you out."

Shivering, Kate waved a thank you and hustled back into the house. She closed the front door and watched as Kevin climbed into the van and tossed his overnight bag into the back.

She went back to the tree. She had already put the tiny white lights way in the back by the trunk, and she was artfully arranging the beautiful colored bulbs on the ends of the branches. The weight always pulled them down a bit and made it look like the tree was holding out arms, brilliantly decorated, beckoning to delight the eye.

This was the first year since Felipe had left her that her father hadn't stopped by with a tree and stayed to decorate it with her and Kevin. It made her sad. His reasons made her angry.

She went into the kitchen and poured herself a frothy glass of eggnog and decided to spike it with a little whiskey. She sprinkled a little bit of nutmeg on the top and made her way back to the tree.

An hour later she had put all the finishing tinsel on the branches, strand by strand. She turned the lights off in the room and turned the lights of the tree on.

It was beautiful. It made her cry.

She decided to move on to the Christmas cards. She

always hung a wide red ribbon around the doorway and pinned the cards to it. Then, remembering that she hadn't gone to the mailbox that day, Kate went to the hall closet for her coat.

It was six o'clock and already quite dark. A luminescent glow from the moon on the snow cast haunting shadows under the branches of the bare trees. Kate trudged down her driveway. The snow was deep and heavy and wet. It had already started to snow again.

She huffed and puffed her way to the mailbox and yanked it open. It was full of cards from friends and friendly acquaintances. She pulled off her mittens and went through them in the street light.

Eileen sending her love and another invitation if she felt up to it. Karen Whelan with stylish greetings from Bloomie's.

She shoved the stack into her deep pockets, slammed the frozen mailbox door shut, and looked up and down the road.

There was a white Volkswagen parked down the road a bit. Its lights were off, but Kate knew that Flynn was in it. Her whole body reacted, the skin over her belly tightened, and tears stung her eyes. He was watching her, never coming near her, just watching her.

She turned away, crossed the icy road, and halfway across the front lawn fell into the deep wet snow.

Black eyes watched as she crossed the road. His heart leapt into his throat when she fell.

She was pregnant. Pregnant with his child. He sat there, the final battle of the war within himself raging to a close.

There was the woman he loved, struggling to get up.

The child inside her body was his. There was no one else to help her rise.

Then why am I sitting here? he screamed to himself. *Because I am afraid,* he answered.

Kate saw the lights of the Volkswagen blink on. She heard the engine start. She heard the squeak of the tires as they moved over the snow in the driveway.

She heard the crunch of his feet as he approached her, slowly, while she lay nearly helpless in the snow.

His hands reached under her, his arms picked her up, and he carried her to the house. The baby moved under the palm of his right hand as he carried her.

Kate could barely breathe. Strong emotions raged through her. She had her arms around his neck. Her head rested on his shoulder. She breathed his scent in and tried not to cry.

He reached down and opened the door, never letting her go. Warm yellow light spilled out onto the snow.

It reminded her of summer sunlight.

It reminded him of her smile.

He stood there holding her, not wanting ever to let her go.

"I left Joan. I took Seamus and Maureen with me."

She didn't say anything. She just kept her arms around his neck and her head burrowed into his shoulder.

"Seamus and I found this two-bedroom apartment. We can move in next week."

She didn't say anything. He gently put her feet down and, holding her away from him, said, "I want to come home."

He had started to cry, and he repeated his plea. "I want to come home. Please let me come home."

She leaned her body into his, and his arms closed around her tightly.

She whispered in his ear, "Do you think we should sell the house or add the bedrooms on? From one child to four is quite a change."

He took her face in his hands and kissed her fiercely.

They entered the house together, finally, together.